PLEASE STAND BY . . . FOR DOOMSDAY

Malibert's heart was leaden. The thing he had given his professional career to—SETI, the Search for Extra-Terrestrial Intelligence—no longer seemed to matter. If the bombs went off, as everyone said they must, then that was ended for a good long time, at least—

Gabble of voices at the end of the bar; Malibert turned, leaned over the mahogany, peered. The *Please Stand By* slide had vanished, was delivering a news bulletin:

"—the president has confirmed that a nuclear attack has begun against the United States. Missiles have been detected over the Arctic, and they are incoming. Everyone is ordered to seek shelter and remain there pending instructions—"

Yes. It was ended, thought Malibert, at least for a good long time.

—from "Fermi and Frost"
by Frederik Pohl

ISAAC ASIMOV'S EARTH

EDITED BY
GARDNER DOZOIS
and SHEILA WILLIAMS

ACE BOOKS, NEW YORK

This book is an Ace original edition,
and has never been previously published.

ISAAC ASIMOV'S EARTH

An Ace Book / published by arrangement with
Davis Publications, Inc.

PRINTING HISTORY
Ace edition / May 1992

ISBN: 0-441-37377-1

Ace Books are published by The Berkley Publishing Group,
200 Madison Avenue, New York, New York 10016.
The name "ACE" and the "A" logo
are trademarks belonging to Charter Communications, Inc.

PRINTED IN THE UNITED STATES OF AMERICA

10 9 8 7 6 5 4 3 2 1

ACKNOWLEDGMENTS

The editors would like to thank the following people for their help and support: Susan Casper, who helped with the scut work involved in preparing the manuscript, and lent the use of her computer; Shawna McCarthy, for having the good taste to buy some of this material in the first place; Tracey French, who suggested the idea; Ian Randal Strock, Charles Ardai, and Scott L. Towner, who did much of the basic research needed; Constance Scarborough, who cleared the permissions; Cynthia Manson, who set up this deal; and thanks especially to our own editor on this project, Susan Allison.

CONTENTS

ISAAC ASIMOV'S
EARTH

FERMI AND FROST

Frederik Pohl

"Fermi and Frost" was purchased by Shawna Mc-
Carthy, and appeared in the January 1985 issue
of IAsfm, with an illustration by John Jinks. Pohl
doesn't appear in the magazine nearly as often as
we'd like him to, but each of his appearances there
has been memorable—and never more so than with
the terrifying story that follows, a frighteningly plausible glimpse of an all-too-probable future . . . one
that we'd better pray won't prove to be prophetic,
for the sake of Planet Earth.

A seminal figure whose career spans almost the
entire development of modern SF, Frederik Pohl has
been one of the genre's major shaping forces—as
writer, editor, agent, and anthologist—for more than
fifty years. He was the founder of the Star series, SF's
first continuing anthology series, and was the editor
of the Galaxy group of magazines from 1960 to 1969,
during which time Galaxy's sister magazine, Worlds
of If, won three consecutive Best Professional Magazine Hugos. As a writer, he has several times won
Nebula and Hugo awards, as well as the American
Book Award and the French Prix Apollo. His many
books include several written in collaboration with

1

the late C. M. Kornbluth—including The Space Merchants, Wolfbane, *and* Gladiator-at-Law—*and many solo novels, including* Gateway, Man Plus, Beyond the Blue Event Horizon, *and* The Coming of the Quantum Cats. *Among his many collections are* The Gold at the Starbow's End, In the Problem Pit, *and* The Best of Frederik Pohl. *His most recent books are* The Gateway Trip *and his non-fiction collaboration with Isaac Asimov,* Our Angry Earth.

On Timothy Clary's ninth birthday he got no cake. He spent all of it in a bay of the TWA terminal at John F. Kennedy airport in New York, sleeping fitfully, crying now and then from exhaustion or fear. All he had to eat was stale Danish pastries from the buffet wagon and not many of them, and he was fearfully embarrassed because he had wet his pants. Three times. Getting to the toilets over the packed refugee bodies was just about impossible. There were twenty-eight hundred people in a space designed for a fraction that many, and all of them with the same idea. Get away! Climb the highest mountain! Drop yourself splat, spang, right in the middle of the widest desert! Run! Hide!—

And pray. Pray as hard as you can, because even the occasional plane-load of refugees that managed to fight their way aboard and even take off had no sure hope of refuge when they got wherever the plane was going. Families parted. Mothers pushed their screaming children aboard a jet and melted back into the crowd before screaming, more quietly, themselves.

Because there had been no launch order yet, or none that the public had heard about anyway, there might still be time for escape. A little time. Time enough for the TWA terminal, and every other airport terminal everywhere, to jam up with terrified lemmings. There was no doubt that the missiles were poised to fly. The attempted Cuban coup had escalated wildly, and one nuclear sub had attacked another with a nuclear charge. That, everyone agreed, was the signal. The next event would be the final one.

Timothy knew little of this, but there would have been nothing he could have done about it—except perhaps cry, or have nightmares, or wet himself, and young Timothy was doing all of those anyway. He did not know where his father was. He didn't know where his mother was, either, except that she had gone somewhere to try to call his father; but then there had been a surge that could not be resisted when three 747s at once had announced boarding, and Timothy had been carried far from where he had been left. Worse than that. Wet as he was, with a cold already, he was beginning to be very sick. The young woman who had brought him the Danish pastries put a worried hand to his forehead and drew it away helplessly. The boy needed a doctor. But so did a hundred others, elderly heart patients and hungry babies and at least two women close to childbirth.

If the terror had passed and the frantic negotiations had succeeded, Timothy might have found his parents again in time to grow up and marry and give them grandchildren. If one side or the other had been able to preempt, and destroy the other, and save itself, Timothy forty years later might have been a graying, cynical colonel in the American military government of Leningrad. (Or body servant to a Russian one in Detroit.) Or if his mother had pushed just a little harder earlier on, he might have wound up in the plane of refugees that reached Pittsburgh just in time to become plasma. Or if the girl who was watching him had become just a little more scared, and a little more brave, and somehow managed to get him through the throng to the improvised clinics in the main terminal, he might have been given medicine, and found somebody to protect him, and take him to a refuge, and live. . . .

But that is in fact what did happen!

Because Harry Malibert was on his way to a British Interplanetary Society seminar in Portsmouth, he was already sipping Beefeater Martinis in the terminal's Ambassador Club when the unnoticed TV at the bar suddenly made everybody notice it.

Those silly nuclear-attack communications systems that the radio stations tested out every now and then, and nobody paid any attention to any more—why, this time it was real! They were serious! Because it was winter and snowing heavily Malibert's flight had been delayed anyway. Before its rescheduled departure time came, all flights had been embargoed. Nothing would leave Kennedy until some official somewhere decided to let them go.

Almost at once the terminal began to fill with would-be refugees. The Ambassador Club did not fill at once. For three hours the ground-crew stew at the desk resolutely turned away everyone who rang the bell who could not produce the little red card of admission; but when the food and drink in the main terminals began to run out the Chief of Operations summarily opened the club to everyone. It didn't help relieve the congestion outside, it only added to what was within. Almost at once a volunteer doctors' committee seized most of the club to treat the ill and injured from the thickening crowds, and people like Harry Malibert found themselves pushed into the bar area. It was one of the Operations staff, commandeering a gin and tonic at the bar for the sake of the calories more than the booze, who recognized him. "You're Harry Malibert. I heard you lecture once, at Northwestern."

Malibert nodded. Usually when someone said that to him he answered politely, "I hope you enjoyed it," but this time it did not seem appropriate to be normally polite. Or normal at all.

"You showed slides of Arecibo," the man said dreamily. "You said that radio telescope could send a message as far as the Great Nebula in Andromeda, two million light-years away—if only there was another radio telescope as good as that one there to receive it."

"You remember very well," said Malibert, surprised.

"You made a big impression, Dr. Malibert." The man glanced at his watch, debated, took another sip of his drink. "It really sounded wonderful, using the big telescopes to listen for messages from alien civilizations somewhere in space— maybe hearing some, maybe making contact, maybe not being alone in the universe any more. You made me wonder why we hadn't seen some of these people already, or anyway heard from them—but maybe," he finished, glancing bitterly at the ranked and guarded aircraft outside, "maybe now we know why."

Malibert watched him go, and his heart was leaden. The thing he had given his professional career to—SETI, the Search for Extra-Terrestrial Intelligence—no longer seemed to matter. If the bombs went off, as everyone said they must, then that was ended for a good long time, at least—

Gabble of voices at the end of the bar; Malibert turned, leaned over the mahogany, peered. The *Please Stand By* slide had vanished, and a young black woman with pomaded hair, voice trembling, was delivering a news bulletin:

"—the president has confirmed that a nuclear attack has begun against the United States. Missiles have been detected over the Arctic, and they are incoming. Everyone is ordered to seek shelter and remain there pending instructions—"

Yes. It was ended, thought Malibert, at least for a good long time.

The surprising thing was that the news that it had begun changed nothing. There were no screams, no hysteria. The order to seek shelter meant nothing at John F. Kennedy Airport, where there was no shelter any better than the building they were in. And that, no doubt, was not too good. Malibert remembered clearly the strange aerodynamic shape of the terminal's roof. Any blast anywhere nearby would tear that off and send it sailing over the bay to the Rockaways, and probably a lot of the people inside with it.

But there was nowhere else to go.

There were still camera crews at work, heaven knew why. The television set was showing crowds in Times Square and Newark, a clot of automobiles stagnating on the George Washington Bridge, their drivers abandoning them and running for the Jersey shore. A hundred people were peering around each other's heads to catch glimpses of the screen, but all that anyone said was to call out when he recognized a building or a street.

Orders rang out: "You people will have to move back! We need the room! Look, some of you, give us a hand with these patients." Well, that seemed useful, at least. Malibert volunteered at once and was given the care of a young boy, teeth chattering, hot with fever. "He's had tetracycline," said

the doctor who turned the boy over to him. "Clean him up if
you can, will you? He ought to be all right if—"

If any of them were, thought Malibert, not requiring her
to finish the sentence. How did you clean a young boy up?
The question answered itself when Malibert found the boy's
trousers soggy and the smell told him what the moisture was.
Carefully he laid the child on a leather love seat and removed
the pants and sopping undershorts. Naturally the boy had not
come with a change of clothes. Malibert solved that with a
pair of his own jockey shorts out of his briefcase—far too big
for the child, of course, but since they were meant to fit tightly
and elastically they stayed in place when Malibert pulled them
up to the waist. Then he found paper towels and pressed the
blue jeans as dry as he could. It was not very dry. He grimaced,
laid them over a bar stool and sat on them for a while, drying
them with body heat. They were only faintly wet ten minutes
later when he put them back on the child—

San Francisco, the television said, had ceased to transmit.

Malibert saw the Operations man working his way toward
him and shook his head. "It's begun," Malibert said, and the
man looked around. He put his face close to Malibert's.

"I can get you out of here," he whispered. "There's an
Icelandic DC-8 loading right now. No announcement. They'd
be rushed if they did. There's room for you, Dr. Malibert."

It was like an electric shock. Malibert trembled. Without
knowing why he did it, he said, "Can I put the boy on instead?"

The Operations man looked annoyed. "Take him with you,
of course," he said. "I didn't know you had a son."

"I don't," said Malibert. But not out loud. And when they
were in the jet he held the boy in his lap as tenderly as though
he were his own.

If there was no panic in the Ambassador Club at Kennedy
there was plenty of it everywhere else in the world. What
everyone in the superpower cities knew was that their lives
were at stake. Whatever they did might be in vain, and yet
they had to do something. Anything! Run, hide, dig, brace,
stow . . . pray. The city people tried to desert the metropolises
for the open safety of the country, and the farmers and the

exurbanites sought the stronger, safer buildings of the cities.

And the missiles fell.

The bombs that had seared Hiroshima and Nagasaki were struck matches compared to the hydrogen-fusion flares that ended eighty million lives in those first hours. Firestorms fountained above a hundred cities. Winds of three hundred kilometers an hour pulled in cars and debris and people, and they all became ash that rose to the sky. Splatters of melted rock and dust sprayed into the air.

The sky darkened.

Then it grew darker still.

When the Icelandic jet landed at Keflavik Airport Malibert carried the boy down the passage to the little stand marked *Immigration.* The line was long, for most of the passengers had no passports at all, and the immigration woman was very tired of making out temporary entrance permits by the time Malibert reached her. "He's my son," Malibert lied. "My wife has his passport, but I don't know where my wife is."

She nodded wearily. She pursed her lips, looked toward the door beyond which her superior sat sweating and initialing reports, then shrugged and let them through. Malibert took the boy to a door marked *Snirting,* which seemed to be the Icelandic word for toilets, and was relieved to see that at least Timothy was able to stand by himself while he urinated, although his eyes stayed half closed. His head was very hot. Malibert prayed for a doctor in Reykjavik.

In the bus the English-speaking tour guide in charge of them—she had nothing else to do, for her tour would never arrive—sat on the arm of a first-row seat with a microphone in her hand and chattered vivaciously to the refugees. "Chicago? Ya, is gone, Chicago. And Detroit and Pittis-burrug—is bad. New York? Certainly New York too!" she said severely, and the big tears rolling down her cheek made Timothy cry too. Malibert hugged him. "Don't worry, Timmy," he said. "No one would bother bombing Reykjavik." And no one would have. But when the bus was ten miles farther along there was a sudden glow in the clouds ahead of them that made them squint. Someone in the USSR had decided that it was time for neatening up loose threads. That someone, whoever remained in whatever remained of their central missile control, had realized that no one had taken out that supremely, insultingly dangerous bastion of imperialist American interests in the North Atlantic, the United States airbase at Keflavik.

Unfortunately, by then EMP and attrition had compromised the accuracy of their aim. Malibert had been right. No one would have bothered bombing Reykjavik—on purpose—but a forty-mile miss did the job anyway, and Reykjavik ceased to exist.

They had to make a wide detour inland to avoid the fires and the radiation. And as the sun rose on their first day in Iceland, Malibert, drowsing over the boy's bed after the Icelandic nurse had shot him full of antibiotics, saw the daybreak in awful, sky-drenching red.

It was worth seeing, for in the days to come there was no daybreak at all.

The worst was the darkness, but at first that did not seem urgent. What was urgent was rain. A trillion trillion dust particles nucleated water vapor. Drops formed. Rain fell—torrents of rain; sheets and cascades of rain. The rivers swelled. The Mississippi overflowed, and the Ganges, and the Yellow. The High Dam at Aswan spilled water over its lip, then crumbled. The rains came where rains came never. The Sahara knew flash floods. The Flaming Mountains at the edge of the Gobi flamed no more; a ten-year supply of rain came down in a week and rinsed the dusty slopes bare.

And the darkness stayed.

The human race lives always eighty days from starvation. That is the sum of stored food, globe wide. It met the nuclear winter with no more and no less.

The missiles went off on the 11th of June. If the world's larders had been equally distributed, on the 30th of August the last mouthful would have been eaten. The starvation deaths would have begun and ended in the next six weeks; exit the human race.

The larders were not equally distributed. The Northern Hemisphere was caught on one foot, fields sown, crops not yet grown. Nothing did grow there. The seedlings poked up through the dark earth for sunlight, found none, died. Sunlight was shaded out by the dense clouds of dust exploded out of the ground by the H-bombs. It was the Cretaceous repeated; extinction was in the air.

There were mountains of stored food in the rich countries of North America and Europe, of course, but they melted swiftly. The rich countries had much stored wealth in the form of their livestock. Every steer was a million calories of protein and fat. When it was slaughtered, it saved thousands of other calories of grain and roughage for every day lopped off its life in feed. The cattle and pigs and sheep—even the goats and horses; even the pet bunnies and the chicks; even the very kittens and hamsters—they all died quickly and were eaten, to eke out the stores of canned foods and root vegetables and grain. There was no rationing of the slaughtered meat. It had to be eaten before it spoiled.

Of course, even in the rich countries the supplies were not equally distributed. The herds and the grain elevators were not located on Times Square or in the Loop. It took troops to convoy corn from Iowa to Boston and Dallas and Philadelphia. Before long, it took killing. Then it could not be done at all.

So the cities starved first. As the convoys of soldiers made the changeover from seizing food for the cities to seizing food for themselves, the riots began, and the next wave of mass death. These casualties didn't usually die of hunger. They died of someone else's.

It didn't take long. By the end of "summer" the frozen remnants of the cities were all the same. A few thousand skinny, freezing desperadoes survived in each, sitting guard over their troves of canned and dried and frozen foodstuffs.

Every river in the world was running sludgy with mud to its mouth, as the last of the trees and grasses died and relaxed their grip on the soil. Every rain washed dirt away. As the winter dark deepened the rains turned to snow. The Flaming Mountains were sheeted in ice now, ghostly, glassy fingers uplifted to the gloom. Men could walk across the Thames at London now, the few men who were left. And across the Hudson, across the Whangpoo, across the Missouri between the two Kansas Cities. Avalanches rumbled down on what was left of Denver. In the stands of dead timber grubs flourished. The starved predators scratched them out and devoured them. Some of the predators were human. The last of the Hawaiians were finally grateful for their termites.

A Western human being—comfortably pudgy on a diet of 2800 calories a day, resolutely jogging to keep the flab away or mournfully conscience-stricken at the thickening thighs and the waistbands that won't quite close—can survive for forty-five days without food. By then the fat is gone. Protein reabsorption of the muscles is well along. The plump housewife or businessman is a starving scarecrow. Still, even then care and nursing can still restore health.

Then it gets worse.

Dissolution attacks the nervous system. Blindness begins. The flesh of the gums recedes, and the teeth fall out. Apathy becomes pain, then agony, then coma.

Then death. Death for almost every person on Earth. . . .

For forty days and forty nights the rain fell, and so did the temperature. Iceland froze over.

To Harry Malibert's astonishment and dawning relief, Iceland was well equipped to do that. It was one of the few places on Earth that could be submerged in snow and ice and still survive.

There is a ridge of volcanoes that goes almost around the Earth. The part that lies between America and Europe is called the Mid-Atlantic Ridge, and most of it is under water. Here and there, like boils erupting along a forearm, volcanic islands poke up above the surface. Iceland is one of them. It was because Iceland was volcanic that it could survive when most places died of freezing, but it was also because it had been cold in the first place.

The survival authorities put Malibert to work as soon as they found out who he was. There was no job opening for a radio astronomer interested in contacting far-off (and very likely non-existent) alien races. There was, however, plenty of work for persons with scientific training, especially if they had the engineering skills of a man who had run Arecibo for two years. When Malibert was not nursing Timothy Clary through the slow and silent convalescence from his pneumonia, he was calculating heat losses and pumping rates for the piped geothermal water.

Iceland filled itself with enclosed space. It heated the spaces with water from the boiling underground springs.

Of heat it had plenty. Getting the heat from the geyser fields to the enclosed spaces was harder. The hot water was as hot as ever, since it did not depend at all on sunlight for its calories, but it took a lot more of it to keep out a -30°C chill than a +5°C one. It wasn't just to keep the surviving people warm that they needed energy. It was to grow food.

Iceland had always had a lot of geothermal greenhouses. The flowering ornamentals were ripped out and food plants put in their place. There was no sunlight to make the vegetables and grains grow, so the geothermal power-generating plants were put on max output. Solar-spectrum incandescents flooded the trays with photons. Not just in the old greenhouses. Gymnasia, churches, schools—they all began to grow food under the glaring lights. There was other food, too, metric tons of protein baaing and starving in the hills. The herds of sheep were captured and slaughtered and dressed—and put outside again, to freeze until needed. The animals that froze to death on the slopes were bulldozed into heaps of a hundred, and left where they were. Geodetic maps were carefully marked to show the location of each heap.

It was, after all, a blessing that Reykjavik had been nuked. That meant half a million fewer people for the island's resources to feed.

When Malibert was not calculating load factors, he was out in the desperate cold, urging on the workers. Sweating navvies tried to muscle shrunken fittings together in icy foxholes that their body heat kept filling with icewater. They listened patiently as Malibert tried to give orders—his few words of Icelandic were almost useless, but even the navvies sometimes spoke tourist-English. They checked their radiation monitors, looked up at the storms overhead, returned to their work and prayed. Even Malibert almost prayed when one day, trying to locate the course of the buried coastal road, he looked out on the sea ice and saw a gray-white ice hummock that was not an ice hummock. It was just at the limits of visibility, dim on the fringe of the road crew's work lights, and it moved. "A polar bear!" he whispered to the head of the work crew, and everyone stopped while the beast shambled out of sight.

From then on they carried rifles.

When Malibert was not (incompetent) technical advisor to the task of keeping Iceland warm or (almost incompetent, but learning) substitute father to Timothy Clary, he was trying desperately to calculate survival chances. Not just for them; for the entire human race. With all the desperate flurry of survival work, the Icelanders spared time to think of the future. A study team was created, physicists from the University of Reykjavik, the surviving Supply officer from the Keflavik airbase, a meteorologist on work-study from the University of Leyden to learn about North Atlantic air masses. They met in the gasthuis where Malibert lived with the boy, and usually Timmy sat silent next to Malibert while they talked. What they wanted was to know how long the dust cloud would persist. Some day the particles would finish dropping from the sky, and then the world could be reborn—if enough survived to parent a new race, anyway. But when? They could not tell. They did not know how long, how cold, how killing the nuclear winter would be. "We don't know the megatonnage," said Malibert, "we don't know what atmospheric changes have taken place, we don't know the rate of insolation. We only know it will be bad."

"It is already bad," grumbled Thorsid Magnesson, Director of Public Safety. (Once that office had had something to do with catching criminals, when the major threat to safety was crime.)

"It will get worse," said Malibert, and it did. The cold deepened. The reports from the rest of the world dwindled. They plotted maps to show what they knew to show. One set of missile maps, to show where the strikes had been— within a week that no longer mattered, because the deaths from cold already began to outweigh those from blast. They plotted isotherm maps, based on the scattered weather reports that came in—maps that had to be changed every day, as the freezing line marched toward the Equator. Finally the maps were irrelevant. The whole world was cold then. They plotted fatality maps—the percentages of deaths in each area, as they could infer them from the reports they received, but those maps soon became too frightening to plot.

The British Isles died first, not because they were nuked but because they were not. There were too many people alive there. Britian never owned more than a four-day supply of food. When the ships stopped coming they starved. So did Japan. A little later, so did Bermuda and Hawaii and Canada's off-shore provinces; and then it was the continents' turn.

And Timmy Clary listened to every word.

The boy didn't talk much. He never asked after his parents, not after the first few days. He did not hope for good news, and did not want bad. The boy's infection was cured, but the boy himself was not. He ate half of what a hungry child should devour. He ate that only when Malibert coaxed him.

The only thing that made Timmy look alive was the rare times when Malibert could talk to him about space. There were many in Iceland who knew about Harry Malibert and SETI, and a few who cared about it almost as much as Malibert himself. When time permitted they would get together, Malibert and his groupies. There was Lars the postman (now pick-and-shovel ice excavator, since there was no mail), Ingar the waitress from the Loftleider Hotel (now stitching heavy drapes to help insulate dwelling walls), Elda the English teacher (now practical nurse, frostbite cases a specialty). There were others, but those three were always there when they could get away. They were Harry Malibert fans who had read his books and dreamed with him of radio messages from weird aliens from Aldebaran, or worldships that could carry million-person populations across the galaxy, on voyages of a hundred thousand years. Timmy listened, and drew sketches of the worldships. Malibert supplied him with dimensions. "I talked to Gerry Webb," he said, "and he'd worked it out in detail. It is a matter of rotation rates and strength of materials. To provide the proper simulated gravity for the people in the ships, the shape has to be a cylinder and it has to spin—sixteen kilometers is what the diameter must be. Then the cylinder must be long enough to provide space, but not so long that the dynamics of spin cause it to wobble or bend—perhaps sixty kilometers long. One part to live in. One part to store fuel. And at the end, a reaction chamber where hydrogen fusion thrusts the ship across the Galaxy."

"Hydrogen bombs," said the boy. "Harry? Why don't the bombs wreck the worldship?"

"It's engineering," said Malibert honestly, "and I don't know the details. Gerry was going to give his paper at the Portsmouth meeting; it was one reason I was going." But, of course, there would never be a British Interplanetary Society meeting in Portsmouth now, ever again.

Elda said uneasily, "It is time for lunch soon. Timmy? Will you eat some soup if I make it?" And did make it, whether the boy promised or not. Elda's husband had worked at Keflavik in the PX, an accountant; unfortunately he had been putting in overtime there when the follow-up missile did what the miss had failed to do, and so Elda had no husband left, not enough even to bury.

Even with the earth's hot water pumped full velocity through the straining pipes it was not warm in the gasthuis. She wrapped the boy in blankets and sat near him while he dutifully spooned up the soup. Lars and Ingar sat holding hands and watching the boy eat. "To hear a voice from another star," Lars said suddenly, "that would have been fine."

"There are no voices," said Ingar bitterly. "Not even ours now. We have the answer to the Fermi paradox."

And when the boy paused in his eating to ask what that was, Harry Malibert explained it as carefully as he could:

"It is named after Enrico Fermi, a scientist. He said, 'We know that there are many billions of stars like our sun. Our sun has planets, therefore it is reasonable to assume that some of the other stars do also. One of our planets has living things on it. Us, for instance, as well as trees and germs and horses. Since there are so many stars, it seems almost certain that some of them, at least, have also living things. People. People as smart as we are—or smarter. People who can build space-ships, or send radio messages to other stars, as we can.' Do you understand so far, Timmy?" The boy nodded, frowning, but—Malibert was delighted to see—kept on eating his soup. "Then, the question Fermi asked was, 'Why haven't some of them come to see us?' "

"Like in the movies," the boy nodded. "The flying saucers."

"All those movies are made-up stories, Timmy. Like Jack and the Beanstalk, or Oz. Perhaps some creatures from space have come to see us sometime, but there is no good evidence that this is so. I feel sure there would be evidence if it had happened. There would have to be. If there were many such visits, ever, then at least one would have dropped the Martian equivalent of a McDonald's Big Mac box, or a used Sirian flash cube, and it would have been found and shown to be from somewhere other than the Earth. None ever has. So there are only three possible answers to Dr. Fermi's question. One, there is no other life. Two, there is, but they want to leave us alone. They don't want to contact us, perhaps because we frighten them with our violence, or for some reason we can't even guess at. And the third reason"—Elda made a quick gesture, but Malibert shook his head—"is that perhaps as soon as any people get smart enough to do all those things that get them into space—when they have all the technology we do—they also have such terrible bombs and weapons that they can't control them any more. So a war breaks out. And they kill themselves off before they are fully grown up."

"Like now," Timothy said, nodding seriously to show he understood. He had finished his soup, but instead of taking the plate away Elda hugged him in her arms and tried not to weep.

The world was totally dark now. There was no day or night, and would not be again for no one could say how long. The rains and snows had stopped. Without sunlight to suck water up out of the oceans there was no moisture left in the atmosphere to fall. Floods had been replaced by freezing droughts. Two meters down the soil of Iceland was steel hard, and the navvies could no longer dig. There was no hope of laying additional pipes. When more heat was needed all that could be done was

to close off buildings and turn off their heating pipes. Elda's
patients now were less likely to be frostbite and more to be the
listlessness of radiation sickness as volunteers raced in and out
of the Reykjavik ruins to find medicine and food. No one was
spared that job. When Elda came back on a snowmobile from a
foraging trip to the Loftleider Hotel she brought back a present
for the boy. Candy bars and postcards from the gift shop; the
candy bars had to be shared, but the postcards were all for
him. "Do you know what these are?" she asked. The cards
showed huge, squat, ugly men and women in the costumes
of a thousand years ago. "They're trolls. We have myths in
Iceland that the trolls lived here. They're still here, Timmy,
or so they say; the mountains are trolls that just got too old
and tired to move any more."

"They're made-up stories, right?" the boy asked seriously,
and did not grin until she assured him they were. Then he made
a joke. "I guess the trolls won," he said.

"Ach, Timmy!" Elda was shocked. But at least the boy was
capable of joking, she told herself, and even graveyard humor
was better than none. Life had become a little easier for her
with the new patients—easier because for the radiation-sick
there was very little that could be done—and she bestirred
herself to think of ways to entertain the boy.

And found a wonderful one.

Since fuel was precious there were no excursions to see the
sights of Iceland-under-the-ice. There was no way to see them
anyway in the eternal dark. But when a hospital chopper was
called up to travel empty to Stokksnes on the eastern shore
to bring back a child with a broken back, she begged space
for Malibert and Timmy. Elda's own ride was automatic, as
duty nurse for the wounded child. "An avalanche crushed
his house," she explained. "It is right under the mountains,
Stokksnes, and landing there will be a little tricky, I think.
But we can come in from the sea and make it safe. At least in
the landing lights of the helicopter something can be seen."

They were luckier than that. There was more light. Nothing
came through the clouds, where the billions of particles that
had once been Elda's husband added to the trillions of trillions
that had been Detroit and Marseilles and Shanghai to shut out

the sky. But in the clouds and under them were snakes and sheets of dim color, sprays of dull red, fans of pale green. The aurora borealis did not give much light. But there was no other light at all except for the faint glow from the pilot's instrument panel. As their eyes widened they could see the dark shapes of the Vatnajökull slipping by below them. "*Big* trolls," cried the boy happily, and Elda smiled too as she hugged him.

The pilot did as Elda had predicted, down the slopes of the eastern range, out over the sea, and cautiously back in to the little fishing village. As they landed, red-tipped flashlights guiding them, the copter's landing lights picked out a white lump, vaguely saucer-shaped. "Radar dish," said Malibert to the boy, pointing.

Timmy pressed his nose to the freezing window. "Is it one of them, Daddy Harry? The things that could talk to the stars?"

The pilot answered: "Ach, no, Timmy—military, it is." And Malibert said:

"They wouldn't put one of those here, Timothy. It's too far north. You wanted a place for a big radio telescope that could search the whole sky, not just the little piece of it you can see from Iceland."

And while they helped slide the stretcher with the broken child into the helicopter, gently, kindly as they could be, Malibert was thinking about those places, Arecibo and Woomara and Socorro and all the others. Every one of them was now dead and certainly broken with a weight of ice and shredded by the mean winds. Crushed, rusted, washed away, all those eyes on space were blinded now; and the thought saddened Harry Malibert, but not for long. More gladdening than anything sad was the fact that, for the first time, Timothy had called him "Daddy."

In one ending to the story, when at last the sun came back it was too late. Iceland had been the last place where human beings survived, and Iceland had finally starved. There was nothing alive anywhere on Earth that spoke, or invented machines, or read books. Fermi's terrible third answer was the right one after all.

But there exists another ending. In this one the sun came back in time. Perhaps it was just barely in time, but the food had not yet run out when daylight brought the first touches of green in some parts of the world, and plants began to grow again from frozen or hoarded seed. In this ending Timothy lived to grow up. When he was old enough, and after Malibert and Elda had got around to marrying, he married one of their daughters. And of their descendants—two generations or a dozen generations later—one was alive on that day when Fermi's paradox became a quaintly amusing old worry, as irrelevant and comical as a fifteenth-century mariner's fear of falling off the edge of the flat Earth. On that day the skies spoke, and those who lived in them came to call.

Perhaps that is the true ending of the story, and in it the human race chose not to squabble and struggle within itself, and so extinguish itself finally into the dark. In this ending human beings survived, and saved all the science and beauty of life, and greeted their star-born visitors with joy. . . .

But that is in fact what did happen!

At least, one would like to think so.

DYING IN HULL

D. Alexander Smith

*"Dying in Hull" was purchased by Gardner Dozois,
and appeared in the November 1988 issue of IAsfm,
with a beautiful interior illustration by Janet Aulisio.
It is Smith's only sale to IAsfm to date, although
we are keeping hard after him for more. Amazingly
enough, in fact, since it was one of the most eloquent,
bittersweet, and moving stories of the year, it was
also his first short story sale . . . proving, I guess, that
some people start at the top. It is also a story that all
too many of us may find ourselves living through in
years to come, if the trend toward global warming is
not reversed. . . .*

*D. Alexander Smith lives in Cambridge, Mas-
sachusetts, not far from the setting of "Dying in
Hull," and is currently working as co-editor on a
shared-world anthology of Future Boston stories.
His novels include Marathon, Rendezvous, and, most
recently, Homecoming.*

In the wee hours of February 12, 2004, Ethel Goodwin Cobb
clumped down the oak staircase to check the water level in her

dining room. She always checked her floor when the sea was lowest, no matter whether ebb tide came during the day or, as this time, in the dark of night.

Moonlight from the window reflected on the empty hard-wood floor, a pale milky rhombus. A thin glistening sheen of still water lay over the wood, bright and smooth like mir-ror glass.

Blinking sleepily, Ethel sat her chunky body on the next-to-bottom step and leaned forward to press her big square thumb down into the rectangular puddle. She felt the moisture and withdrew her now-wet hand. Water slid in to cover the briefly-bare spot, and in seconds, the surface was motionless and perfect, her mark gone.

She yawned and shook herself like a disgruntled dog.

Gunfire in the harbor had disturbed her rest; she had slept fitfully until the alarm had gone off. Well, she was awake now. Might as well start the day.

The rose-pattern wallpaper was rippled, discolored with many horizontal lines from rising high water marks. It was crusty at eye level but sodden and peeling where it met the floorboards. Above the waterline, Ethel had filled her dining room with photographs of the town of Hull—houses, streets, beaches, the rollercoaster at Paragon Park—and the people who had lived there. Pictures of the past, left behind in empty houses by those who had fled and forgotten.

Ethel carefully touched the floor again, licking her thumb afterwards to taste the brine. "Wet," she muttered. "No doubt about it." For a moment she hung her head, shoulders sagging, then slapped her palms against the tops of her knees. "That's that." She rose slowly and marched back upstairs to dress.

Cold air drafts whiffled through the loose window frames as she quickly donned her checked shirt, denim overalls, and wool socks. The sky outside was dark gray, with just a hint of dawn. Her bedroom walls were adorned with more photo-graphs like those downstairs. As the water rose with the pass-ing months and years, she periodically had to rearrange things, bringing pictures up from below and finding space in the bathroom, on the stairway, or in her makeshift second-floor kitchen.

Crossing to the white wooden mantelpiece, she hefted the letter. Ethel read what she had written, scowling at her spiky penmanship, then folded the paper twice, scoring the creases with her fingernail. She sealed it in an envelope, licked the stamp and affixed it with a thump. Returning to the bed, Ethel stuck the letter in her shirt pocket and pulled on her knee-high wellingtons.

By the time she descended again to the first floor, the tide had risen to cover the bottom step. Ethel waded over to her front door and put on her yellow slicker and her father's oilskin sou'wester, turning up the hat's front brim.

The door stuck, expanded by the moisture. She wrenched it open and stepped out, resolving to plane it again when she returned. Closing the door behind her, she snapped its cheap padlock shut.

Queequeg floated high and dry, tethered to the porch by lines from his bow and stern. Ethel unwrapped the olive-green tarpaulin from his motor and captain's console. When she boarded her boat, the white Boston whaler rocked briefly, settling deeper into the water that filled K Street. After checking the outboard's propeller to verify that no debris had fouled its blades, Ethel pushed *Queequeg*'s motor back to vertical, untied his painters, and poled away from her house.

She turned the ignition and the big ninety-horse Evinrude roared to life, churning water and smoke. Blowing on her hands to warm them, she eased *Queequeg*'s throttle forward and burbled east down K to the ruins of Beach Avenue.

Dawn burnished the horizon, illuminating the pewter-gray scattered clouds. Submerged K Street was a silver arrow that sparkled with a thousand moving diamonds. The air was bright with cold, tangy with the scents of kelp and mussels, the normally rough winter ocean calm now that last night's nor'easter had passed.

She stood at the tiller sniffing the breeze, her stocky feet planted wide against the possibility of *Queequeg* rolling with an ocean swell, her hands relaxed on the wheel. They headed north past a line of houses on their left, Ethel's eyes darting like a general inspecting the wounded after battle.

As the town of Hull sank, its houses had fallen to the Atlantic, singly or in whole streets. These windward oceanfronts, unshielded from the open sea, were the first to go. Black asphalt shingles had been torn from their roofs and walls by many storms. Porches sagged or collapsed entirely. Broken windows and doors were covered with Cambodian territorial chop signs of the Ngor, Pran, and Kim waterkid gangs. Some homes had been burned out, the soot rising from their empty windowframes like the petals of black flowers.

A girl's rusted blue motor scooter leaned against the front stairs of 172 Beach. Barnacles grew on its handlebars. Mary Donovan and her parents had lived here, Ethel remembered, before she moved to downtown Boston and became an accountant. A good student who had earned one of Ethel's few A-pluses, Mary had ridden that scooter to high school every day, even in the snow, until the water had made riding impossible.

Beach Avenue had been vacant from end to end for years. Still, Ethel always began her day here. It was a reminder and a warning. Her tough brown eyes squinted grimly as the whaler chugged in the quiet, chill day.

"I could have told you folks," Ethel addressed the ghosts of the departed owners. "You don't stop the sea."

Sniffling—cold air made her nose run—she turned down P Street. For three hundred years her ancestors had skippered their small open boats into Hull's rocky coastal inlets, its soft marshy shallows, to harvest the sea. In the skeleton of a town, Ethel Cobb, the last in her family, lived on the ocean's bounty—even if it meant scavenging deserted homes.

Like 16 P just ahead. She throttled back and approached cautiously.

16 P's front door was open, all its lights out. The Cruzes have left, Ethel thought with regret. The last family on P Street. Gone.

Cautiously, she circled the building once to verify that no other combers were inside.

Decades of salt winds had silvered its cedar shingles. Foundation cracks rose like ivy vines up the sides of its cement half-basement. Sprung gutters hung loose like dangled fishing rods. She killed the steel-blue Evinrude and drifted silently toward the two-story frame house.

Luisa Cruz had been born in 16 P, Ethel remembered, in the middle of the Blizzard of '78, when Hull had been cut off from the mainland. A daydreamer, Luisa had sat in the fourth row and drawn deft caricatures of rock stars all over her essay questions.

So the Cruz family had moved, Ethel thought sadly. Another one gone. Were any left?

She looped *Queequeg*'s painter over the porch banister and splashed up 16 P's steps, towing a child's oversize sailboat behind her. The front door had rusted open and Ethel went inside.

Empty soda and beer squeezebottles floated in the foyer, and there was a vaguely disturbing smell. Ethel slogged through soggy newspapers to the kitchen. Maria Cruz had made tea in this kitchen, she recalled, while they had talked about Luisa's chances of getting into Brandeis.

An ancient refrigerator stood in a foot and a half of water. She dragged the door open with a wet creak. Nothing.

The pantry beyond yielded a box of moist taco shells and three cans of tomato paste. Ethel checked the expiration dates, nodded, and tossed them into her makeshift barrow.

What little furniture remained in the living room was rotten and mildewed. The bedroom mattress was green-furred and stank. The bureau's mahogany veneer had curled away from the expanding maple underneath. When Ethel leaned her arm on the dresser, a lion's-claw foot broke. It collapsed slowly into the sawdust-flecked water like an expiring walrus.

Out fell a discolored Polaroid snapshot: Luisa and her brother in graduation cap and gown. I was so proud of her I could have burst, Ethel remembered. Drying the photo carefully, she slipped it into her breast pocket.

On an adjacent high shelf, built into the wall above the attached headboard, were half a dozen paperback books, spines frayed and twisted, their covers scalped. Luisa had been a good reader, a child who wanted to learn so much it had radiated from her like heat.

Pleased, Ethel took them all.

In the bathroom, she found a mirror embossed with the Budweiser logo. With her elbow, Ethel cleaned the glass. The round wrinkled face that grinned back at her had fueled rumors that she had been a marine. The mirror would probably fetch a few dollars at the flea market, maybe more to a memorabilia collector.

Only the front bedroom left to comb, she thought. Good combing. Thank you, Cruz family.

A vulture, Joan Gordon had called her once. "You're just a vulture, eating decay," her friend had said, with the certainty of a mainlander.

"I'm a Cobb," Ethel had answered thickly, gripping the phone. "We live on the sea. My grandfather Daniel Goodwin was lobstering when he was nine."

"What you're doing isn't fishing. It's theft. Just like the waterkids."

"It's *not* like the kids!" Ethel had shouted.

"It's *stealing*," Joan had challenged her.

"No! Just taking what the sea gives. Housecombing is like lobstering." She had clung to her own words for reassurance.

"What you take belongs to other people," her friend had said vehemently.

"Not after they leave," Ethel shot back. "Then it's the ocean's."

Joan switched tacks. "It's dangerous to live in Hull."

"Those folks that left didn't have to go. I'm staying where my roots are."

"Your roots are *underwater*, Ethel!" Joan entreated. "Your town is disappearing."

"It is not," Ethel insisted. "Don't say that."

"Come live in our building. We have a community here."

"Bunch of old folks. Don't want to live with old folks."

"Plenty of people here younger than you."

"Living in a tower's not for me. Closed in, a prisoner. Afraid to go out. Wouldn't like it."

"How do you know? You've never visited me."

"Anyhow, I can't afford it."

She seldom spoke with Joan now. The subject had worn her feelings raw.

"Damn it, Joan," she said in 16 P's hallway, "why did you have to leave?"

The front bedroom door was ajar in a foot and a half of water. She pushed and heard it butt against something. Slowly she craned her neck around.

The two oriental corpses floated on their faces, backs arched, arms and legs hanging down into brown water swirled with red. Ethel gagged at the stench. The youths' long black hair waved like seaweed, their shoulders rocking limply. Catfish and eels nibbled on waving tendrils of human skin and guts.

Retching, Ethel grabbed one of the boys under his armpit and hauled him over onto his back. The bodies had been gutted, bullets gouged out of their chests, leaving no evidence. Periwinkle snails crawled in bloody sockets where the killers had cut out their victims' eyes and sliced off their lips. Each youth's left hand had been amputated. Ethel searched the water until she found one, a bloated white starfish with a Pran gang tattoo on its palm.

She remembered last night's gunshots in Hull Bay. You did not deserve this, she thought to the ruined face, letting it slip back into the water. No one deserved this, not even waterkids.

Of course she knew who did it. Everyone knew who executed waterkids. That was the point. The men on Hog Island *wanted* you to know. They wanted Hull to themselves. The bodies were reminders. And incentive.

In the distance she heard the chatter of several approaching engines. More Cambodian waterkids coming. Hastily she wiped vomit from her mouth and rushed out of the house.

Jumping into the whaler, she untied *Queequeg*'s painter and turned his key, shoving the throttle down hard as his engine caught. But not quickly enough. Before she could get away, four dark gray whalers surrounded her, Pran gang chop signs airbrushed beautifully onto their fiberglass gunwales.

"Hey, grandma." Their leader stood cockily in the stern of his boat while his helmsman grinned. He wore immaculate brown leather pants and a World War II flight jacket, unmarked by spray or moisture. "What's your hurry? Seen a ghost?"

Queequeg rocked slightly as the waves from their sudden arrival washed underneath him. "Yes," Ethel answered.

"Find anything valuable?"

"Nothing you'd want." Unconsciously she touched her breast pocket. "Nothing you can fence."

"Really? Let's see." His boat drifted up against hers and he leaped across into her stern, landing on sure sea legs. "You keep your stuff here?" he scornfully pointed at the plastic sailboat, mugging for his guffawing friends. He kicked it over with his boot and rummaged around among the floorboards. "Hey, Wayne! Huang! We got any use for taco shells?" He held them aloft.

"No, man," they answered gleefully.

"All right, grandma, guess we'll have to look elsewhere." He dropped the box and turned. As she started to relax, he wheeled. "What's in your pocket?"

"I beg your pardon?"

"In your pocket," he snapped.

"A letter and a photograph," she said steadily.

"A naked man, maybe?" the Pran leader chortled. "Let's see it." She opened her sou'wester and handed the picture to him. Waving it like a small fan, he stepped back into his own boat. "Worthless." He pointed it at her like a prod. "Pran gang combs *first*, grandma. Understand? Otherwise the next time I won't just tip over your toy boat. You understand?" He tossed the photo over his shoulder.

Ethel watched it flutter down onto the water, and nodded. "I understand."

He gestured and they started their engines, moving down P Street toward the empty house.

Ethel debated with herself. Keeping silent was too risky— they could always find her later. "Check the front bedroom," she called after them.

He stopped the engine and swung back. "What?" he asked ominously.

"Check the front bedroom. Your two missing friends are there."

The Cambodian teenager's broad face whitened. "Dead?"

She nodded mutely.

"Those bastards," he said softly.

"I'm sorry." She clasped her hands before her.

"*Sorry?*" he shrieked in misery, the hurt child suddenly breaking through his tough facade. "What do you know about sorry?" Their boats leapt away. "What do *you* know about sorry?"

As the sounds of their engines receded, Ethel slowly let out her breath. Hands trembling, she engaged *Queequeg*'s throttle and slowly circled. Sure enough, the snapshot was suspended about three feet below the surface. Ethel lifted her gaffing net and dragged it by the spot, scooping up the picture. The water had curled it and she dried it on her thigh, then returned it to her pocket.

Glancing back at the boats now moored at 16 P, she quickly cut in the whaler's engine with a roar, carving a double white plume behind her.

For the rest of the morning Ethel and *Queequeg* combed the alphabet streets on Hull's submerged flatlands. Nearly all of these houses had long since been abandoned, and she neither stopped nor slowed. Frequently she twisted to check behind her, but there was no sign of the waterkids.

By eleven she had finished W, X, and Y, tiny alleyways that butted against Allerton Hill. Trees at its base were gray and leafless, drowned by the rising seawater. Terry Flaherty had lived on W, she remembered. A short chubby boy with big eyes and a giggle that never stopped, he was someplace in Connecticut now, selling mutual funds. Probably forgotten all the eleventh-grade American history she'd taught him.

As she passed Allerton Point, she looked across the harbor to glass-and-steel Boston. The downtown folks were talking about building walls to hold back the sea that rose as the city sank, but with no money, Hull literally could not afford to save itself. Every storm took more houses, washing out the ground underneath so they fell like sandcastles.

Ethel's house at 22 K was on the far leeward side, as safe as you could be on the flatland, but even it had suffered damage and was endangered.

Town government was disintegrating. People no longer paid property taxes, no longer voted. Nobody ran for selectman, nobody cared. For protection, folks relied on themselves or bought it from Hog Island or the Cambodian waterkids. At night, the long black peterborough boats moved sleekly in the harbor, navigating by infrared. Ethel stayed inside then.

Most of Hull High School was submerged, the brick portico columns standing like piers in the shallow water. The football field was a mudflat.

Forty-one years of history students, all gone, all memories.

When she was young, her students had sniggered that Ethel was a dyke. As she aged, firmly single and unromantic, they had claimed she was a transsexual wrestler. When she reached fifty, they had started saying she was eccentric. At sixty, they had called her crazy.

The jibes always hurt, though she concealed it. After each year was over, fortunately, all she could remember were the names and faces of those whose lives she had affected.

Standing at *Queequeg*'s bow, she left a long scimitar of foam as she circled the buildings. The old school was disappearing, windows shattered, corridors full of stagnant water. She had taken *Queequeg* inside once before to her old classroom, but was eventually driven out by the reek of decomposing flesh from a cat that had been trapped inside and starved.

Ethel closed her eyes, hearing once again the clatter of the period bell, the clamor as kids ran through the corridors, talking at the top of their lungs. Mothers whom she taught had sent their daughters to Hull High School. In her last few years, she had even taught a few granddaughters of former students. Made you proud.

The high school was shut down, dark, and noiseless. Seagulls perched on its roof were her only companions.

To break her mood, she swung onto the open sea and opened the throttle for the five-mile run to South Boston.

The water, hard as a rock this morning, pounded into her calves and knees as the Boston whaler's flat bottom washboarded across the harbor. *Queequeg* kicked up spray over his teak and chrome bow as she slalomed among dayglo styrofoam lobster buoys, tasting the salt spume on her lips.

Behind and above her, a cawing flock of gulls followed, braiding the air. *Queequeg*'s wake pushed small fish close to the surface, under the sharp eyes of the waiting gray and white birds. One after another, the gulls swooped like a line of fighter aircraft. Their flapping wings skimming the waves, they dipped their beaks just enough to catch a fish, then soared back into line.

Hunting and feeding, they escorted her across the harbor until she slowed and docked at the pier.

"Hey, Jerry," Ethel said when she entered the store. "Got a letter for you." She unzipped her slicker and pulled it out. "Mail it for me?"

The storekeeper squinted at the address. "Joan Gordon? Doesn't she live in that senior citizen community in Arlington?"

"Old folks home, you mean."

"Whatever." He suppressed a smile. "You could call her."

"Got no phone."

"No, from here."

"Rather write."

"Okay. What are you writing about?"

Ethel shook her head. "None of your beeswax."

"All right," he laughed, "we've been friends too long for me to complain. How you doing?"

"I get by."

He leaned on the counter. "I worry about you."

"Oh, don't start."

"Sorry." He turned away and began rearranging cans.

"I'm okay," she answered, touched as always.

"Hull gets worse every day." He looked at her over his shoulder. "I see the news."

"Nonsense," Ethel replied with bravado, dismissing his fears with a wave of her hand. "Journalists always exaggerate. Besides, one day *Boston* will be underwater too, same as us."

"I know." Jerry sighed. "I go down to the bathhouse every Sunday for my swim. The sea's always higher. Maybe we should move away, like Joan did. Chicago or Dallas. Somewhere. Anywhere with no ocean."

She laughed. "What would I do in Dallas, Jerry? How would I live?"

"You could teach school. You've taught me more right here in this store than all the history books I ever read."

"Thanks, Jerry. But I'm sixty-eight years old. No one would hire me."

He was quiet. "Then I'd take care of you," he said finally, kneading his hands.

She looked through the window at the pier, where *Queequeg* bobbed on the waves. "Couldn't do it, Jerry," she said. It was hard to find breath. "Too old to move."

"Yeah. Sure." He wiped his forehead and cleared his throat. "Got your usual all set." He put two orange plastic bags on the counter.

"Did my check come through?" Ethel looked suspicious. "Can't take your credit."

"Of course it did. It always comes through. It's electronic."

She peered inside, shifting cans and boxes. "All right, where is it?"

He scowled and rubbed his balding head. "Hell, you shouldn't eat that stuff. Rots your teeth and wrecks your digestion and I don't *know* what."

"I want my two-pound box of Whitman's coconut, dammit."

"Ethel, you're carrying too much weight. It'll strain your heart."

"Been eating candy all my life, and it hasn't hurt me yet. Wish you'd stop trying to dictate my diet."

"Okay, okay." He sighed and threw up his hands, then pulled down the embossed yellow box. "No charge." He held it out.

"Can't accept your charity, Jerry. You know that."

"That's not it." He was hurt and offended. "It's my way of saying I'm sorry I tried to keep it away from you." He gestured with the box. "Please?"

Ethel took the chocolates. "Thank you, Jerry," she replied somberly, laying her right hand flat on the cover. "You've been a good friend."

"Don't talk like that!" the grocer said in exasperation. "Every time you come in here, you sound like you got one foot in the grave. It's not wholesome."

"Was different this morning." Ethel sat down, the candy held tightly in her lap. Her voice was faint, distant. "This morning I *saw* it. Saw my future in the water. Sooner or later, I'm going to pass away. No sense denying that." She kicked her right foot aimlessly. "Maybe I should have accepted when you proposed."

"Still could," he said, wistful. "But you won't."

"No." She shook her head just a bit.

"Stubborn."

"Not stubborn." She was gentle. "Wouldn't be fair. You can't live in Hull. You've said so before."

"Ethel." Jerry wiped his hands on his apron. "I read the paper. Houses are falling into the ocean or burning down. Dangerous evil kids are running loose."

"I can handle the waterkids," she said defiantly.

"No, you *can't*," he insisted. "Drugs and crime and I don't *know* what. Why won't you leave?"

"It's my home," Ethel said in a troubled voice. "My family. Friends." She waved her hands. "My world. What I know."

Jerry rubbed his head again. "That world isn't *there* any more. The people you knew—they're all gone. It's past. Over."

"Got no place to go," she muttered, biting her thumbnail. "Cobbs and Goodwins have lived in Hull since colonial times. That's something to preserve. Elijah Goodwin was a merchant captain. Sailed to China in 1820. Put flowers on his grave every Sunday noon after church. Rain or shine or Cambodian kids. Put flowers on all the Cobbs and Goodwins on Telegraph Hill. Telegraph's an island now, but they will still be in that ground when all the flatland has gone under. Somebody has to remember them."

"Cripes, don't be so morbid." He came around behind her, put his arm around her shoulder and rubbed it.

"I suppose." She leaned her head in the crook of his elbow.

Cars and buses passed in the street outside, sunlight reflecting off their windshields. He patted her shoulder.

She covered his hand with hers. "Thanks, Jerry. You're a good man."

After a moment, she rose and kissed his cheek, then hefted the bags, one to an arm. "Well, that's that," she called with returning jauntiness. "See you next Friday."

Lost in memories, she let *Queequeg* take his return trip more slowly. Islands in the harbor were covered with trees and shrubs, reminding her of great submergèd whales. When she neared Hog Island, at the entrance to Hull Bay, she kept a respectful distance. The Meagher boys had lived there—Dennis, Douglas, Dana, Donald, and Dapper. Their mother had always shouted for them in the order of their birth. Five rambunctious Boston-Irish hellions in seven years, usually with a black eye or a skinned knee.

No families lived on Hog now. Castellated gray buildings had grown upward from the old Army fortress underneath. Thieves and smugglers and murderers lived in them, men who drove deep-keeled power yachts without finesse, like machetes through a forest.

Tough sentries carrying binoculars stood lookout as she passed, scanning the horizon like big-eyed insects, their rifles out of sight. Ethel shivered. Delinquent waterkids she could evade, but the organized evil on Hog was shrewd and ruthless.

The fish feeding on that poor child's face, Ethel thought. The people who still lived on Hull. The men on Hog. The Cambodian kids. One way or another, all took their livelihoods from the remains of a town whose time was past. Eventually they would extract Hull's last dollar, and they would all leave. And, in time, the rising sea would engulf everything.

K Street was falling into shadow when she returned. Her house needed a coat of paint, but would last long enough without one, she thought wryly. The dark-green first-floor shutters were closed and nailed shut as a precaution, but her light was still burning in 22 K's bedroom window. Always leave a light on, so everyone knows you're still on guard.

A gang symbol was sprayed on her front door.

Pran chop, she realized with a sick feeling in her gut, remembering the morning's encounter.

Her padlock was untouched, though the waterkids could have easily forced it.

The chop was a message: this is a Pran house.

Perhaps their form of thanks.

Safely inside, Ethel took off her sou'wester and slicker, shook the wet salt spray off them, and hung them on the pegs.

She unloaded her groceries and stacked her day's combings. Tomorrow she would sell them in the Quincy flea market.

All but the photo. Ethel took it from her pocket and smiled at Luisa's young face. She found a spot on the wall barely larger enough and tacked it up, stepping back to admire her work.

As the sun set on the golden bay, she made supper: soup, salad, and cheese sandwiches that she grilled on the woodburning stove she had installed on the second floor. Seagulls wheeled over the marsh flats, snatching clams in their beaks. Rising high over the coastline, the birds dropped their prey to smash open on the wet shoreline rocks. Then the gulls landed and ate the helpless, exposed animal inside the broken shell.

When she was done, Ethel went onto the upper porch and put down her bowl and plate. The birds converged, jostling for the last scraps, hungry and intense, like schoolchildren in gray and white uniforms.

Sitting in her rocking chair, her box of Whitman's coconut firmly on her stomach, Ethel thought about the letter she had mailed that morning.

> Today the ocean took my ground floor. One day it will take my house. It's going to reclaim South Boston and Dorchester and Back Bay. Folks will go on denying it like I've tried to, but it won't stop until it's through with all of us.
>
> Enclosed is my will. Had a Cohasset lawyer write it up so it's legal. You get everything. You don't have to comb for it, Joan. It's yours.
>
> Except *Queequeg*. The boat goes to Jerry. He'll never use it, but he'll care for it, and it's no use to you in your tower.
>
> After I'm gone, burn the place down. With me in it. At high tide so the fire won't spread. Nobody will bother you. Nobody else lives around here anyway. No one else has lived here for years.
>
> 22 K is a Cobb house. Always been a Cobb house. No squatters here. Give it all to the sea.

But take the pictures first. Put them on your walls. Remember me. Remember me.

Should have left years ago. Can't now.

Wish you'd stayed, Joan. Miss you.

Ethel

The houses around her were black hulks, silent like trees. The crescent moon rose, silvering the ocean. Ethel heard the gulls call to one another, smelled the sea as it licked the beach. In the distance, boats moved on the bay, dots of green and red light, thin black lines of wake.

"God, I love it here," she said suddenly, full of contentment.

ON CANNON BEACH

Marta Randall

"On Cannon Beach" was purchased by Shawna McCarthy, and appeared in the April 1984 issue of IAsfm, *with an illustration by Janet Aulisio. Randall is not prolific at shorter lengths, and has only made several sales to the magazine in the last decade— but we keep hoping to see more by her. The little story that follows is a perfect evocation of place and mood, packing a subtle but powerful punch, as a woman travels to the relentlessly progressing edge of the glacial Ice, to bid farewell to the world she knew, which is about to disappear forever. . . .*

Born in Mexico City, Marta Randall now lives with her family in the San Francisco Bay Area. She served two terms as President of the Science Fiction Writers of America, and was the editor, with Robert Silverberg, of the anthologies New Dimensions 11 *and* New Dimensions 12. *Her many novels include* Islands, A City in the North, Journey, Dangerous Games, The Sword of Winter, *and* Those Who Favor Fire.

Toleman found me slumped near my equipment, said he couldn't afford to lose me, too, and gave me a week's leave. Typical of him; a week was not long enough to catch a transport out of the Rainier Ice Station and back again, and certainly not long enough to go anywhere on foot—he wanted me close by, where his generosity could be easily interrupted by the unfortunate press of work. So sorry, my dear. Unavoidable. Here's your cryometer—go.

Of the original fourteen on the crew, only seven of us remained and we knew Toleman well enough to anticipate his acts of generosity and work around them. That night Marti accidentally misplaced the keys to Toleman's LandCat, Jerry accidentally forgot to lock the transport pool door, and Gretch accidentally left two full cans of gas strapped in place. I took off well before dawn. A week of being short-handed would cool Toleman's anger at the theft—it always did.

The drive south was depressing. Small, sad towns littered the sides of the collapsing highway, their empty buildings and icy streets interrupting blasted brown fields or the skeletons of forests. Neither roads nor habitations had been built to withstand great cold, and the ice had come quickly; increasing cloudiness had given us progressively colder summers, until one hard winter laid down the first ice, and the next cool summer had not melted the pack. A second hard winter deflected more of the sun's heat; the next summer the nascent glaciers bounced even more sunlight back to space. The pattern established itself: a colder winter, a colder summer, and now glaciers marched down the sides of mountains, linking one to the other and freezing the northern latitudes. For all our observing and metering and evacuating, this sudden, speedy ice age was upon us and no one, least of all the beleaguered scientists, could tell when, or if, it would end. Hard winters were now a foregone conclusion; cold destroyed the work of hands and by next January this land, too, would be under the ice.

I slept that night in a schoolhouse amid the detritus of evacuation. "MY GREAT-GRANDFATHER BUILT THIS TOWN" read a spray-painted message on the wooden door. I put my fingertips to the words. Salvage crews had been through the area already, taking whatever they found necessary and important and removing it to the increasingly crowded south. But who would save the real memories, the important, mundane trivia of the world before the ice? Not me. My job was to monitor the glaciers, measure the progress of the hungry ice, observe the rubble of broken homes and broken lives swept tidily before the glaciers' skirts. I touched the faded words again, wriggled into my down bag, and tried to sleep.

I crossed into Oregon the next day, on highways pitted and buckled by the cold, and on impulse skirted the dead city of Portland and drove west. Glaciers surrounded the state, the Cascades were impassable, but the ocean's warmth should keep the coast bearable; pines still survived where oak and manzanita once flourished. Evacuation had been more recent and more hasty here, but I expected no other people, and met none.

Glacial streams had washed out the last three miles of road. I switched tires for treads and bumped down the sides of the coast range. The sky was high and white with fog, the road north blocked by fallen trees and bridges. I turned south, looking for a place to stay.

The sign said "Cannon Beach" and two bedraggled, stubborn manzanita grew beside it. I drove toward the sea.

Sagging homes lined the road, roofs caved in by last year's snow or the fall of dead trees. Wind gusted through broken windows along the main street; a door creaked and slammed and creaked again. Cold had killed the ferns, hollyhocks, azaleas, and rhododendrons. Like much of the animal life, these plants would not be replaced by their colder-climate counterparts; the speed of glaciation prevented it. Road and town ended together where a concrete culvert had succumbed to the cold and the torrents of the spring melt, taking the pavement with it. I backed the LandCat, found a side street to the beach, and drove along the tide line. A huge, beehive-shaped rock loomed over the surf. The town looked better from here, less obviously dead. Waves fell against the sand, gray and white beneath a gray sky; I skirted piles of driftwood and the wrack of storms.

Toward evening I selected a house beside one of the clear, non-glacial streams feeding into the ocean; the top story had collapsed but the beach level seemed wind-tight and secure. A huge iron stove stood inside the door, but I didn't know if the flue and chimney were intact and was too tired to check it out. I built a driftwood fire on the beach, ate of the supplies Joshua had accidentally left in the LandCat, staggered back inside and into my sleeping bag, and fell asleep to the noise of surf.

I woke to the smell of frying fish and a high, cracked voice saying, "About time you wake up. Only breakfast I serve, nothing else, just bed and breakfast and breakfast is at dawn. I have too much to do to wait on my people. That your car?"

Without moving, I opened my eyes. A small, gaunt figure bent to chuck more driftwood into the iron stove's firebox. It slammed the door closed and turned to look at me, hands on hips. I blinked, unable to make out the face.

"Been a long time," the figure said. "But I still know what to do. I rent houses here for fifty year, sixty, all types. You don't have dog, do you? I don't mind dogs, but some of my people don't like them, I try to make everybody happy, but . . ." The figure turned back to the stove and I sat up slowly.

"You're not supposed to be here," I said stupidly. The smell of fish made my mouth water.

"Sixty year, seventy, *I'm* not going to leave. Ice Age, humph." The figure pushed a skillet off the burner, flapped most of the sand from a rickety table, and, using both hands, hoisted the skillet from stove to table. "There. No napkin, too busy to all the time wash napkin. I'm Mrs. Vrach, you know that. Who are you?"

"Sandra," I said, pulling my sweater over my head. "Sandra Price."

"Sit," Mrs. Vrach said. "Eat. I clean table soon. You say you have dog?"

We sat on uneven chairs across the table from each other, while Mrs. Vrach ate and talked, and I ate and stared. The fish came from a pool upstream, she had caught them herself. She'd hidden in the woods when the Evac crews came through, she said proudly. Her children and grandchildren had long since gone south. She showed me snapshots indecipherable with age;

she said she had two great-grandchildren but she'd never seen photographs of them. She had reached that androgynous age where the sexes begin to merge: whiskers peppered her chin, and her yellow-white hair was sparse, for all that her eyes and voice were sharp. When the fish had been reduced to bones I licked my fingers clean while Mrs. Vrach hefted the skillet. Her arms shook, but she wouldn't let me near it.

"Part of service," she said. "I treat my people okay." But she didn't object when I insisted on washing the dishes, although she watched me carefully and swooped down once to flick a sliver of fish from the skillet.

I spent the day, and the next, following Mrs. Vrach around the deserted ruins of Cannon Beach, trying to determine just how crazy she was and expostulating on the benefits of moving south. She ignored my arguments; she had been here for sixty years, she said firmly, and wasn't going to leave. "Wars," she told me, shaking her head. "Famine. Political craziness. I, Mrs. Vrach, I live through all. Now to leave my home, and for what? A little cold? Humph." I couldn't convince her that in a year or two her home would be under a glacier, and eventually I gave up.

She knew all the houses, all the stores, and precisely what each one contained. We shopped together through the ruins of the village; Mrs. Vrach carefully counted out shells and agates in payment and I carried her purchases, adding them to the rag-tag pile she kept near the stove. That evening we went to check her fish traps, Mrs. Vrach scurrying before me. As we returned along the broken road, she called greetings to empty doorways, held animated conversations with broken windows, reprimanded a nonexistent dog in the collapse of what had been a garden. I was used to the logic of the ice and this old woman confused me, until I floundered between the reality of my world and the reality of hers. That evening I talked again of the life to the south, the warm weather, the food; she stopped in the midst of a conversation with her favorite grandson and stared at me.

"No," she said flatly. "Here I have come, after long time, many trials. Here I stay." She gathered her dilapidated quilt about her shoulders and went outside. I lay in my sleeping bag, thinking about abduction, while tears ran down my nose.

I woke well past dawn. The room was empty and no fish sizzled on the stove; the iron barely retained the heat of last night's fire. I dressed hastily and ran onto the beach, still zipping my parka, shouting her name. A figure stood far down the beach near the great triangular rock. I ran toward her, cursing the sand underfoot.

When I reached her, she had settled again in the lee of a driftwood pile. I stopped, gasping for air, while she gestured toward the sea.

"That," she said. "It is what?"

I squinted through the fog, barely making out a darker mass looming off the northern point, beyond the rock with the ruined lighthouse. I rubbed my eyes and looked again. Mrs. Vrach was uncharacteristically silent.

"An iceberg," I said finally. "It's an iceberg."

"Ah." She put her hands on her knees. "I watch it get bigger, it comes close. It is far away, yes?"

"Yes."

"It come closer?"

"No. The ice will come down from the mountains."

She nodded. "Then it is time to go."

But she made no gesture toward leaving, even after I had run back to the house, thrown her possessions and mine into the LandCat, and driven it down the beach to her. I pleaded, argued, cajoled, shouted, and threatened until, exhausted, I sat at her feet. She took my hand and pressed it between her twisted fingers. She started to talk, then: to me, her grandchildren, her husband, her friends. She told folk stories and personal stories, she sang in a language I didn't know. Toward dusk I built a fire and the talking lessened, then stopped. I looked at her, but she patted my hair and pulled my head against her knee. Eventually I slept.

I woke a few hours later. The fire was a bed of sullen embers and Mrs. Vrach, relaxed in the arms of the driftwood, faced the ocean with her eyes open and a tiny, wrinkled smile on her lips. I wanted to close her eyes, I wanted to carry her back to her house, I wanted to bury her far from the threat of the ice, but in the end I did none of these things. Instead I took her possessions from the LandCat and arranged them around her: the skillets and pans, the empty fish traps, the ancient photographs, the tattered quilt tucked about her shoulders. I took my thick woolen muffler and wrapped it around her neck, and I got into the LandCat and left her there, staring toward the coming ice. I was crying so hard I almost missed the road.

On the way back north, I took an axe and chopped free the plank that said "MY GREAT-GRANDFATHER BUILT THIS TOWN." It hung outside my hut, facing the ice, until the day we had to leave.

For the students of Haystack '83

TERMITES

Dave Smeds

"Termites" was purchased by Gardner Dozois, and appeared in the May 1987 issue of IAsfm, with an illustration by Daniel R. Horne. It is Smeds's only sale to IAsfm to date, although quite a handsome debut— a brilliant and disturbing story that postulates an ingenious cure for humankind's oldest enemy, hunger . . . but one that must be purchased at a cost that is perhaps too high to pay.

Before turning to writing, Dave Smeds made his living as a commercial artist. He made his first fiction sale in 1980, and has subsequently sold stories to IAsfm, Far Frontiers, Dragons of Light, In the Field of Fire, and to various men's magazines. He has published two novels, The Sorcery Within *and* The Talisman of Alemar, *and is at work on several more. He lives with his family in Santa Rosa, California.*

August, 2011

When I first arrived in the Cherangani Hills of northwestern Kenya as a young woman, the mountains had been green and tawny, cloaked in lush bush, dotted with the cultivated plots of the Pokot tribe that I had come to study. Now I could hardly recognize the place where I had lived my life between the ages of twenty-two and twenty-eight. The drought had turned the Great Rift Valley into blistered, lunarlike terrain; the hills reminded me of Ethiopia back in the eighties—steep mounds unintended for human habitation, withered, eroded, and above all, dry. Greg stopped the Land Rover and let me examine the scenery more carefully. But it was no use.

"I'm lost," I said.

He brushed a cloud of flies away from his face, callused fingers rasping against a four-day growth of tough, white beard. "I believe it's around the next promontory," he said, his clipped British inflections making the statement unequivocal, though in truth he knew the region far less than I.

His confidence made me try one more time. "Yes. Yes, I think you're right," I said.

When we rounded the flank of the hills, we saw the remnants of a village. All that remained of the huts were the firepits, the packed-earth floors, and ruptured holes where the branches that formed the walls had been anchored. And, of course, the sitting stones—it was improper for a man of the Pokot to sit on naked ground. In their stead were three hovels constructed of piled dung and animal hides, not true dwellings at all; merely places to get out of the sun. I saw a dozen or more people, all lying or sitting listlessly in the shade.

We felt the impact of their eyes, but aside from the stares, most of them did not react to our arrival. A single boy stood and began to approach the Land Rover. He was suffering from the early stages of marasmus, his limbs painfully thin, stomach bloated, skin hanging slack from his bones so that his face resembled that of an old man and not, so I estimated, a boy well short of puberty. His only garment was a pair of threadbare, stained khaki shorts.

Greg pulled out the .45 as we stopped rolling, keeping it

in obvious view. But the boy emitted not even a flicker of belligerence; he was past those emotions. He gazed at us blankly, like a retardate. Only the fact that he had risen of his own accord gave me hope of obtaining a response from him.

"Do you know KoCherop?" I asked. I used the Pokot dialect, though the words came haltingly, with a bittersweet tang. The boy, if he had been schooled, could speak English or Swahili, but use of his home tongue might ingratiate me. "Do you know where she is?"

He turned his prematurely old eyes toward me, and I saw, to my surprise, a mind still capable of activity and calculation. "You are Chemachugwo," he said, using my Pokot name, his voice raspy but energetic.

"Yes." I did not know him, but I was not surprised that he had guessed my identity. There were no other middle-aged white women alive who could speak his language.

"I will tell you where to find KoCherop if you give me a piece of paper," he stated.

I hesitated a moment, then reached into a compartment under the seat and withdrew the bribe. I gave him a whole sheet. The boy ran his hands over it, apparently pleased with the rough, pulpy texture and sawdust-yellow color. He rolled it into a funnel, and with his empty hand pointed to a terrace plot far up the nearest mountain. "She is there."

I could make out a tendril of smoke. I signaled Greg to drive on.

I could see the boy and his piece of paper in the side mirror for a full thirty seconds. Just before the dust and the turns in the track obscured him I saw him bite off the end of the funnel and begin to chew it. I wanted to weep, but the past few days had left me incapable of tears. It was the village, I told myself. It had been so much like the one in which I had built my hut, almost forty years back.

The road narrowed and grew more steep, until the Land Rover would go no further. We faced a dilemma, for we couldn't leave the vehicle unattended.

"I'll stay," Greg said, handing me the .45. He pulled out one of the rifles for himself.

I hadn't reckoned on this development. I needed his plucky

humor and stiff upper lip. But I had gone alone into the wilderness of East Africa before. I buckled on my holster and started up the path.

Climbing these hills had been easier in younger days. I stopped often, until I could no longer bear to gaze out over the valley, where I had once watched the herdsmen and their cattle. The air became cooler, though not enough to compensate for my exertion. I estimated it would take me two hours to reach the terrace. I thought of KoCherop.

January, 1978

"Now we are like sisters," she said, touching my belly. I jumped. The tattoo was still tender from the artist's needle. She jerked back her hand. "I'm sorry."

"It's all right. I was just surprised."

"It will only hurt for a little while," she said encouragingly. "Then you will be happy because you have become more beautiful." She pointed at the spectacular, star-shaped design carved around her navel. The blood still congealed around it. "All the other girls will be jealous of me," she said firmly. "Now that I am a woman, I will add more all along here." She brushed her fingers up and down her midriff.

I concealed my shiver. KoCherop—she still used her childhood name, Chesinen, at that point—had a sleek body and perfect, rich brown complexion. It needed no accentuation. Along with clitoridectomy, scarification was one of the practices that tempted me to drop my anthropologist's reserve.

"Many of the girls nowadays are leaving their bellies smooth," I said.

"Those girls must be looking for Kikuyu husbands," she said with disdain. She smeared her face with red ocher and ghee, and offered to do the same for me. I accepted.

She lavished it over my nose and cheeks. "Trust me. One day a handsome man with much land will look at your belly and admire what you have had done."

I chuckled, staring down at the tattoo. I had to admit it was pretty. It was a tiny butterfly, etched in six colors of ink, excellent artistry considering that it had been performed by a traveling craftsman. In my own way, I *would* enjoy owning it; otherwise I would never have done something so permanent to my body. But it most certainly had not been done to attract a husband. I had done it for my Pokot sister, because her father had become like my own, and because she, though ten years my junior, had made me feel instantly welcome in a sea of strange black faces.

"Oh, no one will marry me," I said. "I always burn the porridge."

August, 2011 (continued)

I passed terrace after terrace of abandoned land. The farms extended far up the slope ahead of me, each family tilling parcels at not one but several elevations, the better to guard against crop failure. Some could be found as high as seven or eight thousand feet, among the peaks where, in former times, the mist would gather, moistening the land, dispelling the aridity of the Great Rift Valley. Now all I could see growing were gnarled hardwoods whose resins made them impossible to eat, or thorn thickets and brambles not worth the pain to molest. Dust crawled up my shoes and into the cuffs of my trousers.

Breathless, aching in my calves, I reached the terrace that the boy had indicated. Nothing was left of the fields but irrigation channels waiting for water that had not come. KoCherop was seated on a flat stone beside a firepit. An empty porridge kettle sat over dying coals. Beside her was a gourd of water and small sack of maize or millet.

She stared at me with wide eyes, perhaps thinking that she had died and met a ghost. I spoke her name.

She bowed her head. "I am called only Ko, now."

"Ko" means grandmother. Her full name meant Grandmother of Daughter of Rain, which she had adopted upon the birth of her first granddaughter. It was a declaration that Cherop was dead.

KoCherop, in her typically Pokot way, did not display overt grief. It was enough to have made the statement. In a culture in which the lives of the women of the tribe revolve so deeply around those of their children that they rename themselves each time a new generation is established, no loss could have been sharper.

"I'm sorry," I said, trying to keep my voice steady. "Lokomol told me."

"He sent you, didn't he? I told him not to do that." Her voice softened. "He is well? And the little ones?"

"There is food in the refugee camp, for the moment. He wouldn't accept help. But he did beg me to come to you."

"And you have come. What will you do now?"

"Greg and I plan to take you to back to Kampala," I said. "We want you to live with us."

"I live here," she said, standing up. She had always been thin and spare; now the effect was more extreme, but the vigor— and determination—in her body was still obvious.

"What happens when that sack is empty?" I asked, pointing at her food supply. It was nearly depleted already.

She ground a toe into the dust, and dislodged a hidden stick. She tossed it in the firepit. "I am waiting for the government workers, coming to tell me that now I can eat dirt."

I started to speak, lost my momentum, paused.

"What is there for me in Kampala, Chemachugwo?" she continued. "Do they have grindstones? Can you farm there?"

"Can you farm *here?*" I found my tongue. "Do you remember the time you had the fever? I started to leave the hut one night, but you begged me not to go. Do you remember what you said?"

She faced me for the first time. "You are not fair, Janet."

"You said you didn't want to die alone. Have you changed your mind after all these years?"

The flies were devils. KoCherop, with her African composure, paid them no mind, even when they sipped fluid from the rim of her eyelids. "Lokomol should not have sent you."

"But he did." I reached out and clasped her shoulder. She leaned into my hand. "We won't have to stay in the city all the time. You can come with us when I do my field work in the Ituri forest. The pygmies will call you a giant."

KoCherop, who was rather short, smiled faintly, then lost it. I could feel her tremble through my palm. "Yes. Yes, Janet, I will come. But give me one more night. I must say goodbye to Cherop."

I am ashamed to say that, for an instant, I did not believe her. I envisioned her hiding from us when the time came to leave. But if she did, I would have to respect that choice, so I told her where the truck was and climbed down the mountain.

February, 1988

KoCherop was giving her two-year-old son Lokomol a bath Pokot style: squirting water out of her mouth in a pencil-thin stream and scrubbing him with her fingers. The baby wailed, watching forlornly as the mud he'd so diligently splattered over his skin was rinsed away. Not far away his slightly older sister laughed at his discomforture, while KoCherop's three other children clambered up and down the acacia tree under which we sat.

"You have been married for half a year, Chemachugwo," she said. "Why aren't you pregnant?" I knew she was scolding me; she reserved use of my Pokot name for times when she wanted to lecture or argue.

I paused, keeping my glance on Lokomol, marveling at how much he had grown in the year and a half since I had last visited my tribal friends. "Greg and I don't plan to have any children just yet."

"You are over thirty years—well over. You could be a grandmother by now."

I thought of the crow's feet in the corners of my eyes and the strands of gray hair that I'd found a couple of months back. I didn't need KoCherop's reminder.

"What about you?" I asked. "Are you going to stop at five?"

"Oh, no!" she said emphatically, sending Lokomol off to his siblings with an affectionate pat on the butt. "Seven, eight, nine—whatever luck brings me. I am already behind. KamaChepkech already has six," she said of her younger sister.

KoCherop was twenty-four years old.

August, 2011 (continued)

Morning arrived with the suddenness of the tropics. I, lying awake on the bed of the Land Rover, watched the sun illuminate the tracks of the snakes that had crawled past the vehicle in the night. I heard footsteps scuffing the path and my heart began to pound.

KoCherop had come.

She had brought her sack and her gourd. She stood like a statue, her wide, Nilo-Hamitic features impassive. She was dressed in the traditional style: a skirt of thick brown muslin covering her from the base of her rib cage to her knees, huge hoop earrings, and a cornucopia of bright, multi-colored beads in the form of belts, anklets, bracelets, armbands, a headband, and row after row of necklaces draping her collar, shoulders, and upper chest, leaving her breasts bare. This was her best outfit, and a rare sight in days when most Pokot women had long since begun to mimic Western fashions.

"When we get to Kampala, they will know I am a Pokot," she explained.

I pursed my lips. They would know, all right.

I saw her glance wistfully at the hills. "It will be temporary," I said rapidly. "The rain will come. It has to come. Lokomol and his brothers will plant new crops. You can return then."

"And maybe my granddaughter will be born again," she replied.

I sighed. It was hard not to agree with her pessimism. The rain *would* come again—no doubt far more of it than the vegetationless soil could withstand—and some of the million Pokot refugees would reestablish their homes, but for vast numbers, the old way of life had ended forever.

Greg grumbled up out of his sleep, saw KoCherop, and gave me a questioning glance.

"Start her up," I said. "There's no reason to stay here."

July, 1990

As I watched the first news broadcast concerning the Termite bacteria, I remembered Grape Nuts. In a flashback to my childhood Euell Gibbons appeared, white-haired, fatherly, pouring a bowlful of cereal. "Ever eat a pine tree?" he asked in his backwoods accent.

The geneticists explained how they had developed a strain of *E. coli* capable of converting cellulose into sugar. Doctors calculated that the effects, though disconcerting, would not be dangerous in the long term. Politicians justified its release into test populations in East Africa and Bangladesh on the grounds that it hailed the end of world hunger, a new chance for the stricken nations of the Third World.

I kept thinking of Marie Antoinette. *Let them eat wood.*

August, 2011 (continued)

We made our way to the main road, a dirt track that would take us down the valley, past Mt. Elgon to Lake Victoria, and eventually across the border into Uganda. The grimy windshield showed us a view of bleak mountains and dust, broken by an occasional cactus or bit of scrub brush.

KoCherop sat between Greg and me, taking no note of the surroundings, a contagious gloom that kept my husband and me from saying more than ten words to each other all morning. It was as if each mile enervated her, until it was all she could do to simply sit.

We approached Sigor, the district's marketing center, the only "big town" KoCherop had ever visited. It was little more than a collection of dung huts with tin sheet roofs. Nowhere on the wind-whipped ground was there a tree or a blade of grass, only dust, rusting oil drums, black requiem birds, a scent of human poverty. In temperate climates, poverty smells sour, but in hot regions it is sickeningly sweet. Small knots of people gathered at the periphery of the street as we rolled through: sad black faces, pleading eyes.

We kept our weapons visible, but here, as with the boy the day before, no one had the energy to threaten us. They simply stood with the passivity of the starving, hoping that perhaps we were famine relief workers. I did not look at their faces. Though we had an ample supply of food in the Land Rover, we didn't dare stop and try to share it, or the spell holding them back would have been broken. Our food stayed hidden inside plastic, metal, and canvas, as inconspicuous as we could make it.

I couldn't save them. There were too many. What mattered now was KoCherop. I could, God willing, rescue one person, if she would let me.

She paid no attention to the audience, though they stared at her beads and naked breasts, which in their minds marked her as more primitive, and therefore poorer, than they. Perhaps they were wondering why she, and not they, deserved to ride. We didn't stop until long after the village had merged with the dust of the horizon.

February, 1992

"You don't have to do that anymore," I said.

KoCherop continued picking bits of stems and stalks out of the sorghum she was grinding. She looked at me with skepticism.

"You don't have to separate the chaff," I clarified. "Just grind it in. The bacteria will allow you to digest it, just like the grain."

"It is meant for cattle, not people," she said firmly. "You talk like the government workers."

"The crop's been very poor this year. You don't have much to waste."

"Do they eat chaff in California?" she asked. She knew that I had just returned from a visit to my hometown in the San Joaquin Valley.

"No. North America hasn't been infected yet. But it will be. There's no way to stop *E. coli*. Eventually it'll get everyone. We'll all be Termites. I'm one already. So are you."

"No, I am not."

"Yes, you are. It's even gotten into your cattle. That's why the dung burns so poorly," I said, pointing at the smoldering fire underneath the kettle of porridge. There wasn't enough fiber left in the cow pies to serve as fuel. "Don't tell me you haven't noticed a big difference in how food passes through your system."

Not being Caucasian, her blush didn't show, but the expression was the same. I, too, had been embarrassed by the sudden, violent cycles of diarrhea and constipation, and most of all by the methane, though more recently my body had begun to adjust.

"I will keep doing it this way," she insisted. "This is the way my mother taught me."

August, 2011 (continued)

We began to catch up with the refugee caravans by midafternoon. The first contained about fifty people, shuffling along at a pace of perhaps a kilometer an hour. It was much worse than in Sigor, for they made no effort to get out of the way of the Land Rover—many, I suspected, would not have cared if they had been run over—and it took a considerable length of time to weave our way through them, all the while aware of their eyes an arm-length outside the windows. Their lighter coloring and thinner features told me that they were Samburu. They had come even further than we, from the vicinity of Lake Turkana, where the normally bountiful supplies of fish had become exhausted from the excessive demand.

At least they were away from the water and its mosquitoes. Fewer would die from malaria.

In due course we came upon another, somewhat larger group, readily distinguishable because some of them still carried significant possessions, either in carts, on packs, or slung on poles. They even drove a pair of oxen and a few bony cows ahead of them. I noticed four men huddled around a bowl of milk and blood, a traditional meal of the pastoralists of the Rift Valley, while a knot of women and children watched, quiet with envy. My hands, lubed with perspiration, slid along the stock of my rifle. Greg gave me a glance, and I knew he saw what I did: these tribesmen had enough strength left to cause trouble should they wish.

Three young men, painfully lean but still muscular, were very slow to get out of our path. They glowered at us as we passed. I pretended to be distracted by the constant bouncing from the ruts and chuck holes, but I could feel their eyes riveted to us. It was like the sensation a woman gets when a man blatantly undresses his in her mind.

The last obstacle was a boy who strode behind one of the

oxen with a thin whip. For a full two minutes, though it was obvious he knew we were behind him, he refused to move himself or his animal out of the way. Finally the track widened and Greg began to pull around. Suddenly the boy began lashing at us. The sound of leather on metal made me jump. The boy shouted—a guttural, wordless roar. The tip of his lash struck the steering wheel.

Greg stepped firmly on the throttle, shooting us into the clear, and didn't let up until the irregularity of the road shook us more than our aging bones could tolerate. He eased off, put the .45 back into its holster on the dash, got out his handkerchief, and wiped his forehead. The boy, his image shrinking out of sight in the mirror, was laughing that his whip had spurred us so well. His poor ox could not have been so vigorous.

"Bloody little blighter," Greg cursed.

My hands were shaking. I turned to share a sigh of relief with KoCherop, only to find her gazing ahead, lips pursed, as if nothing of importance had occurred. Greg noticed and, like me, his eyebrows drew together.

Ahead in the distance, well away from the Samburu, an escarpment loomed. "We'll pull over when we reach that," Greg announced, pointing. "Time for a rest."

September, 2001

We were walking down a trail between two plots of farmland, one belonging to KoCherop's uncle, the other to her brother. For once, the rain had come in full vigor, and neither locusts nor the flocks of marauding queleas had come to steal the grain. Dozens of tribesmen worked the fields, the glistening brown backs of both men and women happily bending down to harvest a bumper crop.

"Why do you do what you do?" KoCherop asked suddenly.

The question had come from out of the blue. "You mean, why am I an anthropologist?"

She nodded. "See my people with their scythes? See this mountain? I am in my place. Why do you live so far from your parents? Why do you go to the forest to study the pygmies, instead of having children? You are too old now to start a family. How can you be happy?"

There were occasional times, as menopause approached and I wondered what would have happened if I had married my college sweetheart and stayed in the United States, that I wasn't totally content with the alternative I'd chosen. But I was able to answer KoCherop honestly. "I do what I do because I want to. My work fulfills me."

She shook her head, mystified. "I could never be like that. Take me from my clan and this dirt and I would die."

August, 2011 (continued)

We stopped in the shade of the escarpment, where we were relatively inconspicuous but nevertheless had an unobstructed view of the road. Greg got out quickly, looked toward the rear of the truck, and groaned.

"I thought that last mile was a mite rough," he said. I walked around to his side, and saw that we had a flat tire.

"A gift from the Samburu?" I suggested.

"Could be. Most likely the frigging road." He opened up the rear of the Land Rover. "Last spare," he said, which we both knew already. I checked the map to measure the distance to Lake Victoria, and gnawed at my inner lip.

I began to help him, but he convinced me to relax, and in exchange I would drive the remaining short leg until sundown. KoCherop and I found a relatively comfortable spot in the talus a few yards away, where I spread out the last of our fresh fruit, as well as bread and, most important of all, a jug of water. The flies were overjoyed at the repast.

KoCherop ate a piece of fruit, a treat even in good seasons and a part of her diet of which she had surely been totally deprived lately, drank her fill, and turned to look at the plain.

"Have more," I said.

She didn't answer. Occasionally her glance would dart toward the north, where we had now left the last of the Pokot lands behind. She began taking apart her headband, running the beads off the ends of their threads one by one and flicking them away.

I am ashamed to confess that my own appetite was ravenous,

and when I was certain my friend was not going to touch another bite, I saw to it that the ants had nothing more than stems and gleaned rinds to attack. The sand at the edge of the talus was now vivid with specks of color, an inadvertent piece of artwork created by KoCherop's cast-off beads, each one a particle of the life she knew, gone. I made sure not to disturb it as I walked back to check on Greg.

He was cinching the last nut. I handed him his canteen. He drained it. "Next time we bring a chauffeur," he joked, slightly breathless.

"We're losing her," I told him. "She's just waiting until the wind calls her name and takes her away."

He stowed the tire iron. "Well," he murmured, "the choice is hers now, isn't it? You can't make it for her."

The words seemed callous, but I had no answer for them at the time. KoCherop was waiting for the world to conform to her desires, not unlike the scientists who had created the Termite bacteria. But the world has ways of turning the tables back around. Now it was man's, and KoCherop's, turn to adapt, and she was refusing.

Brooding, I assisted Greg in lifting the flat tire into the Land Rover. The winds of upper Kenya had arrived with their usual vigor, hurrying us toward the next leg of our journey.

March, 2007

We were walking along the bank of a river. The drought had been severe for three years, and now the watercourse contained only sand, pocked with pits where the tribespeople had dug to reach the watertable. Now even those holes were desiccated. Thirty years before, when I had still lived here, the river had been lined with grass and overhung by broad, leafy acacias. Now even the stumps were gone.

Ironically, it was the industrialized nations that had benefited from the modified *E. coli*. The sugar industry no longer had to boil away ninety percent of the raw cane during refining. Grains no longer had to be as thoroughly processed. But in the Third World bureaucrats became dangerously lax in educating the people about the need for population control, and the added demand for wood exacerbated the already severe deforestation problem. The climate had rebelled.

Cherop, the granddaughter for whom my friend had been renamed, skipped along ahead of us, always alert for a sunning lizard or a pretty stone. We were solemn in spite of the child's exuberance. KoCherop's husband had died two months before. This was my first visit since that event, and our conversation had awakened some of KoCherop's sense of loss. Now we just walked, thinking about the changes brought by time. It was young Cherop who broke the silence.

"Look!" she cried, pointing. Not far off the path, partially hidden in a thorn bramble, stood a termite mound.

Assured that we were watching, she ran over to it and began climbing. The mound was nearly three times as tall as she, rising into a dozen eroded towers. A hyena or aardwolf had dug a burrow at its base; birds had done the same, on a smaller scale, in its heights. The termites themselves had abandoned the site. Cherop explored the structure as much as the thorns would allow, no doubt hoping that one of the nests would still contain something interesting.

I smiled. The girl gave me a big, toothless grin, breaking off a small projection to demonstrate her strength, offering the dust to the wind.

I turned to KoCherop, and stage by stage my smile faded. I had never seen such a bitter look on her face.

"What's wrong?"

"I wish that all the termites had died ten thousand years ago. Then maybe your people would never have thought of a way to make us like insects."

It felt like I had been stung. The worst part of it was that she seemed unaware that she was hurting me. I could not avoid blurting out a response.

"Maybe if your people had stopped having so many babies, my people wouldn't have tried to solve your problems."

August, 2011 (continued)

We reached an armed checkpoint shortly before dusk. An overweight minor officer, skin so oily it gleamed, examined our papers with a frown, peering repeatedly at our vehicle's contents. He spared KoCherop a disinterested glance, mostly toward her breasts. Greg bribed him with two packs of American cigarettes and we were on our way. "Wish it could be that easy at the border," said my husband. We camped not far down the road, reasoning that bandits might be discouraged by the proximity of the checkpoint.

It was crowded in the back of the Land Rover. I slept between Greg and KoCherop, listening to the wind moan and the crickets trill, unable to sleep. KoCherop's scent evoked memories. It is strange that an entire tribe can have an identifiable essence. When I had lived with them year-round I had become oblivious to it.

I thought about the city, trying to picture KoCherop walking to the supermarket, wearing a cotton smock, smelling the civilized odors of cement and auto exhaust. What kind of fool was I to think that, simply because I loved her, I could succeed in transferring a human being from her culture into mine?

Greg woke and crawled out of the vehicle. Soon I heard the muffled, rain-on-the-roof sound of urine splattering dust. I glanced at KoCherop. Even in the dim illumination I could see the determined, stubborn tension in her shoulders, and I became angry.

"Damn it," I murmured. "What more do you want me to do? *It's not my fault.*"

She didn't stir, but something in the stillness of her breathing hinted that she was awake. But after Greg returned and began snoring, I convinced myself that I had imagined it.

In the distance, I was certain I heard a hyena laughing, like a ghost of Africa of old.

July, 2011

The refugee camp was a sea of humanity. Our guide was a young doctor who, judging from his haggard cheeks and the red in his eyes, had not slept in four days. Somehow he kept his humor as we threaded through the crowd from checkpoint to checkpoint, trying to find Lokomol and the rest of KoCherop's family.

A little girl, bloated with kwashiorkor, stared at me as I passed. I turned away—from her and from all the faces, keeping my glance on the doctor. Here and there sat a lucky family with a tent or blanket to shade themselves; for the most part the refugees simply lay on the packed ground beneath an open sky, waiting until the next shipment of food arrived at the distribution point, or until the doctors received a fresh supply of basic medicines.

Some attempt had been made to funnel members of various tribal groups into specific areas of the camp. Otherwise we might never have found Lokomol.

He was sitting with his youngest daughter propped in his lap. I spotted him immediately; his lean features and long fingers closely resembled his mother. He was, much to my relief, apparently in good health.

"We came as soon as we got your message," I said. "We've arranged for transportation to take you to the camp near Kampala. It's much better supplied than this one."

"You have always been good to us, Chemachugwo," he answered pensively. "But it is for my mother that I sent for you."

"Why isn't she with you?"

He shrugged.

Knowing KoCherop, I understood completely. "You want me to try to bring her?"

He nodded. "I am ashamed to ask this of you, but you are the only person I have ever known who can make my mother listen."

August, 2011 (continued)

"Wake up, Janet."

It was Greg's voice, coming from the other end of a long tunnel. I peeled my eyes open. The morning light was unforgivably bright.

"Time for breakfast," Greg said for the second time. "I want to get to the border well before dusk."

I moaned, rubbed the grit from my lashes, and went about the meal like a zombie, hoping that my headache would soon go away. KoCherop sat nearby. I noticed that she ate a full share this time, but otherwise I avoided paying much attention to her. The border crossing was enough to think about, I told myself.

"You are sad, Janet," KoCherop said during a moment when Greg was out of hearing range.

"That's true," I replied, and turned to clean my bowl.

"Janet?"

"Yes?"

"I am sorry."

I looked at her, frowned, and climbed into the Land Rover. I was sorry, too, but what good was that? I didn't answer her. She had nothing to add, and we didn't speak for the rest of the morning.

By noon we began to see grass and brush. The air closed in, a sign of humidity. Greg spotted a flamingo in flight. Suddenly we crested a hill and saw Lake Victoria sprawling into the distance.

KoCherop's eyes went wide. It was easy to understand why.

"Where is the other side?" she whispered.

The shore to which she referred was over two hundred miles away, lost over the horizon. The lake was so vast that it could generate its own climate, moistening the adjacent countryside that would otherwise have been as arid as the region from which we had emerged.

It was one more new thing to overwhelm her, I thought bitterly.

KoCherop stared at the lake for almost an hour, while I stayed locked in my own preoccupations. She startled me when she called for us to stop.

"I want to look at that," she said.

We had reached a particularly good vantage point from which to view the lake. KoCherop got out of the vehicle and walked to the edge of the road. Just in front of her the land dropped off abruptly. I could see jagged rocks down below.

My friend stood where one more step would send her tumbling over the edge. Suddenly my insides clenched.

"Greg!" I cried.

"Give her a moment," he said in a voice that struck me as far too calm.

I held my breath, prepared at any time to shut my eyes and cover my ears. Again Greg, though observing carefully, seemed much too unruffled. Then, bit by bit, I began to see it as he did.

Her posture was no longer stiff. She stared at the lake not as if overwhelmed or contemplating suicide, but as I had the first time I had seen this, the second largest body of fresh water in the world—with awe and delight. I realized then that her demeanor had been different all day, but I, in my melancholy, had failed to notice.

She turned and walked toward me, her back straight, her eyes bright.

"Will I have my own room in Kampala?" she asked.

I felt a smile tugging at my lips. This was the KoCherop I had once known, someone with hopes for the years to come. "Yes," I replied. "A big one."

"Good," she said crisply, and climbed into the Land Rover. I thought back to the beads she had cast away the previous day. Not particles of life, thrown away in order to embrace Death, but bits of the past, dropped by the wayside to make room for the future. KoCherop was willing to adapt. The tightness in my throat melted away.

"Let's go home," I told Greg.

TOUCHDOWN

Nancy Kress

"Touchdown" was purchased by Gardner Dozois,
and appeared in the October 1990 issue of IAsfm,
with an illustration by Janet Aulisio. It is the latest
in a long sequence of elegant and incisive stories
by Kress that have appeared in IAsfm under four
different editors over the last decade, since her first
IAsfm sale to George Scithers in 1979—stories that
have made her one of the most popular of all the
magazine's writers. Here she gives us a suspenseful
look at a very unusual (and very dangerous) high-
tech competition, played out across the gameboard of
a deserted and devastated Earth—and in the process
gives us some clues as to how it got that way in the
first place. . . .

Born in Buffalo, New York, Nancy Kress now lives
with her family in Brockport, New York. Her books
include the novels The Prince of Morning Bells, The
Golden Grove, The White Pipes, and An Alien Light,
and the collection Trinity and Other Stories. Her
most recent books are the novel Brain Rose and the
novella-length chapbook Beggars in Spain. She has
frequently been a finalist for science fiction's major

awards, and she won a Nebula Award for her story
"Out of All Them Bright Stars."

Maria told me that Team B had found Troy. It took me a
moment to find the right answer (all we had found was Tokyo),
and in that moment there was no way to tell how unprotected
my expression had been. But I did find the answer. "That's
impossible. Troy was *early*."

"Nonetheless, Team B found it. Excavated ruins."

"It wouldn't be big enough to carry any points!"

"It's on the exception list."

"I don't believe it."

Maria shrugged, watching (what had my face shown?). "So
access the channel."

"But there wasn't anything *there*."

"There were enough exposed excavations or whatever to
be on the list. Three hundred points. Leader just made the
official acceptance." She smiled at me sweetly. "He said he
was pleased."

Bitch. She knew I didn't access the open channel as often as
she did; I work best with uninterrupted team-channel access.
She also knew that Team B Leader had been my second husband. Her background psych research was always thorough. I
toggled my 'plant to "record" and made a note to bid for her
next season.

Tokyo was worth only forty-five points. *Anybody* can identify Tokyo, even starting from a fucking Pacific Island.

My Team Leader's voice buzzed in my 'plant. "Time's up,
Cazie. Come on in."

"We have another four hours!"

"Touchdown city by Team A. Quarter's over."

Maria smirked; she was on Team A. Her 'plant had of course
already told her about the touchdown. No appeal; someone on
Team A had actually done it, gone out and touched an artifact
from one of their cities. I turned away from her and pretended
to study my console, my face under careful control. *She'll say*

it, my 'plant said, programmed for this. The programming had been expensive, but worth it: No point in giving away rage if you can be warned those few seconds in advance that let you get your reactions under control. A few times the 'plant had even been wrong, audio context analysis being as uncertain as it is. A few times no one had even said it.

Maria said it.

"Don't be too upset. After all, Cazie—it's just a game."

Flying back is the part I hate the worst. Going out for the first quarter, of course, you can't see anything. The portholes are opaqued; even a loose chair strap could disqualify you in case it might let you glimpse something. During actual play, you're concentrating on the console readings, the team chatter as it comes over your 'plant, the hunches about where to search next, the feints to keep your flyer-mate off-balance. Especially the feints. You hardly notice the actual planet at all, even when you play in what passes for daylight.

But flying back to base, the quarter's over, the tension's broken, and there's nothing much going on over the 'plant to distract you from the place. And God, it was depressing. Even Maria felt it, she of the alloy sensitivity. We had been playing a day game in Tokyo; the computer flew us west, into the dying light. Ocean choked with slime or else just degree after degree of gray water, followed by great barren dusty plains howled over by winds of unbreathable air. Continents' worth of bare plains. Nothing hard, nothing bright or shiny, nothing cozy and compact. Just the bare huge emptiness. And overhead, the constant thick clouds that make it impossible to even guess where the sun is.

Once I told Ari—now Team Leader B—I wasn't sure the game was worth the aftermath, it was so depressing. He stared at me a long time and then asked, in that sweet voice that meant attack, whether the openness frightened me? And we were still married at the time. I said of course it didn't frighten me, what was there about such a dead world that was frightening? I kept my voice bored and disdainful. But he went on watching me anyway. And that was when we were even still *married*.

"Nothing," Maria said. She stood deliberately staring out the porthole as we whizzed over some dead plain. Showing off. Thinking she was out-psyching me. She even made a little song of it: "No-thing, no-thing, no-thing."

I didn't look at her. Maria smiled.

At the base we all gathered in the dome while the computer reffed the first quarter. The four members of Team A had found Sydney, Newcastle, Wollangong, Capetown, Oudtshoorn, Port Elizabeth, Shanghai, Beijing, and Hong Kong. The touchdown was for Sydney, but it was only a piece of bent metal, not a whole artifact, so it wasn't worth a lot of points. They had a lot of cities but the team had concentrated on coastal cities, which aren't worth as much overall because they're easier to find and to identify (although they did get extra points for Hong Kong, because it had sunk so deep).

Team B found Troy, Istanbul, Thessaloniki, New York, Yonkers, Greenwich, Stamford, Norwalk, Edmonton, Calgary, and Chikon: high initial points but a big loss after reffing because the North American cities were so close together and because they had misidentified Chikon—*twice*. I watched while the computer announced the adjusted score, but Maria went on smiling and her face gave away nothing. Neither did Ari's, damn him.

Team C found Rio de Janeiro, Santos, Campinas, Ouriphos— the actual Ouriphos, or what had been left of it after the earthquake—Bujumbura, Kigall, Dallas, Fort Worth, Waco, Austin, Leningrad, Tallinn, and Helsinki. An impressive score—and for nine of the cities they had been playing in the dark. The floating cameras zoomed in for close-ups of their smiles.

Team D found Tokyo, Jakarta, Bandung, Herat, Ferah, and (at the last minute, thanks to Nikos), Wichita. But we were saved from last place by Team E, who had found only *two* cities, Saskatoon and Kifta, and had misidentified Kifta. They couldn't hide their embarrassment, not even the Team Leader, not even when the cameras targeted him. The glances that went around the dome were almost compensation for our losing the quarter. Team Leader E stared straight ahead, mottled color rising on the back of his neck; unless he made a fast recovery

in the next quarter, he'd be fucking his hand for *months*. And
the fan reaction and betting back home on his orbital didn't
even bear thinking about—let alone the sponsor's reaction. The
team ended with only twenty-eight points adjusted.

Team C won the quarter, of course, 480 adjusted. Team
Leader instructed me through my 'plant to try to find out their
I.D. tactics in the coffee hour.

Larissa always does that to me. As if I were some kind
of tactical genius, just because once I'd been quarterback
for the team that racked up the record, 996 points in a single quarter. We'd found Pax. But you can't find Pax every
quarter—after all this time, the accursed place is still floating
around the Pacific—and underneath I'm always afraid some
flyer-mate will psych out how bad I really am at team tactical
programs.

What had Maria seen on my face?

I didn't find out. I didn't find out Team C's I.D. tactics
either, because the coffee hour is only fifty-six minutes by
strict rule before the blackout period, and Team B Leader had
taken the risk of doping all of his people on Impenetrables set
to kick in right after the ref announcements. God, he was self-
confident. I looked at him sideways, when I was sure Maria or
the cameras weren't watching. He hadn't changed much in the
two years since our divorce. Short, muscled, smiling. Ari.

Then the coffee hour was over and the Leaders took the
dome field down and Maria and I went back to the flyer and
shot each other with the time-release knock-out drugs. The
camera hovered close as we laid the strips on each other's
necks, and stayed close afterward. There's a hazy period while
the stuff takes effect. Players are vulnerable: it's a warm sweet
letting go, sometimes of words as well as consciousness. But
I was pretty sure I didn't give anything away. Maria finally
stopped talking to me and rolled over in her bunk, and I smiled
to myself in the darkness.

Preparation for second quarter.

When I woke, Maria was blinking sleepily. The camera was
already on. I felt rested, but of course that was no clue to how
much time had elapsed—the drug made me feel rested. Had

we been out two hours or twenty? However long it had been, the computer had moved all the flyers for the second round. I knew the latitude and longitude of where we had been, but now we could be literally anywhere in the world. Again.

Adrenaline surged, and my stomach tightened with pleasure.

We strapped ourselves into the kick-off chairs. The portholes were shallow opaque caves. "Tallyho," Maria said. I ignored her. The computer kept us waiting for ten minutes. When the seat straps finally unlocked, Maria tried a direct run for her console (she's strong), but I was ready for her and made a flying tackle. She went down. I scrambled over her, reached my console, and activated it. The first half-hour control of the flyer was mine.

Maria got up slowly. She wasn't hurt, of course, but she made a show of rubbing her shoulder for the camera. She's a high-ranked player on a number of orbitals. Very dramatic.

The portholes de-opaqued. Daylight. More barren plain, more dust blown by unbreathable air, some scraggly plant stuff in dull olive. Not much rock. No coast. No snow or frost, but of course with the greenhouse effect worsening every year that ruled out less than fifteen degrees of latitude. We could still be anywhere. You always hope the random patterns generated by the computer will set you down right at the edge of a qualifiable city, but that has only happened to me once. And it was Moscow, only ninety points unreffed.

I lifted the flyer for an aerial view, taking it up as high as the rules allowed. Maria and I both peered through every single porthole. Nothing but plain. Then I saw it, a quick flash of silver on the right horizon. Water. I headed right.

"Water over there!" I said excitedly, jazzing it up for the camera. It was watching Maria for the reaction shot, of course, but she just looked thoughtful: the serious young player concentrating for the fans back home.

A small river meandered across the dust. Along its banks, plants were a little greener, a little fuller. They disgusted me; pitiful things, trying to actually grow in this place. God knew what chemicals were in the river.

I followed it at top speed, needing to reach a city before my half-hour was up. With speed limited during play to sixty-five miles per hour, every minute counted. I didn't want to arrive at a city just as Maria's console cut in and mine shut down.

We flew for twenty minutes. Ruins appeared below us, some broken concrete and the mound pattern that means structures under the dust. But visual was enough to tell me that the place was too small to qualify as a city. Some stupid little town, not even enough left of it to get a fix on the architecture and make a guess what continent we were on.

Then the alarm bells went off.

"Lift! For God's sake lift the fucking flyer!" Maria screamed. I thought she was over-reacting for the camera until I saw her face. She was terrified.

Maria was—or rather, somewhere along the line had become—toxiphobic.

The computer had removed the aerial ceiling the second the radiation detectors had registered the toxic dump. I took the flyer up to forty thousand feet. It was the one time the rules allowed a major overview during a quarter, but Maria didn't even glance at a porthole. She stood breathing hard, eyes on the deck, pale as dust. By the time she had control of herself again, we had shot forward and I was dropping back to legal height.

Maria was toxiphobic.

And she hadn't even seen the ruins over the horizon at 342 degrees.

I used the five minutes I had left to take us as far in the other direction as I could. Five minutes would never be enough time to fly there and do an I.D. My best bet was to hope she didn't fly that way during her half-hour.

She didn't. She veered off at twenty-eight degrees, and I kept careful track on my compass of everything she did after that. We came across three more polluter towns, but nothing big enough to qualify for points. When my console came back on, I headed straight back to my ruins, flying with that cocky grin that alerts fans that something is going to happen. Maria watched me sourly, at least when the camera was off her. "Know where we're going, do we?" I didn't answer. I didn't have to.

The city ruins were extensive, with roads leading in from all directions and a downtown´section of fallen concrete and steel poking above the blowing dust. There were no clues, however, in the architecture, or at least none that I could identify. Ari had been the architectural whiz.

I started the chatter on the 'plant. "Cazie on. I've found one. Daylight, doesn't seem to be waxing or waning. No architectural clues to describe. Central downtown core, roads leading in from all directions, collapsed overpasses, plain with a 1.62-degree incline, small river flowing outside the city but not through it, no other still-existing visible waterways."

"Team Leader on. What's the diameter?"

"Crossing it now . . . I estimate three miles metropolitan . . . hard to be sure."

"Regular perimeter?"

"Circling now . . ." The detector shrilled.

I started to take the flyer up and to the right, but after a minute the alarm shut down.

"Cazie on. There's a toxic dump, but it's small—a few seconds moved me out of range."

"Did you see anything significant while you were lifting?"

"No. I'll circle in the other direction, try to get a shape for the perimeter."

By now the fans would be glued to their sets. They, of course, already knew what city we had. The name would be shimmering across their screens. The question now was, how would we players identify it? And who would get the points? I had 14.3 minutes left. Maria stood at her console, jaw clenched so tight her lips flared out slightly, like a flower.

"Cazie on. The shape is pretty regular. No, wait, it flattens out into a sort of corridor of ruins extending out at 260 degrees. There's a *river* here. Another one. A big one, but really muddy, clogged, and sluggish. . . ." Not for the first time, I wished that soil analysis from inside the flyer was legal. Although then where would the challenge be?

"Jack on," he said through the 'plant. "Do the city ruins go right to the edge of the river or was there a park?"

"Cazie on. Seems to be extensive flat area between even the smallest ruins and the river."

"Team leader on. Vestigial vegetation?"

"None. The . . ." The alarm shrilled again.

This time the computer let me take the flyer all the way up. Maria started to tremble, clutching the edge of her console with both hands. Even over the alarms I could hear her: "Near cities. In their water, by their parks, goddamn fucking polluters, toxic dumps all over the place they *deserved* to all die . . ." But I didn't have time to gloat over her loss of control. Over twenty thousand feet the high-altitude equipment kicked in, all per game rules, and I got it all: aerial photos before we broke the cloud cover, sonar dimensions, sun position above the clouds, steel density patterns. Of course we couldn't access the computer banks, but we didn't have to. We had Jack, who had been a first-draft pick for his phenomenal memory. I passed him the figures right off the console, such a sweet clean information pass it almost brought tears to my eyes, and in less than a minute Jack said, "Syracuse, United States, North America!" Team Leader filed it, the computer confirmed, and the news went out over 'plants and cameras. The first score of the quarter. 185 points, plus points for initial continent identification, and no fouls for holding too long in toxic range. Mine.

I took the flyer down and grinned at Maria.

Once we knew where we were, the plays became a cinch. Chatter flew heavy over team channels: if you're in waning light and Cazie is in full light at 76 20' W 43 07' N, where might I be in what seems to be dawn? I pictured fans flipping channels, listening, arguing, the serious betters plotting flyer trails on map screens.

Maria found Rochester, United States. Her time ran out and I got Buffalo, United States, and Niagara Falls, Canada, which barely qualified for size and wasn't very many points, given that the falls are still there, torrents of water over eroded rock. Ari once told me that those falls are one of the few places on earth with relatively clean water because water going that fast through rapids cleanses itself every hundred yards. He was probably teasing.

Time was called a few hours after we reached dusk. Maria looked tired and angry, the anger probably because she'd given away so much. She was behind in points, behind in psych-out, undoubtedly down in the betting back home.

I whistled some Mozart.

Maria stared at me coldly. "Did you know they buried him in an open grave for outcasts? With lime over him so the body wouldn't smell? Just threw him in like garbage?"

I shrugged. I couldn't see that it mattered. His music is glorious, but he was probably just as morally guilty as all the rest of them. Polluters do not deserve to live. That's the first thing children are taught: Do not foul the life systems. I had a sudden flash of memory: Myself at four or five, marching around kindergarten, singing the orbital anthem and fingering the red stitching on my uniform: MY BODY, MY ORBITAL.

I said maliciously, "At least limestone isn't toxic." But she didn't even react. She really was depressed.

The screen in the corner suddenly flashed to life: Team Leader A. It startled both of us so much we turned in unison, like mechanical dolls. Only Team Leader A can use the screen to contact everyone during a game, and then only for game called, for an emergency, or for important news from home. He's the only one allowed direct orbital contact. My stomach tightened.

"Team Leader A. News flash. Don't panic, anyone, it's *not* an orbital. Repeat, no orbital is in danger. But something has happened: They've opened warfare on the moon."

Maria and I looked at each other. She was breathing hard. Not that she knew anybody on the moon, of course; it's been two generations since anybody but diplomats have made contact with those maniacs. Generations before that their ancestors chose their way off planet, ours chose ours. To qualify for an orbital, you had to be a certain kind of person: non-violent, non-polluting, no criminal record of any kind, clearly self-supporting (you had to have money, of course, but money alone wouldn't do it), intelligent, and *fair*. You had to be able to respect rules.

Nobody else got in, not even relatives of qualifiers. Our founders knew they were choosing the future of the human race.

Everybody else with enough money but not enough decency tried to get to a moon colony.

"As far as orbital diplomats can tell, the war started when one underground moon colony mined another and detonated by remote. We don't yet know how many colonies are involved. But the orbitals agree that there is no danger to us. This war, if it is a war, is confined to themselves."

Team Leader A looked at us a minute longer. I couldn't read his expression. Then the screen went blank.

"Oh, God," Maria said. "All those people."

I looked at her curiously. "What do you care? There's no threat to any orbital."

"I *know* that. But even so, Cazie . . . that's not a game. It's real. Dying trapped underground while everything explodes around you. . . ."

I got out the third set of black-out strips. To tell you the absolute truth, I find attitudes like Maria's tiresome. She can't really care about moonies; how could she? They're no different from the maniacs who ruined Earth in the first place. She was just pretending because it made her look sensitive, cosmopolitan . . . to me it looked flabby. Moonies weren't like us. They didn't understand moral obligations. They didn't follow the rules. If they all blew each other up, it would just make space that much safer for the orbitals.

And her depression was ruining my triumph in the game.

That was when I realized that she must be doing it deliberately. And pretty neat it was. I had almost lost my edge for the game, thinking about moonies trapped underground . . . there's nothing so terrible about being underground anyway. It probably wasn't that much different from the coziness of an orbital. It was wide, open, unprotected spaces that were scary.

Unless you were scoping them from thirty thousand feet, making a high, clean information pass, the first one of the quarter and a total of two hundred points. . . .

I opened her black-out drug, grinning.

In the third quarter the computer set us down in darkness, on sand. Blowing sand as far as the high beams could see at maximum altitude. Miles and miles of blowing sand. Over

my 'plant Nikos, our broad-base geography offense, ran me
through the most likely deserts. Maria used a sweet triple-feint
to get to her console first, and she called the first play.

We didn't find *anything* for hours. Team C reported Glasgow
just as our sky began to pale in the east, and that gave us an
approximate longitude. Jack found Colombo. Team A reported
Managua and Baghdad. Then, slowly, mountains began to rise
on our horizon. I calculated how far away they must be; they
were *huge*.

"Nikos on," he said. "All right, I have to make this quick,
Cazie, my play starts in forty-five seconds and we're coming
into something. The mountains are part of the Rockies, and
you're between them and the Mississippi River in the Great
Central Desert of North America. Fly close enough to describe
specific mountain profiles with degree separations to Jack and
he'll take it from there. Jack, can you take it now?"

"Jack on. Got it. Cazie, go."

I described for three minutes and he suggested where I
should look. I did, but not quick enough. Maria got La Junta,
United States, North America. I got Pueblo, just barely. Then
we hit a toxic dump and an announcement from Team Leader
A simultaneously.

"Team Leader A. News flash. Orbital diplomats in three
moon colonies have ceased communicating: Faldean, Troi-
ka, and Alpha. The assumption is that all three colonies are
destroyed and our . . . our diplomats are dead."

His image stared straight ahead. After a minute he added,
"I'll let you all know if they call the game."

Call the game.

"They won't do that, will they, do you think?" I said to
Maria.

She said, "I don't know."

I found Colorado Springs.

But how many fans were even watching?

They didn't call the game. We finished the day almost dead
even. Right after we took the black-out drug, Maria crawled
into my bunk. I was surprised—flabbergasted. But it turned
out she didn't even want to fuck, just to be held. I held her,

wondering what the hell was going on, if she thought I'd
fall for some kind of sexual psych-out. The idea was almost
insulting; I'd been a pro for nearly eight years. But she just
lay there quietly, not talking, and when black-out was over she
again seemed focused and tough, ready for the last quarter.

"Tallyho."

I never did learn what that meant. But I wasn't about to ask.
I knew Maria had finished most of the two-year Yale software,
and I've never even accessed a college program.

We de-opaqued in rocky hills, in daylight. Twenty minutes
later we found a saltwater coast. After that it was almost too
easy: Algiers. Bejaia. Skikda. Bizerte. Tunis. Not even any
toxic dumps to speak of.

Too easy. And Maria and I were almost even in pre-reffed
points.

"My play!"

"Take it, asshole. You won't reach Kalrouan or Monastir by
the time the quarter ends."

"The hell I won't."

Of course I didn't. It was too far. But I reached something
else.

The light had begun to fail. I gambled on sticking to the
coast rather than flying inland towards Kalrouan. Out of the
gathering darkness loomed red cliffs. Piles of rubble clung
to their sides, banked on terraces and ledges that had been
folded by earthquakes and eroded by wind. From the sides
of the cliffs twisted steel beams bristled like matted hair.
"Cazie on. There's a city—maybe not a city—just below me.
We're twenty-two minutes out of Tunis following the coast.
Jack?"

"Jack on. Too small to qualify."

"Team Leader on. Sorry, Cazie. Come on in."

"It doesn't look too small!"

"It's too small."

"Maybe it's in the supplementary d-base." Nobody memo-
rizes the supplementary database; it's all those cities and towns
that don't qualify for points. Unless, of course, there's a tie, or
a field goal at endgame. . . .

Seventeen minutes left.

"Team Leader on. We don't have any reason to think we're that close to a tie, Cazie. And if you earn a penalty by calling it wrong—"

Nobody can call in advance how the computer will ref points. Base points are of course known, but there are too many variables altering base points. If there's a flash of sunshine that the flyer registers as strong enough to count as a latitude clue, you lose points, even if you didn't notice that the fucking clouds parted. There are penalties assessed against other teams that you don't hear about until the quarter's over. There are points added for plays in darkness, subtracted for nuclear-radiation clues above certain level, multiplied by a fractional constant for the number of cities already found during the quarter, factored for dozens of other things. But against all that, I *knew*. I did. We were close to a tie. You don't play this game for eight years without developing a sixth sense, a feeling. A hunch.

Sixteen minutes.

"Cazie on. I got a hunch. I just do. Let me try for a touchdown."

"Team Leader on. Cazie, last time you . . ."

"Larissa—*please*."

She didn't say anything. Neither did Jack or Nikos. Last time I tried for an endgame touchdown I froze. Just froze, out there alone in the howling unbreathable desert with no walls, no life support, unprotected under that naked angry sky. . . . We were disqualified. Disgraced. Odds on us lengthened to the moon, all four of us slept alone for a month. It took three flyers to get me in.

"Please. I have the hunch."

"Team Leader on. Go."

Fifteen minutes.

I slammed my fist onto the console code and struggled into my suit. The camera floated in for close-ups. Maria watched me through narrowed eyes. My 'plant said, *She's going to say it.*

"Cazie, it's only a game. It's not worth risking your life for a game."

I sealed the suit.

"You'll be exposed right at the edge of the ocean. God knows what toxins you'll be exposed to, even through the suit. You know that. We went right over that dump down the coast, and that ocean looks terrible. When your field's off, you'll be completely exposed."

I reached for my helmet. She was talking her fears, not mine.

"*And* you'll be right there in the *open*. God, all that open space around you, desolate, winds blowing—completely *exposed*. Unprotected. The winds could blow you off the—"

I sealed my helmet, shutting out her words.

The airlock took one minute to empty and open. Eleven minutes. The second the door opened, I was out.

The winds hit me so hard I cried out and fell against the flyer. The camera, buffeted by winds, was right behind me. I straightened and started away from the flyer. Almost immediately the fear was there, clawing at me from inside.

Open. Unprotected. Poisoned. Life systems fouled, death in the air and soil and water. . . . Twenty-eight years of conditioning. And the fact that my conscious mind knew it was conditioning didn't help at all. Dead, foul, exposed, dead, dead, unprotected. . . .

I made myself keep walking. Nine minutes.

The city—town, village—had been built down the cliff and, probably, along a coastal strip that was now all underwater. When they had built like that, often "richer" people lived higher up, in sturdier structures. Ahead of me the cliff turned in on itself a little, giving more shelter to whatever structures had been there. I made for the bend, running as fast as I could, the wind at my back, fighting the desire to scream. To fall. To freeze.

Around the curve of rock were twisted steel beams, welded together and extending back inside the rock. I wrenched at them, which was stupid; they were huge, and nothing was going to break off a piece that could be carried into a flyer. There were chunks of concrete all around, but concrete doesn't count. Below me, the poisoned ocean howled and thrashed.

I worked my way between the steel beams. Whatever walls had been here had long since fallen down, the rubble blown away or washed away or just disintegrated. Dust blew all over everything; the steel and concrete were pitted by grit. It was the ugliest place I had ever seen. And it could shift under my feet any second. But between the steel beams a kind of cave, still roughly rectangular, led back into the cliff. The polluters had built into the earth before they destroyed it.

Three minutes.

I climbed over fallen rocks and rubble to get deeper into the cave house. For a moment I remembered the underground war on the moon and my breath stopped, but at the same moment I passed some kind of threshold and the sound from the horrible winds diminished abruptly. I kept on going.

Two minutes.

At the very back of the house I found it.

There was a loose fall of rock from the ceiling in the most protected corner; smashed wood stuck out from under it. Some piece of furniture. I tugged at the rocks; when they wouldn't move, I scrabbled with my hands behind them. Oh God don't tear the suit, don't let the ground shift or more rocks fall from the ceiling, don't . . . my fingers closed on something smooth and hard.

And whole.

It was a keyboard, wedged between two rocks, slimy with some kind of mold but in one piece. I wiggled it free and started to run. For the first time in many minutes I became aware of the camera, floating along behind me. Not slowing, I held the keyboard in front of it, screaming words it couldn't hear and I couldn't remember. The winds hit me like a blow, but if I was clear enough of the cave for wind, I was clear enough for transmission.

"Cazie on! Larissa? Fuck it—*Larissa!*"

"Go!"

"I got it! A touchdown! A whole! A touchdown!"

"Touchdown by Team D!" Larissa screamed, on what I assumed to be all channels. "Touchdown!"

Thirty seconds.

The earth moved under me.

I screamed. I was going to die. The game was over but I was going to die, exposed unprotected poisoned dead on the fucking earth. . . .

The quake was small. I wasn't going to die. I swayed, sobbed, and began to fight my way back against the wind. Darkness was falling fast. But I could see the flyer, I was almost there, I had the whole, I was not going to freeze, and the treacherous earth was not going to take its revenge on me. On someone, almost certainly, eventually, but not on me.

Touchdown.

We won.

The reffed score among three teams—not just two, but *three*—was close enough to make the endgame play legal. We got 865 points adjusted, and beat the closest team, C, by 53 points. My keyboard gave us Sidi Bou Said, Tunisia, North Africa, from the supplementary database—a town no one had scored before.

The party at the base was wild, with fans at home flashing messages on the screen so fast you could barely read them. Drink flowed. I got pounded on the back so often I was sore. I had five whispered bids for the traditional post-game activity, *three* of them from Team Leaders. High on victory, I chose Ari. He had always been the best lover I had, and we even, in drunken pleasure, talked about getting together again back home. It was an astonishing party. Fans will talk about it for years.

Team Leader A says they'll put the keyboard in a museum in one of the orbitals, after the thing is cleaned up and detoxed. I don't care what they do with it. It served its purpose.

The moon war apparently was brief and deadly. No transmissions from any colony. They're assumed all dead. But while I was downing my third victory drink and Larissa and I were laughing it up for the cameras, I got a great idea. All the moon colonies were underground, so it won't take long for the surface marks to disappear: Collapse the energy domes and in a few years meteors will make the surface look pretty much like the rest of the moon. But the colonies will still be there underground, or their ruins will, detectable to sonar or maybe new heatseekers. As long as the heat lasts, anyway. Looking for them will be a tremendous challenge, a new kind of challenge, with new plays and feints and tactics and brand new rules.

I can hardly wait.

WATER BRINGER

Mary Rosenblum

*"Water Bringer" was purchased by Gardner Dozois,
and appeared in the March 1991 issue of IAsfm,
with an evocative cover painting and interior illustration by Broeck Steadman. A brand-new writer,
Mary Rosenblum made her first sale, to IAsfm, in
1990, but she is a pleasingly prolific writer, and
soon made a half dozen more sales to us, as well
as sales to* The Magazine of Fantasy and Science
Fiction, Pulphouse, *and elsewhere; we are happy to
say that we have a number of new stories by her in
inventory. Among her stories to appear in IAsfm in
1991 were a linked series of three stories about the
Drylands, the first of which, "Water Bringer," follows. In it, she takes us out West—not to the familiar
American West that we know, but instead to a near
(and all-too-probable) future West where the water
has finally and irrevocably run out, the aquifers and
watertables have run dry, and deserts have eaten
the former farms and towns and ranches of Oregon
and Washington and Montana and Wyoming . . . and
against this bleak background, she spins a stark but
poignant story of human hopes and fears, of love and
betrayal and the power of dreams.*

A graduate of Clarion West, new writer Mary Rosenblum lives with her family in Portland, Oregon. She has just completed her first novel, based on her Drylands stories, and is at work on another.

Sitting with his back against the sunscorched rimrock, Jeremy made the dragonfly appear in the air in front of him. It hovered in the hot, still air, wings shimmering with bluegreen glints. Pretty. He looked automatically over his shoulder, as if Dad might be standing there, face hard and angry. But Dad was down in the dusty fields. So were Jonathan, Mother, Rupert, even the twins—everyone but him.

It was safe.

Jeremy hunched farther into his sliver of shade, frowning at his creation. It was a little too blue—that was it—and the eyes were too small. He frowned, trying to remember the picture in the insect book. The dragonfly's bright body darkened as its eyes swelled.

Bingo. Jeremy smiled and sat up straight. The dragonfly hovered above a withered bush, wings glittering in the sunlight. He sent it darting out over the canyon, leaned over the ledge to watch it.

Far below, a man was leading a packhorse up the main road from the old riverbed. A stranger! Jeremy let the dragonfly vanish as he squinted against the glare. Man and horse walked with their heads down, like they were both tired. Their feet raised brown puffs of dust that hung in the air like smoke.

Jeremy held his breath as the stranger stopped at their road. "Come *on*," Jeremy breathed. "There's nowhere else for two miles."

As if they'd heard him, the pair turned up the rutted track. The man didn't pull on the horse's lead rope—they moved together, like they'd both decided together to stop at the farm.

Jeremy scrambled up over the rimrock and lurched into a

shambling run. You didn't see strangers out here very often. Mostly, they stopped at La Grande. The convoys stuck to the interstate, and nobody else went anywhere. Dead grass stems left from the brief spring crackled and snapped under Jeremy's feet, and the hard ground jolted him, stabbing his twisted knees with bright slivers of pain.

At the top of the steep trail that led down to the farm, Jeremy had to slow up. He limped down the slope, licking dust from his lips, breathing quick and hard. They'd hear it all first—all the news—before he even got there. The sparse needles on the dying pines held the heat close to the ground. Dry branches clawed at him, trying to slow him down even more. They wouldn't wait for him. They never did. Suddenly furious, Jeremy swung at the branches with his thickened hands, but they only slapped back at him, scratching his face and arms.

Sure enough, by the time he reached the barnyard the brown-and-white horse was tethered in the dim heat of the sagging barn, unsaddled and drowsing. Everyone would be in the kitchen with the stranger. Jeremy licked his lips. At least there'd be a pitcher of fresh water out. He crossed the sunburned yard and limped up the warped porch steps.

" . . . desertification's finally reached its limit, so the government's putting all its resources into reclamation."

Desertification? Jeremy paused at the door. The word didn't have a clear meaning in his head, but it felt dusty and dry as the fields. He peeked inside. The stranger sat in Dad's place at the big table, surrounded by the whole family. He wore a stained tan shirt with a picture of a castle tower embroidered on the pocket. He had dark curly hair and a long face with a jutting nose. Jeremy pushed the screen door slowly open. The stranger's face reminded him of the canyon wall, all crags and peaks and sharp shadows.

The door slipped through his fingers and banged closed behind him.

"Jeremy?" His mother threw a quick glance at Dad as she turned around. "Where have you been? I was worried."

"He snuck up to the rimrock again," Rupert muttered, just loud enough.

Jeremy flinched, but Dad wasn't looking at him at all. He'd heard, though. His jaw had gotten tight, but he didn't even turn his head. Jeremy felt his face getting hot, and edged toward the door.

"Hi." The stranger's smile pinned Jeremy in place; it crinkled the sunbrowned skin around his eyes. "I'm Dan Greely," the stranger said.

"From the Army Engineers!" ten-year old David announced.

"To bring *water*!" Paulie interrupted his twin.

"You're not supposed to go up there, Jeremy." Mother gave Dad an uneasy, sideways glance. "You could fall."

"So, just how does the Corps of Engineers plan to irrigate the valley when the river's dry as a bone?" Jeremy's father spoke as if no one else had said a word. "God knows, you can't find water when it ain't there to be found."

"Don't be so hard on him, Everett." Mother turned back to Dad.

"I ain't even heard any solid reasons for *why* the damn country's drying up," Dad growled. "Desertification!" He snorted. "Fancy word for no damn water. Tell me *why*, surveyor."

"At least someone's trying to do something about it." Mother was using her soothing tone.

They weren't paying any attention to him any more, not even tattletale Rupert. Jeremy slipped into his favorite place, the crevice between the wood-box and the cold kitchen cookstove.

"We'll be glad to put you up while you're about your business," Mother went on. "It would be like a dream come true for us, if you folks can give us water again. We've all wondered sometimes if we did right to stay here and try to hang on."

"What else *could* we do?" Dad said harshly. "Quit and go work in the Project fields like a bunch of Mex laborers?"

"I can't promise you water," the stranger said gravely. "I'm just the surveyor. I hear that some of these deep-aquifer projects have been pretty successful, though."

"It's enough to know that there's hope." Mother's voice had gone rough, like she wanted to cry.

Jeremy started to peek around the stove, but froze as Dad's hand smacked the tabletop.

"He ain't dug any wells *yet*. You kids get back to work. Those beans gotta be weeded by supper,'cause we're not wasting water on weeds. Jonathan, I know you and Rupert ain't finished your pumping yet."

"Aw, come on," Rupert whined. "We want to hear about stuff. Are people really eating each other in the cities?"

"You heard your father," Mother said sharply. "The washbucket's too dirty for supper dishes. Rupert, you take it out to the squash—the last two hills in the end row—and bring me a fresh bucket."

"Aw, Mom!" Rupert said, but he pushed back his chair.

Jeremy scrunched down, listening to the scuffle of his brothers' bare feet as they filed out of the kitchen.

"We don't have much in the way of hay for your pony," Jeremy's father grumbled. "How long are you planning on staying, anyway?"

"Not long. I can give you a voucher for food and shelter. When they set up the construction camp, you just take it to the comptroller for payment."

"Lot of good *money*'ll do me. There wasn't enough rain to make hay worth shit this season. Where'm I going to buy any?"

The screen door banged. Dad was angry. Jeremy frowned and wiggled into a more comfortable position. Why should Dad be angry? The stranger talked about water. Everyone needed water.

"Never mind him." From the clatter, Mother was dishing up bean-and-squash stew left over from lunch. "You have to understand, it's hard for him to hope after all these years." A plate clunked on the table. "You keep pumping water, trying to grow enough to live on, praying the well holds out and watching your kids go to bed hungry. You don't have much energy left for hoping. When you're done, I'll show you your room. The twins can sleep with Jeremy and Rupert."

She sounded like she was going to cry again. Jeremy looked down at his loosely curled fists. The thick joints made his fingers look like knobby tree roots. The stranger said something, but Jeremy didn't catch it. He'd only heard Mother cry once before—when the doctor over in La Grande had told her that there wasn't anything that could be done about his hands or his knees.

This stranger made Dad angry and Mother sad. Jeremy thought about that while he waited, but he couldn't make any sense of it at all. As soon as the stranger and Mother left the kitchen, Jeremy slipped out of his hiding place. Sure enough, the big plastic pitcher stood on the table, surrounded by empty glasses. You didn't ask for water between meals. Jeremy listened to the quiet. He lifted the pitcher, clutching it tightly in his thick, awkward grip.

The water was almost as warm as the air by now, but it tasted sweet on his dusty throat. He never got enough water. No one did—not when the crops needed it, too. Jeremy swirled the pitcher, watching the last bit of water climb the sides in a miniature whirlpool.

Absently, he made it fill clear to the brim. What would it be like to live in the old days, when it rained all the time and the riverbed was full of water and fish? He imagined a fish, made it appear in the water. He'd seen it in another book, all speckled green with a soft shading of pink on its belly. He made the fish leap out of the pitcher and dive back in, splashing tiny droplets of water that vanished as they fell. Jeremy tilted his head, pleased with himself. Trout—he remembered the fish's name, now.

"Jeremy!"

Jeremy started at his mother's cry and dropped the pitcher. Water and fish vanished as the plastic clattered on the linoleum. Throat tight, he stared at the small puddle of real water. The stranger stood behind Mother in the doorway.

"Go see if there are any eggs." His mother's voice quivered. "Do it right now!"

Jeremy limped out the door without looking at either of them.

"Don't mind him," he heard his mother say breathlessly. "He's clumsy, is all."

She was afraid that the stranger had seen the fish. Jeremy hurried across the oven glare of the barnyard. What if he *had*? What if he said something in front of Dad? His skin twitched with the memory of the last beating Dad had given him, when he'd gotten to daydreaming and made the dragonfly appear in the church. Jeremy shivered.

The stranger's horse snorted at him, pulling back against its halter with a muffled thudding of hooves. "Easy boy, easy." Jeremy stumbled to a halt, stretched out his hand. The pinto shook its thick mane and stretched its neck to sniff. Jeremy smiled as the velvety lips brushed his palm. "You're pretty," he said, but it wasn't true. It wasn't even a horse, really—just a scruffy pony with a thick neck and feet big as dinnerplates.

He was ugly. Jeremy sat down stiffly, leaning his back against the old, smooth boards of the barn. "Hey." He wiggled his toes as the pony sniffed at his bare feet. "It's not *your* fault you're ugly." He stroked the pony's nose. "I bet you can run like the wind," he murmured.

The pony's raspy breathing sounded friendly, comforting. Eyes half-closed, Jeremy imagined himself galloping over the sunscorched meadows. His knees wouldn't matter at all. . . . He drifted off into a dream of wind and galloping hooves.

"Jeremy! It's supper time. Where the hell are you?"

Rupert's voice. Jeremy blinked awake, swallowing a yawn. It was almost dark. Straw tickled his cheek, and he remembered. He was in the barn, and a stranger had seen him make something.

"I know you're in here." Rupert's footsteps crunched closer.

By now, Dad probably knew about the trout. Jeremy rolled onto his stomach and wriggled under the main beam beneath the wall. There was just enough space for his skinny body.

"I hear you, you brat." Rupert's silhouette loomed against the gray rectangle of the doorway. "You think I want to play hide and seek after I work all day? If I get in trouble, I'll *get* you."

The pony laid back its ears and whinnied shrilly.

"Jesus!" Rupert jumped back. "I hope you get your head kicked off!" he yelled.

Jeremy listened to Rupert stomp out of the barn. "Thanks, pony," he whispered as he scrambled out of his hiding place.

He shook powdery dust out of his clothes, listening for the slam of the screen door.

Better to face Rupert later than Dad right now.

The pony nudged him, and Jeremy scratched absently at its ear. A bat twittered in the darkness over his head. Jeremy looked up, barely able to make out the flittering shadows coming and going through the gray arch of the doorway. He'd sneak in later. Jeremy's stomach growled as he curled up against the wall of the barn. The pony snuffled softly and moved closer, as if it was glad he was there.

The barn was full of dry creaks and whispers. Something rustled loudly in the loft above Jeremy's head and he started. Funny how darkness *changed* the friendly barn, stretched it out so big. Too big and too dark. "Want to see a firefly?" Jeremy asked the pony. The darkness seemed to swallow his words. It pressed in around him, as if he had made it angry by talking.

He hadn't been able to find a picture . . . The firefly appeared, bright as a candleflame in the darkness. It looked sort of like a glowing moth. That didn't seem right, but its warm glow drove back the darkness. Jeremy examined it thoughtfully. Maybe he should make the wings bigger.

"So I wasn't seeing things," a voice said.

The pony whinnied and Jeremy snuffed out the firefly. Before he could hide, a dazzling beam of light flashed in his eyes. He raised a hand against the hurting glare.

"Sorry." The light dipped, illuminating a circular patch of dust and Jeremy's dirty legs. "So, this is where you've been. Your brother said he couldn't find you." The beam hesitated on Jeremy's lumpy knees.

The surveyor patted the pony and bent to prop the solar flashlight on the floor. Its powerful beam splashed back from the wall, streaking the straw with shadows. "Can you do it again?" he asked. "Make that insect appear, I mean."

Jeremy licked his dry lips. He *had* seen the trout. "I'm not supposed to . . . make things."

"I sort of got that impression." The man gave him a slow, thoughtful smile. "I pretended I didn't notice. I didn't want to get you in trouble."

Jeremy blinked. This stranger—a grown-up—had worried about getting *him* in trouble? The bright, comforting light and the surveyor's amazing claim shut the two of them into a kind of private, magic circle.

Why *not* let him see? He'd already seen the trout, and he hadn't told Dad. The firefly glowed to life in the air between them. "What does a firefly really look like?" Jeremy asked.

"I don't know." The surveyor reached out to touch the making, snatched his hand away as his finger passed through the delicate wings.

"It isn't real. It doesn't even *look* right." Disappointed, Jeremy let it fade and vanish.

"Wow." The surveyor whistled softly. "I've never seen anything like *that*."

He made it sound like Jeremy was doing something wonderful. "Don't tell I showed you, okay?" Jeremy picked at a thread in his ragged cutoffs.

"I won't." The man answered him seriously, as if he was talking to another grown-up. "How old are you?" he asked, after a minute.

"Twelve. I'm small for my age." Jeremy watched him pick up his marvelous light and swing its bright beam over the old pony.

"You look pretty settled, Ezra. I'll get you some more water in the morning." The surveyor slapped the pony on the neck. "Come on," he said to Jeremy. "Let's go in. I think your mom left a plate out for you." He gave Jeremy a sideways look. "Your dad went to bed," he said.

"Oh." Jeremy scrambled to his feet, wondering how the stranger knew to say that. If Dad was asleep, it was safe to go back in. Besides, this ungrownuplike man hadn't told on him. "Are you going to bring us water?" he asked.

"No," the man said slowly. "I just make maps. I don't dig wells."

"I bet you're good," Jeremy said. He wanted to say something nice to this man, and that was all he could think of.

"Thanks," the surveyor said, but he sounded more sad than pleased. "I'm pretty good at what I do."

No, he didn't act like a grown-up. He didn't act like anyone Jeremy had ever met. Thoughtfully, he followed the bright beam of the surveyor's flashlight into the house.

Next morning was church-Sunday, but the family got up at dawn as usual, because it was such a long walk into town. Jeremy put on his good pair of shorts and went down to take on Mother in the kitchen.

"You can't go." She shoved a full water-jug into the lunch pack. "It's too far."

She was remembering the dragonfly. "I won't forget. I'll be good," Jeremy said. "Please?"

"Forget it." Rupert glared at him from the doorway. "The freak'll forget and do something weird again."

"That's enough." Mother closed the pack with a jerk. "I'll bring you a new book." She wouldn't meet Jeremy's eyes. "What do you want?"

"I don't know." Jeremy set his jaw. He didn't usually care, didn't like church-Sundays, with all the careful eyes that sneaked like Rupert when they looked at his hands and knees. But this time, the surveyor was going. "I want to *come*," he said.

"Mom . . ."

"I said that's enough." Mother looked past Rupert. "Did you get enough breakfast, Mr. Greely?" she asked too cheerfully.

"More than enough, thanks." The surveyor walked into the kitchen and the conversation ended.

When Jeremy started down the gravel road with them, Mother's lips got tight and Rupert threw him a look that promised trouble, but Dad acted like he wasn't even there, and no one else dared say anything. Jeremy limped along as fast as he could, trying not to fall behind. He had won. He wasn't sure why, but he had.

It was a long, hot walk to town.

Rupert and Jonathan stuck to the surveyor like burrs, asking about the iceberg tugs, the Drylands, Portland, and L.A. The surveyor answered their questions gravely and politely. He wore a fresh tan shirt tucked into his faded jeans. It was clean, and the tower on the pocket made it look like it meant something special.

It meant *water* . . .

Everyone was there by the time they reached the church—except the Menendez family who lived way down the dry creekbed and sometimes didn't come anyway. The Pearson kids were screaming as they took turns jumping off the porch, and Bev LaMont was watching for Jonathan, like she always did.

As soon as they got close enough for people to count the extra person, everyone abandoned their picnic spreads and made for the porch.

"This is Mr. Greely, a surveyor with the Army Corps of Engineers," Mother announced as they climbed the wide steps.

"Pleased to meet you." The surveyor's warm smile swept the sun-dried faces. "I've been sent to make a preliminary survey for a federal irrigation project." He perched on the porch railing, like he'd done it a hundred times before. "The new Singhe solar cells are going to power a deepwell pumping operation. We think we've identified a major aquifer in this region."

"How come we ain't heard of this before?" It was bearded Ted Brewster, who ran the Exxon station when he could get gas, speaking up from the back of the crowd.

"Come on, Ted." Fists on her bony hips, gray-haired Sally Brandt raised her voice. "By the time news makes it here from Boise, it's gone through six drunken truckers. They're lucky if they can remember their names."

"No. That's a good question." The surveyor looked around at the small knot of dusty faces. "You don't get any radio or TV?"

"No power, out here." Sally shook her head. "Anyway, we couldn't get TV after Spokane quit. There's too many mountains to pick up Boise, and I don't think there's anything big broadcasting anymore this side of Portland."

The surveyor nodded and reached inside his shirt. "I have a letter from the regional supervisor." He pulled out a white rectangle. "I'm supposed to deliver it to the mayor, city supervisor, or whoever's in charge." He raised his eyebrows expectantly.

A gust of wind whispered across the crowded porch, and no one spoke.

"Most people just *left*." Jeremy's father finally stepped forward, fists in the pockets of his patched jeans. "This was wheat and alfalfa land, from the time the Oregon Territory became a state. You can't farm wheat without water." His voice sounded loud in the silence. "The National Guard come around and told us to go get work on the Columbia River project. That's all the help the *government* was gonna give us. If we stayed, they said, we'd dry up and starve. They didn't really give a shit." He paused. "We don't have a mayor anymore," he said. "There's just us."

The surveyor looked at the dusty faces, one by one. "Like I told Mr. Barlow last night," he said quietly, "I can't promise that we'll find water, or that you'll grow wheat again. I'm only the surveyor."

For a long moment, Jeremy's father stared at the envelope. Then, with a jerky, awkward gesture, he reached out and took it. He pried up the white flap with a blunt thumb, and squinted at the print, forehead wrinkling with effort.

Without a word, he handed the paper to Ted Brewster. Jeremy watched the white paper pass from hand to hand. People held it like it was precious—like it was water. He listened to the dry rustle of the paper. When it came around to Dad again, he stuck it into the glass case beside the door of the church. "I hope to God you find water," he said softly.

"Amen," someone said.

"Amen." The ragged mutter ran through the crowd.

After that, everyone broke up. After the Reverend had died in the big dust storm, they'd moved the pews outside. Families spread cloths on the long, rickety tables inside. There weren't any more sermons, but people still came to eat together on church-Sundays. The surveyor wandered from group to group in the colored shadows of the church, eating the food people pressed on him. They crowded him, talking, brushing up against him, as if his touch would bring good luck, bring water to the dead fields.

Jeremy hung back, under the blue-and-green diamonds of the stained-glass window. Finally, he went down the narrow stairs to the sparse shelves of the basement library. He found a little paperback book on insects, but it didn't have a picture of a firefly. He tossed it back onto the shelf. When it fell onto the dusty concrete floor, he kicked it, feeling both guilty and pleased when it skittered out of sight under a shelf. Upstairs, the surveyor was giving everyone the same warm grin that he'd given to Jeremy in the barn last night.

It made Jeremy's stomach ball up into an angry knot.

He wandered outside and found little Rita Menendez poking at ants on the front walk. Mrs. Menendez was yelling at the older kids as she started to unpack the lunch, so Jeremy carried Rita off into the dappled shade under the scraggly shrubs. She was too little to mind his hands. Belly still tight, Jeremy made a bright green frog appear on Rita's knee.

Her gurgly laugh eased some of the tightness. *She* liked his makings. He turned the frog into the dragonfly and she grabbed at it. This time, Jeremy heard the surveyor coming. By the time the man pushed the brittle branches aside, the dragonfly was gone.

"Do you always hide?" He reached down to tickle Rita's plump chin.

"I'm not hiding." Jeremy peeked up through his sun-bleached hair.

"I need someone to help me." The surveyor squatted, so that Jeremy had to meet his eyes. "I talked to your father and he said I could hire you. If you agree. The Corps' only paying crisis-minimum," he said apologetically.

Jeremy pushed Rita gently off his lap. This man wanted to hire *him*—with his bad knees and his lumpy, useless hands? Hiring was something from the old days, like the flashlight and this man's clean, creased shirt.

Jeremy wiped his hands on his pants, pressing hard, as if by doing so he might straighten his bent fingers. "I'd like that, Mr. Greely," he said breathlessly.

"Good." The man smiled like he meant it. "We'll get started first thing tomorrow." He stood, giving Rita a final pat that made her chuckle. "Call me Dan," he said. "Okay?"

"Okay, Dan," Jeremy said softly. He watched the man walk away, feeling warm inside.

• • •

Jeremy didn't see much of Dan Greely before the next morning.
It seemed like everyone had to talk to Dan about watertables,
aquifers, deep wells, and the Army Corps of Engineers. They
said the words like the Reverend used to say prayers. *Army
Corps of Engineers*.

Dan, Dad, and Jonathan stayed in town. Mother shepherded
the rest of them home. The twins were tired, but Rupert was
pissed because he couldn't stay, too. He shoved Jeremy whenever Mother wasn't looking.

"I hope you work hard for Mr. Greely," Mother said when
she came up to say goodnight. The twins were already snoring
in the hot darkness of the attic room.

"Waste of time to hire *him*," Rupert growled from his bed.
"The pony'd be more use."

"That's enough." Mother's voice sounded sharp as a new
nail. "We can't spare either you or Jonathan from the pumping,
so don't get yourself worked up. You don't *have* to go with
him," she said to Jeremy. Her hand trembled just a little as she
brushed the hair back from his forehead.

She was worried. "It'll be okay," Jeremy murmured. He
wondered why. He almost told her that Dan already knew
about the making and wouldn't tell, but Rupert was listening.
"I'll do good," he said, and wished he believed it.

It took Jeremy a long time to fall asleep, but, when he did,
it seemed like only moments had passed before he woke up
again. At first, he thought Mother was calling him for breakfast. It was still dark, but the east window showed faint gray.

There it was again—Mother's voice. Too wide awake to fall
back to sleep, Jeremy slipped out of bed and tiptoed into the
dark hall.

"Stop worrying." Dad's low growl drifted through the half-
open door. "What do you think he's gonna do? Eat the kid?"

"I don't know. He said he needed a helper, but what . . ."

"What can Jeremy do? He can't do shit, but Greely's gonna
pay wages, and we can use anything we can get." Dad's voice
sounded like the dry, scouring winds. "How do you think I felt
when I had to go crawling to the Brewsters and the Pearsons
for food last winter?"

"It wasn't Jeremy's fault, Everett, the well giving out."

"No one *else* has an extra mouth to feed. No one but me, and I've gotta go begging."

"I lost three babies after Rupert." Mother's voice sounded high and tight. "I couldn't of stood losing another."

Jeremy fumbled his way down the hall, teeth clenched so hard they felt like they were going to break. *No one else has an extra mouth to feed.* His father's cold words chased him down the stairs. *No one but me.*

A light glowed in the barn's darkness. "Hi." Dan pulled a strap tight on the pony's packsaddle. "I was just going to come wake you. Ezra and I are used to starting at dawn." He tugged on the pack, nodded to himself. "Have you eaten yet?" he asked Jeremy.

"Yeah," Jeremy lied.

Dan gave him a searching look, then shrugged. "Okay. Let's go."

It was just light enough to see as they started down the track. The pony stepped over the thin white pipe that carried water from the well to the field. Above them, the old bicycle frame of the pump looked like a skeleton sticking up out of the gray dirt. In an hour, Jonathan would be pedaling hard to get his gallons pumped. Then Rupert would take over. The twins would be carrying the yoked pails, and dipping out precious water to each thirsty plant.

"Did your dad make that?" Dan nodded at the metal frame.

"Uh huh." Jeremy walked a little faster, trying not to limp.

He had had a thousand questions about the outside world to ask, but the sharp whispers in the upstairs hall had dried them up like the wind dried up a puddle. He watched Ezra's big feet kick up the brown dust, feeling dry and empty inside.

"We'll start here." The surveyor pulled Ezra to a halt. They were looking down on the dry riverbed and the narrow, rusty bridge. The road went across the riverbed now. It was easier.

The pony waited patiently, head drooping, while Dan unloaded it. "This machine measures distance by bouncing a beam of light off a mirror." Dan set the cracked plastic case down on the ground. "It sits on this tripod and the reflector goes on the other one." He unloaded a water jug, lunch, an axe, a steel tape measure and other odds and ends. "Now, we get to work," he said when he was done.

Sweat stuck Jeremy's hair to his face as he struggled across the sunbaked clay after Dan. They set up the machine and reflector, took them down and set them up somewhere else. Sometimes Dan hacked a path through the dry brush. It was hard going. In spite of all he could do, Jeremy was limping badly by mid-morning.

"I'm sorry." Dan stopped abruptly. "You keep up so well, it's easy to forget that you hurt."

His tone was matter of fact, without a trace of pity. There was a knot in Jeremy's throat as Dan boosted him onto Ezra's back. He sat up straight on the hard packsaddle, arms tight around the precious machine. It felt heavy, dense with the magic that would call water out of the ground. Jeremy tried to imagine the gullied dun hills all green, with blue water tumbling down the old riverbed.

If there was plenty of water, it wouldn't matter so much that he couldn't pump or carry buckets.

Jeremy thought about water while he held what Dan gave him to hold, and, once or twice, pushed buttons on the distance machine. He could manage that much. It hummed under his touch and bright red numbers winked in a tiny window. He had to remember them, because his fingers were too clumsy to write them down in Dan's brown notebook.

Dan didn't really need any help with the measuring. Jeremy stood beside the magic machine, watching a single hawk circle in the hard blue sky. Mother had been right. Dan wanted something else from him.

Well, that was okay. Jeremy shrugged as the hawk drifted off southward. No one else thought he had *anything* to offer.

The sun stood high overhead when they stopped for lunch. It poured searing light down on the land, sucking up their sweat. Dan and Jeremy huddled in a narrow strip of shade beneath the canyon wall. Ezra stood in front of them, head down, tail whisking.

They shared warm, plastic-tasting water with the pony, and Dan produced dried apple slices from the lunch pack. He had stripped off his shirt, and sweat gleamed like oil on his brown shoulders. His eyes were gray, Jeremy noticed. They looked bright in his dark face.

"Why do you have to do all this stuff?" Awkwardly, Jeremy scooped up a leathery disc of dried apple. The tart sweetness filled his mouth with a rush of saliva.

"I'm making a map of the ground." Dan shaded his eyes, squinting into the shimmering heat-haze. "They have to know all the humps, hollows, and slopes before they can decide how to build a road or plan buildings."

"I was trying to imagine lots of water." Jeremy reached for another apple slice. "It's hard."

"Yeah," Dan said harshly. "Well, don't start counting the days yet." He shook himself and his expression softened. "Tell me about your fireflies and your fish that jump out of pitchers."

"Not much to tell." Jeremy looked away from Dan's intent gray eyes. Was *that* what he wanted? "If I think of something hard enough, you can see it. It's not real. It's not any *good* for anything." Jeremy drew a zig-zag pattern in the dust with his fingers. "It . . . bothers people," he said.

"Like your mom and dad."

"Dad doesn't like it." Jeremy smoothed the lines away.

"What about your mother? What about the other folk?" Dan prodded.

"Dad doesn't let us talk about it. I don't make things where people can see." Mostly. Jeremy shifted uneasily, remembering the dragonfly.

"Is that why you hide?" Dan was looking at him.

"The Pearsons had a baby with joints like mine. So did Sally Brandt—from the dust or the water, or something in it." Jeremy spread his thick, clumsy hands. "They . . . died," he said. "There isn't enough water for extra mouths."

"Who said that?" Dan asked in a hard, quiet voice.

I lost three babies Mother had cried in that scary voice. *I couldn't stand to lose another.*

Their old nanny goat had had a kid with an extra leg last spring. Dad had taken the biggest knife from the kitchen and cut its throat by a bean hill, so that the blood would water the seedlings. The apple slice in Jeremy's mouth tasted like dust. Feeling stony hard inside, he made the dragonfly appear, sent it darting through the air to land on Dan's knee with a glitter of wings.

"Holy shit." Dried apples scattered in the dust as Dan flinched. "I can almost believe that I feel it," he breathed.

He wasn't angry. Jeremy sighed as the shimmering wings blurred and vanished.

"I don't believe it." Dan stared at the space where the making had been. "Yes, I *do* believe it, but it's fantastic!" He slapped Jeremy lightly on the shoulder, a slow smile spreading across his face. "We could be the hottest thing in this whole damn dry country, kid. *Think* of it. The hicks would fall all over themselves to come see a show like that! *Hoo . . . ey.*" His grin faded suddenly.

"You're afraid of doing it, aren't you?" Dan asked softly. "Because it scares your Dad?"

Scared? Not Dad. Jeremy shook his head. Rupert was scared of the brown lizards that lived under the rocks out back. He killed them all the time. But Dad wasn't scared of the makings. He *hated* them.

"Look at this." Dan yanked a grubby red bandana out of his pocket and dangled it in front of Jeremy's eyes. He stuffed the cloth into his closed fist. "Abracadabra . . ." He waved his hand around. "Watch closely, and . . . ta da." He snapped open his hand.

Jeremy stared at his empty palm.

"Your handkerchief, sir." With a flourish, Dan reached behind Jeremy's head and twitched the bandana into view.

"Wow." Jeremy touched the handkerchief. "How did you do that?"

"It's pretty easy." Dan looked sad as he stuffed the bandana back into his pocket. "The card tricks, juggling—it's not enough to keep you in water out here in the Dry. The sun's baked all the *belief* out of people. It would take a miracle to get some attention." He stared solemnly at Jeremy. "*You're* that kind of a miracle," he said.

Dan acted like the making was a wonderful thing, not something shameful, not something that made Dad have to ask the

Brewsters for food. Suddenly unsure, Jeremy bent to scoop up the apples that Dan had dropped. "You don't want to waste these."

"I'd give a lot for your talent." Dan's eyes gleamed like water.

Talent? Jeremy dumped the withered rings of apple into the pack, struggling to understand Dan's tone. "You're a surveyor," he said. "You don't *need* to do tricks."

"I guess I am." Dan's laugh sounded bitter. "So I guess we'd better get back to surveying." He got to his feet.

Strange feelings fluttered in Jeremy's chest. Could Dan be right? Would people really look at him like Dan had looked at him, all excited and envious? What if Dan was *wrong*? What if everyone looked at him like *Dad* did, instead?

He could find out. If he went with Dan.

Jeremy thought about that—going with Dan—for the rest of the day, while he steadied the machine and pushed buttons. It excited him and scared him shitless at the same time, but he didn't say anything to Dan.

Dan might not want him to come along.

It seemed like everyone within walking distance was waiting at the house when they plodded back to the farm that evening. People had brought food and water, because you didn't ask for hospitality, not anymore. Covered dishes and water jugs cluttered the kitchen table, and Dan was swept into the crowd and out of Jeremy's reach.

Dan didn't belong to him here, in the dusty house. Here, Dan belonged to the grown-ups and the Army Corps of Engineers. It was only when they were out in the dry hills with Ezra that Dan would be his. Jeremy slipped away to his barn sanctuary to pet Ezra and think.

What would happen if he walked away from the peeling old house? Dad wouldn't have to ask the Brewsters for food then, Jeremy thought, and he pulled at the pony's tangled mane until the coarse horsehair cut his fingers.

After the first three days, the crowd waiting at the farm had thinned out. They'd heard what news Dan had to tell. They'd sold him the food and supplies that he'd asked for, taking his pale-green voucher slips as payment. Now they were waiting for the construction crews to arrive. Even Dad was waiting. He whistled while he carried water to the potato plants, and he smiled at Dan.

Dan was the water bringer. *Everyone* smiled at Dan.

It made Jeremy jealous when they were at home, but they weren't home very often. He and Dan trudged all over the scorched hills along the river. Dan talked about cities and about the Dryland beyond the fields, with its ghosts and the bones of dead towns. He told Jeremy unbelievable stories about the shrinking sea and the ice getting thicker up north, maybe getting ready to slide southward and bury the Dry. He taught Jeremy how to describe the land in numbers. He asked Jeremy to make things every day, and he laughed when Jeremy made a frog appear on Ezra's head.

Jeremy tried hard to make Dan laugh. His face and hands got scratched by the brittle scrub and his knees hurt all the time, but it was worth it. Dan never asked him outright, but he talked like Jeremy was going to come with him to the cities and the sea. Both of them understood it, and the understanding was a comfortable thing between them.

"Where did you come from?" Jeremy asked on Saturday afternoon. They were eating lunch under the same overhang where they'd stopped the first day out.

"The Corps' regional office at Bonneville."

"No, I don't mean that." Jeremy swallowed cold beans. "I mean *before* that—before the surveying. Where were you born?"

"South." Dan looked out toward the dead river. His gray eyes looked vague, like he was looking at something far away or deep inside his head.

"Everyone thought it would be a war," he said, after a while. "No one really believed that the *weather* could do us in." He gave a jerky shrug. "We came north from L.A., running from the Mex wars and the gangs." His eyes flickered. "California was dying, and if anyone had water in the Valley, they weren't sharing, so we kept on going. You leave everything behind you when you're dying of thirst—one piece at a time. Everything."

He was silent for a moment. The wind blew grit across the rocks with a soft hiss and Jeremy didn't make a sound.

"I ended up with the Corps," Dan said abruptly.

The transition from *we* to *I* cut off Jeremy's questions like a knife. He watched Dan toss a pebble down the slope. It bounced off an elk skull half-buried in drifted dust.

"I won't kid you about things." Dan tossed another pebble at the bleached skull. "If you come with me, you're going to find out that things aren't always what they should be. When you're on the road, you don't have any options. You do what it takes to stay alive. Sometimes you don't like it much, but you *do* it."

The sad bitterness in Dan's tone scared Jeremy a little, but it didn't matter. Dan had said *if you come with me*.

If you come with me.

"Can you make a face?" Dan asked suddenly.

"I don't know." Jeremy looked into Dan's bleak, hungry eyes. "I'll try," he said uncertainly.

"She was about sixteen, with brown eyes and black hair. It was straight, like rain falling." His eyes focused on that invisible something again. "She looked a little like me, but prettier," he said. "Her nose was thin—I used to kid her about it—and she smiled a lot."

Straight black hair; thin nose . . . Jeremy shaped a face in his mind, watched it take shape in the air. No. That was *wrong*. He didn't need Dan's look of disappointment to tell him so.

"Stupid to play that kind of game." Dan laid his hand on Jeremy's shoulder. "Thanks for trying."

Jeremy shook his head, wanting to do this more than he'd ever wanted to do anything in his life. The face was wrong, but barely wrong. He could *feel* it. If he just changed it a little, maybe smoothed the forehead like *so*, widened the nose, it might be . . .

Right.

She smiled, face brimming with warmth and sadness. Jeremy stared at her, sweat stinging his eyes. She was *right* in a way that no bird or fish or animal had ever been right.

"Amy!" Dan cried brokenly. "Oh God, Amy!"

The sound of Dan's voice scared Jeremy. He felt the making slip and tried to hang on, but the face wavered, blurred, and vanished. "I'm sorry," he whispered.

Dan buried his face in his hands. That was scarier than if he'd cried or yelled. Hesitantly, Jeremy reached out and touched him.

"It's all right." Dan raised his head, drew a long breath. "You did what I asked, didn't you?" His eyes were dry as the riverbed. "I didn't know. . . ." He got up suddenly. "Let's go back." He looked down the dead valley. "I'm through here."

"You mean all through? Like you're leaving?" Jeremy forced the words through the sudden tightness in his throat.

"Yeah." Dan looked down at him. "The job's finished. I didn't expect to be here this long. I shouldn't have stayed this long." His shoulders lifted as he took a long, slow breath. "Are you coming?"

"Yes." Jeremy stood up as straight as he could. There was nothing for him here. Nothing at all. "I'm coming," he said.

"Good." Dan boosted him onto Ezra's back. "I'm leaving early," he said. "You better not tell your folks."

"I won't," Jeremy said.

No one was pumping on the bicycle frame as they plodded past. Jeremy looked up at the brown hillside, imagining it all green with grass, like in pictures. Water would come, Dad would be happy, and *he* would be with Dan. Mother would cry, but she wouldn't have to protect him from Dad any more.

The green landscape wouldn't take shape in his mind. Ezra broke into a jouncing trot, and Jeremy had to grab the saddle as the pony headed for the barnyard and the watertub there.

"Mr. Greely," Dad called from the porch.

Jeremy stiffened. Dad sounded cold and mad, like when he caught Jeremy making.

"We want to talk to you."

Mr. Brewster stepped onto the porch behind him. Rupert and Jonathan followed, with Mr. Mendoza, Sally Brandt, and the Deardorf boys.

Mr. Mendoza had his old deer rifle. They all looked angry.

"My brother got into town last night." Sally's voice was shrill. "He told me about this scam he heard of back in Pendleton. Seems this guy goes around to little towns pretending to be a surveyor. He buys things with vouchers from the Army Corps of Engineers."

"We searched your stuff." Ted Brewster held up a fist full of white. "You carry a few spare letters, don't you?" He opened his hand. "You're a fake," he said harshly.

The white envelopes fluttered to the dusty ground like dead leaves. Stunned by the anger of the crowd, Jeremy turned to Dan, waiting for him to explain, waiting for Dan to tell them how they were wrong, waiting for him to remind them about the *water*.

"Dan?" he whispered.

Dan looked at him finally, his head moving slowly on his neck, and Jeremy felt his insides going numb and dead. "Mother gave you dried apples." Jeremy swallowed, remembering the tears and hope in her voice. "Dried apples are for birthdays."

For one instant, Dan's gray eyes filled with hurt. Then he looked away, turning a bland smile on the approaching adults. "I heard about some bastard doing that." He spread his hands. "But *I'm* legit." He plucked at the black insignia on his sweaty shirt.

Dad took one long step forward and smashed his fist into Dan's face. "He described you." He looked down as Dan sprawled in the dirt. "He described you real well."

Dan got up very slowly, wiping dust from his face. Blood smeared his chin. He shrugged. They took him into town, walking around him in a loose ring. Jeremy stood in the road, watching the dust settle behind them. Even if Mr. Mendoza didn't have the gun, Dan couldn't run. The dry hills brooded on every side. Where would he run *to*? Jeremy climbed up onto the rimrock, and didn't come down until it got dark.

"I wondered about that guy," Rupert sneered as they got ready for bed that night. "Federal survey, huh? The feds couldn't even hang onto the Columbia Project! I don't know how anybody could believe him."

"Hope is a tempting thing." Jeremy's mother leaned against the doorway. She hadn't scolded Jeremy for running off. "If there was any water around here, no matter how deep, someone would have drilled for it a long time ago." Her voice was tired. "I guess we all just *wanted* to hope."

Jeremy climbed onto his cot without looking at her.

"I'm sorry," she murmured. "I'm sorry for us, and I'm sorry for him, too."

"They'll *hang* him—like they did to that trucker over in La Grande."

"Shame on you, Rupert." Her voice caught a little.

Jeremy buried his face in his pillow. She was feeling sorry for him, and he didn't want anyone to feel sorry for him. I hate him, too, he thought fiercely. Why couldn't Dan have been what he said? He could have gone with Dan, *made* things for him. Now, they'd always have to pump, and he would always be an extra mouth to Dad. A *useless* mouth.

"They're gonna *hang* him," Rupert whispered to Jeremy after Mother had left. He sounded smug. "No wonder that jerk wanted *you* to help him. You're too damn dumb to figure out he was a fake!"

Jeremy pressed his face into the pillow until he could barely breathe. If he made a sound, if he moved, he'd kill Rupert. Rupert might be almost sixteen and Jeremy's hands might not work very well, but he'd kill Rupert, somehow.

Rupert was right. They were going to hang Dan. He'd seen it in their eyes when they walked up to him. It wasn't just because he'd tricked them. They hated Dan because the government, the Army Corps of Engineers, didn't *really* care about them.

No one cared. And Dan had made them see it.

He lied to me, too. Jeremy burrowed deeper into the pillow, but he kept hearing Dan's sad-bitter voice. *You do what it takes to stay alive. Sometimes you don't like it much, but you do it.*

Dan hadn't lied to *him*.

Jeremy must have fallen asleep, because he woke up from a dream of the woman with the black hair. Like rain, Dan had said. Jeremy opened his eyes. His throat hurt, as if he had been crying in his sleep. Amy, Dan had cried. She was dead, whoever she had been. Dan's *we* had turned into *I*.

Rupert snored, arm hanging over the side of his mattress. The sloping roof pressed down on Jeremy, threatening to crush him, trying to smear him into the dry darkness, dissolve him. Where was Dan now? In the church? Jeremy sat up, pushing against the heavy darkness, heart pounding with the knowledge of what he had to do. The house creaked softly to itself as he tiptoed down the steep stairs.

"Who's there?" his father said from the bottom of the stairway.

"Me." Jeremy froze, clutching the railing with both hands. "I . . . had to pee," he stammered. It was a feeble lie—the pot in the bedroom was never full.

"Jeremy?" His father bulked over him, a tower of shadow. "It's late. I just got back from town." He ran a thick hand across his face. "You liked Greely."

It was an accusation. "I still like him." Jeremy forced himself to stand straight. "He's not a bad man."

His father grunted, moved down a step. "He's a parasite," he said harshly. "His kind live on other people's sweat. You got to understand that. You got to understand that there's no worse crime than that."

"Isn't there?" Jeremy's voice trembled. "Who's going to share with *him?* Who's going to let him have a piece of their orchard or a field? He was just trying to live, and he didn't hurt anybody, not really . . ."

"He lied to us and he stole from us." His tone dismissed Dan, judged and sentenced him. "You get back to bed. Now!"

"No." Jeremy's knees were shaking and he clung to the railing. "If it doesn't help the crops, it's bad, isn't it? Nothing else matters to you but the land. *Nothing.*"

His father's hand swung up and Jeremy turned to flee. His knee banged the riser and he fell, crying out with the hot pain, sprawling on the steps at his father's feet.

All by itself, the firefly popped into the air between them, glowing like a hot coal.

With a hoarse cry, Dad flinched backward, his hand clenching into a fist, ready to smash him like he'd smashed Dan. He *was* scared. Dan was right. Jeremy stared up at his father through a blur of pain tears. "It's not *bad!*" he screamed. "It's just *me.*

Me! I make things because they're pretty! Doesn't that count?"
He cringed away from his father's fist.

His father hesitated, lowered his hand slowly. "No," he said
in a choked voice. "It doesn't count. It doesn't count, either,
that a man's just trying to stay alive. I . . . I wish it did." He
stepped past Jeremy and went on up the stairs.

Jeremy listened to his slow, heavy tread on the floorboards
over his head. His pulse pounded in his ears and he felt dizzy.
It doesn't count, his father had said. *I wish it did.* Jeremy put
his forehead down on his clenched fists, and his tears scalded
his knuckles.

Jeremy was right. Dan was in the church basement. Yellow
light glowed dimly from one of the window wells along the
concrete foundation, the only light in the dark, dead town.
Jeremy lay down on his stomach and peered through the
glassless window. Yep. Mr. Brewster was sitting on an old
pew beside a wooden door, flipping through a tattered hunting
magazine by the light of a hissing gasoline lantern.

He looked wide awake.

Jeremy looked at the sky. Was it getting light? How long
until dawn? Desperate, he leaned over the cracked lip of the
well. Mr. Brewster wasn't going to fall asleep. Not in time.

The firefly had scared Dad. Jeremy lay flat in the dust, face
pressed against his clenched fists. Mr. Brewster didn't know
about the makings, *probably* didn't, anyway. Cold balled in
Jeremy's belly, so bad that he almost threw up. *Bigger* would
be scarier, but bigger was harder. What if he couldn't do it?

The firefly popped into the air two feet from Mr. Brewster's
magazine, big as a chicken.

"Holy shit!" Mr. Brewster's chair banged over as he scrambled to his feet. "Mother of *God*, what's *that?*" His voice
sounded strange and squeaky. Nails biting his palms, Jeremy
made the firefly dart at Mr. Brewster's face. It moved slug-
gishly, dimming to a dull orange. Oh God, don't let it fade!
Sweat stung Jeremy's eyes.

Mr. Brewster yelled and threw his magazine at it. His footsteps pounded up the wooden stairs, and, a moment later, the
church door thudded open. Jeremy lay flat in the dust as Mr.

Brewster ran past him. The ground felt warm, as if the earth had a fever. Sweat turned the dust on Jeremy's face to mud, and he was shaking all over. He couldn't hear Mr. Brewster's footsteps any more.

Now!

He scrambled down through the window. A fragment of glass still stuck in the frame grazed his arm, and he landed on the broken chair. It collapsed with a terrible crash. Panting, Jeremy scrambled to his feet. Oh God, please don't let Mr. Brewster come back. He struggled with the bolt on the storeroom door, bruising his palm. It slid back, and he pushed the heavy door open.

Dan was sitting on the floor between shelves of musty hymnals and folded choir robes. The yellow light made his skin look tawny brown, like the dust. His face was swollen and streaked with dried blood.

"Jeremy?" Hope flared in Dan's eyes.

"Hurry." Jeremy grabbed his arm.

Dan staggered to his feet and followed Jeremy up the steps, treading on his heels. Someone shouted behind them and Jeremy's heart lurched.

"That way." He pointed.

Dan threw an arm around him and ran, half-carrying Jeremy as they ducked behind the dark Exxon station. They scrambled under the board fence in the back, lay flat while someone ran and panted past. Mr. Brewster? This was like a scary game of hide-and-seek. Gray banded the eastern horizon as Jeremy led Dan across the dusty main street, listening for footsteps, stumbling on the rough pavement. They turned left by the boarded-up restaurant, cut through a yard full of drifted dust, dead weeds, and a gasless car.

Jeremy had left Ezra tethered behind the last house on the street. The pony gave a low, growling whinny as they hurried up. Dan stroked his nose to quiet him, his eyes running over the lumpy bulges of the pack.

"It's all there, food, water, and everything," Jeremy panted. "It's not a very good job—I didn't know how to fix a pack. The ground's pretty hard along the river, so you won't leave many tracks. Willow creekbed'll take you way south. It's the first creekbed past the old feed mill. You can't miss it."

"I thought you were coming with me." Dan looked down at Jeremy.

"I was." Jeremy looked at the old nylon daypack he'd left on the ground beside Ezra. It wasn't very heavy because he didn't have much. "I changed my mind."

"You can't." Dan's fingers dug into his shoulders. "They'll know you let me out. What'll happen then?"

"I don't know." Jeremy swallowed a lump of fear. His father was part of the land, linked to it. If the land dried up and died, Dad would die. "I got to stay," he whispered.

"Why? You think you'll make peace with your father?" Dan shook him—one short, sharp jerk that made Jeremy's teeth snap together. "You've got magic in your hands. Real magic. You think that's ever going to matter to *him?*"

"I don't know." Tears clogged Jeremy's nose, burned his eyes.

"Hell, my own choices haven't turned out so hot. Who am I to tell you what you should do?" Dan wiped the tears away, his fingers rough and dry on Jeremy's face. "Just don't let them kill your magic." He shook Jeremy again, gently this time. "He needs it. They *all* need it." He sighed. "And I'd better get going. Keep making things, kid." He squeezed Jeremy's shoulder hard, grabbed Ezra's lead rope, and walked away into the fading night.

Jeremy stood still, the last of his tears drying on his face, listening to Ezra's muffled hoofbeats fade in the distance. He listened until he could hear nothing but the dry whisper of the morning breeze, then he started back. He thought about cutting across the dun hills and down through the riverbed to get home. Instead, his feet carried him back into town and he let them.

They might have been waiting for him in front of the church—Mr. Brewster, Sally Brandt, Mr. Mendoza and . . . Dad. Jeremy faltered as they all turned to stare at him, wishing in one terrible, frightened instant that he had gone with Dan after all. They looked at him like they had looked at Dan yesterday, hard and cold. Mr. Brewster walked to meet him, slow and stifflegged, and Jeremy wondered suddenly if they'd hang *him* instead of Dan.

Maybe. It was there, in their faces, back behind their cold eyes.

"You little snot." Mr. Brewster's hand closed on Jeremy's shirt, balling up the fabric, lifting him a little off his feet. "You let Greely out! I saw you. Where's he headed?"

"I don't know," Jeremy said.

"Like *hell*." Brewster slapped him.

Red-and-black light exploded behind Jeremy's eyelids, and his mouth filled with a harsh, metallic taste. He fell, hard and hurting, onto his knees, dizzy, eyes blurred with tears, belly full of sickness.

"Knock it off, Ted."

Dad—amazingly, *Dad*—was lifting him to his feet, hands under his arms, gentle, almost.

"*I* lay hands on my kids," he said harshly. "No one else."

"He knows where that bastard's headed!" Mr. Brewster was breathing heavy and fast. "You beat it out of him or *I* do."

"He said he doesn't know. That's the end of it, you hear me?"

Jeremy breathed slow, trying not to throw up. Silence hung between the two men, heavy and hot. It made the air feel thick and hard to breathe. Dad was angry, but not at him. He was angry at Mr. Brewster. For hitting him? Jeremy held his breath, tasting blood on his swelling lip, afraid to look up.

"You talk pretty high and mighty," Mr. Brewster said softly. "Considering you had to come crawling for help last winter. Seems like you ought to shut up."

Jeremy felt his father jerk, as if Mr. Brewster had kicked him. He felt his father's arms tremble and held his breath, wondering if Dad was going to let go, turn his back and walk away.

"Seems like *we* all pitched in, when mice got into *your* seed stock a few years back," Dad said quietly.

Mr. Brewster made a small, harsh sound.

"Come *on*, Ted!" Sally's shrill exasperation shattered the tension of the moment. "While you're standing around arguing, Greely's making tracks for Boardman."

"We got to split up," Mr. Mendoza chimed in.

Legs spread, shoulders hunched, Mr. Brewster glowered at
Jeremy. Abruptly, he spun on his heel. "Shit." He jerked his
head at Mr. Mendoza. "I bet the bastard headed west," he
snarled. "We'll go down the riverbed, cut his tracks." He
stalked off down the street with Mr. Mendoza.

Sally Brandt pushed tousled hair out of her face, sighed. "I'll
go wake up the Deardorfs," she said. "We'll spread north and
east. You can take the south."

He felt his father's body move a little, as if he had nodded
at her. Jeremy stared down at the dust between his feet, heart
pounding so hard that it felt like it was going to burst through
his ribs. He felt Dad's hands lift from his shoulders, cringed a
little as his father moved around in front of him, blocking the
rising sun, but all he did was lift Jeremy's chin, until he had
to meet his father's eyes.

"I thought you'd gone with him," he said.

Jeremy looked at his father's weathered face. It looked like
the hills, all folded into dun gullies—not angry, not sad, just
old and dry.

"If we find Greely, we have to hang him," Dad said heavily.
"Right or wrong, we voted—you got to know that, son."

"I was going to go." Jeremy swallowed, tasted dust. "You
had to ask for food," he whispered. "Because of me."

His father's face twitched, as if something hurt him inside.

Without warning, the firefly popped into the air between
them again, pale this time, a flickering shadow in the harsh
morning light. Jeremy sucked in his breath, snuffed it out as
his father flinched away from it.

"I'm sorry," he cried. "I didn't *mean* to make it, it just . . .
happened. It makes Rita Menendez laugh." He took a deep,
hurting breath. "I won't do it anymore," he whispered, struggling to get the words past the tightness in his throat. "Not
ever."

"Do it again." His father's hand clamped down on Jeremy's
shoulder. "Right now."

Trembling, afraid to look at his father's face, Jeremy made
the firefly appear again.

His father stared at it, breathing hard. With a shudder, he
thrust his fingers into the firefly, yanked his hand back as

if it had burned him. "It scares me." His voice was a harsh whisper. "I don't understand it." He stared at his hand, closed his fingers slowly into a fist. "It's like this crazy drought." His voice shook. "I don't understand that, neither." He looked at Jeremy suddenly. "Not everyone's going to laugh. You scared the shit out of Ted. He ain't going to forgive you for that."

Dad talked like he could keep on making things. Jeremy sneaked a look at him, heart beating fast again, throat hurting.

"Hell," his father said softly. "I don't have any answers. Maybe there *aren't* any answers any more—no good ones, anyway." He met Jeremy's eyes. "I've got to look south for Greely," he said. "Which way do you think he headed? Down Willow creekbed—or by the main road to La Grande?"

Jeremy hesitated for a moment, then straightened his shoulders with a jerk. "I think he went down the main road," he said, and held his breath.

His father shaded his eyes, stared at the dun fold of Willow creekbed in the distance. "There aren't any good answers." He sighed and put his hand on his son's shoulder. "We'll look for Greely on the main road," he said.

THE DRAGON LINE

Michael Swanwick

"The Dragon Line" was purchased by Gardner
Dozois, and appeared in the June 1989 issue of
IAsfm, with an illustration by N. Taylor Blanchard.
Swanwick has published a long string of stories in
the magazine, under two different editors, and has
always been one of our most popular writers—being,
for instance, the only writer ever to have two different novels serialized in our pages. In the evocative
and mysterious story that follows, he takes us down
some mean streets in modern-day Philadelphia for
an encounter among the oil refineries and tank farms
with some very ancient magic—an encounter that may
decide whether the Earth itself lives or dies. . . .

Michael Swanwick made his debut in 1980, and
has gone on to become one of the most popular and
respected of all the decade's new writers. He has
several times been a finalist for the Nebula Award,
as well as for the World Fantasy Award and for the
John W. Campbell Award, and has won the Theodore
Sturgeon Award and the Davis Readers Award poll.
His first novel, In the Drift, was published in 1985
as part of the resurrected Ace Specials line. His next
novel, the popular Vacuum Flowers, was serialized

in IAsfm, *as was his critically acclaimed new novel,*
Stations of the Tide. *His most recent books are the
hardcover novella* Griffin's Egg; *a collection of his
collaborative work,* Slow Dancing Through Time;
and a collection of his solo short fiction, Gravity's
Angels. *Swanwick lives in Philadelphia with his wife,
Marianne Porter, and their young son, Sean.*

Driving by the mall in King of Prussia that night, I noticed
that between the sky and earth where the horizon used to be
is now a jagged-edged region, spangled with bright industrial
lights. For a long yearning instant, before the car topped the
rise and I had to switch lanes or else be shunted onto the
expressway, I wished I could enter that dark zone, dissolve
into its airless mystery and cold ethereal beauty. But of course
that was impossible. Faerie is no more. It can be glimpsed, but
no longer grasped.

At the light, Shikra shoved the mirror up under my nose,
and held the cut-down fraction of a McDonald's straw while
I did up a line. A winter flurry of tinkling white powder stung
through my head to freeze up at the base of the skull, and the
light changed, and off we went. "Burn that rubber, Boss-man,"
Shikra laughed. She drew up her knees, balancing the mirror
before her chin, and snorted the rest for herself.

There was an opening to the left, and I switched lanes,
injecting the Jaguar like a virus into the stream of traffic,
looped around, and was headed back toward Germantown.
A swirling white pattern of flat crystals grew in my left eye,
until it filled my vision. I was only seeing out of the right
now. I closed the left and rubbed it, bringing tears, but still
the hallucination hovered, floating within the orb of vision. I
sniffed, bringing up my mouth to one side. Beside me, Shikra
had her butterfly knife out and was chopping more coke.

"Hey, enough of that, okay? We've got work to do."

Shikra turned an angry face my way. Then she hit the window controls and threw the mirror, powder and all, into the

wind. Three grams of purest Peruvian offered to the Goddess.

"Happy now, shithead?" Her eyes and teeth flashed, all sinister smile in mulatto skin, and for a second she was beautiful, this petite teenaged monstrosity, in the same way that a copperhead can be beautiful, or a wasp, even as it injects the poison under your skin. I felt a flash of desire and of tender, paternal love, and then we were at the Chemical Road turnoff, and I drifted the Jag through three lanes of traffic to make the turn. Shikra was laughing and excited, and I was too.

It was going to be a dangerous night.

Applied Standard Technologies stood away from the road, a compound of low, sprawling buildings afloat on oceanic lawns. The guard waved us through and I drove up to the Lab B lot. There were few cars there; one had British plates. I looked at that one for a long moment, then stepped out onto the tarmac desert. The sky was close, stained a dull red by reflected halogen lights. Suspended between vastnesses, I was touched by a cool breeze, and shivered. How fine, I thought, to be alive.

I followed Shikra in. She was dressed all in denim, jeans faded to white in little crescents at the creases of her buttocks, trade beads clicking softly in her cornrowed hair. The guards at the desk rose in alarm at the sight of her, eased back down as they saw she was mine.

Miss Lytton was waiting. She stubbed out a half-smoked cigarette, strode briskly forward. "He speaks modern English?" I asked as she handed us our visitors' badges. "You've brought him completely up to date on our history and technology?" I didn't want to have to deal with culture shock. I'd been present when my people had dug him, groggy and corpseblue, sticky with white chrysalid fluids, from his cave almost a year ago. Since then, I'd been traveling, hoping I could somehow pull it all together without him.

"You'll be pleased." Miss Lytton was a lean, nervous woman, all tweed and elbows. She glanced curiously at Shikra, but was too disciplined to ask questions. "He was a quick study—especially keen on the sciences." She led us down a long corridor to an unmanned security station, slid a plastic card into the lockslot.

"You showed him around Britain? The slums, the mines, the factories?"

"Yes." Anticipating me, she said, "He didn't seem at all perturbed. He asked quite intelligent questions."

I nodded, not listening. The first set of doors sighed open, and we stepped forward. Surveillance cameras telemetered our images to the front desk for reconfirmation. The doors behind us closed, and those before us began to cycle open. "Well, let's go see."

The airlock opened into the secure lab, a vast, overlit room filled with white enameled fermentation tanks, incubators, autoclaves, refrigerators, workbenches, and enough glass plumbing for any four dairies. An ultrafuge whined softly. I had no clear idea what they did here. To me AST was just another blind cell in the maze of interlocking directorships that sheltered me from public view. The corporate labyrinth was my home now, a secure medium in which to change documentation, shift money, and create new cover personalities on need. Perhaps other ancient survivals lurked within the catacombs, mermen and skinchangers, prodigies of all sorts, old Grendel himself; there was no way of telling.

"Wait here," I told Shikra. The lab manager's office was set halfway up the far wall, with wide glass windows overlooking the floor. Miss Lytton and I climbed the concrete and metal stairs. I opened the door.

He sat, flanked by two very expensive private security operatives, in a chrome swivel chair, and the air itself felt warped out of shape by the force of his presence. The trim white beard and charcoal grey Saville Row pinstripe were petty distractions from a face as wide and solemn and cruel as the moon. I shut my eyes and still it floated before me, wise with corruption. There was a metallic taste on my tongue.

"Get out," I said to Miss Lytton, the guards.

"Sir, I—"

I shot her a look, and she backed away. Then the old man spoke, and once again I heard that wonderful voice of his, like a subway train rumbling underfoot. "Yes, Amy, allow us to talk in privacy, please."

When we were alone, the old man and I looked at each other for a long time, unblinking. Finally, I rocked back on my heels. "Well," I said. After all these centuries, I was at a loss for words. "Well, well, well."

He said nothing.

"Merlin," I said, putting a name to it.

"Mordred," he replied, and the silence closed around us again.

The silence could have gone on forever for all of me; I wanted to see how the old wizard would handle it. Eventually he realized this, and slowly stood, like a thunderhead rising up in the western sky. Bushy, expressive eyebrows clashed together. "Arthur dead, and you alive! Alas, who can trust this world?"

"Yeah, yeah, I've read Malory too."

Suddenly his left hand gripped my wrist and squeezed. Merlin leaned forward, and his face loomed up in my sight, ruthless grey eyes growing enormous as the pain washed up my arm. He seemed a natural force then, like the sun or wind, and I tumbled away before it.

I was on a nightswept field, leaning on my sword, surrounded by my dead. The veins in my forehead hammered. My ears ached with the confusion of noises, of dying horses and men. It had been butchery, a battle in the modern style in which both sides had fought until all were dead. This was the end of all causes: I stood empty on Salisbury Plain, too disheartened even to weep.

Then I saw Arthur mounted on a black horse. His face all horror and madness, he lowered his spear and charged. I raised my sword and ran to meet him.

He caught me below the shield and drove his spear through my body. The world tilted and I was thrown up into a sky black as wellwater. Choking, I fell deep between the stars where the shadows were aswim with all manner of serpents, dragons, and wild beasts. The creatures struggled forward to seize my limbs in their talons and claws. In wonder I realized I was about to die.

Then the wheel turned and set me down again. I forced myself up the spear, unmindful of pain. Two-handed, I swung

my sword through the side of Arthur's helmet and felt it bite
through bone into the brain beneath.

My sword fell from nerveless fingers, and Arthur dropped
his spear. His horse reared and we fell apart. In that last
instant our eyes met and in his wondering hurt and innocence
I saw, as if staring into an obsidian mirror, the perfect image
of myself.

"So," Merlin said, and released my hand. "He is truly dead,
then. Even Arthur could not have survived the breaching of
his skull."

I was horrified and elated: He could still wield power,
even in this dim and disenchanted age. The danger he might
have killed me out of hand was small price to pay for such
knowledge. But I masked my feelings.

"That's just about fucking enough!" I cried. "You forget
yourself, old man. I am still the Pen-dragon, *Dux Bellorum
Britanniarum* and King of all Britain and Amorica and as such
your liege lord!"

That got to him. These medieval types were all heavy on
rightful authority. He lowered his head on those bullish shoulders and grumbled, "I had no right, perhaps. And yet how was I
to know that? The histories all said Arthur might yet live. Were
it so, my duty lay with him, and the restoration of Camelot."
There was still a look, a humor, in his eye I did not trust, as
if he found our confrontation essentially comic.

"You and your fucking Camelot! Your bloody holy and ideal
court!" The memories were unexpectedly fresh, and they hurt
as only betrayed love can. For I really had loved Camelot when
I first came to court, an adolescent true believer in the new
myth of the Round Table, of Christian chivalry and glorious
quests. Arthur could have sent me after the Grail itself, I was
that innocent.

But a castle is too narrow and strait a space for illusions. It
holds no secrets. The queen, praised for her virtue by one and
all, was a harlot. The king's best friend, a public paragon of
chastity, was betraying him. And everyone knew! There was
the heart and exemplar of it all. Those same poetasters who
wrote sonnets to the purity of Lodegreance's daughter smirked

and gossiped behind their hands. It was Hypocrisy Hall, ruled over by the smiling and genial Good King Cuckold. He knew all, but so long as no one dared speak it aloud, he did not care. And those few who were neither fools nor lackeys, those who spoke openly of what all knew, were exiled or killed. For telling the truth! That was Merlin's holy and Christian court of Camelot.

Down below, Shikra prowled the crooked aisles dividing the workbenches, prying open a fermenter to take a peek, rifling through desk drawers, elaborately bored. She had that kind of rough, destructive energy that demanded she be doing something at all times.

The king's bastard is like his jester, powerless but immune from criticism. I trafficked with the high and low of the land, tinsmiths and rivergods alike, and I knew their minds. Arthur was hated by his own people. He kept the land in ruin with his constant wars. Taxes went to support the extravagant adventures of his knights. He was expanding his rule, croft by shire, a kingdom here, a chunk of Normandy there, questing after Merlin's dream of a Paneuropean Empire. All built on the blood of the peasantry; they were just war fodder to him.

I was all but screaming in Merlin's face. Below, Shikra drifted closer, straining to hear. "That's why I seized the throne while he was off warring in France—to give the land a taste of peace; as a novelty, if nothing else. To clear away the hypocrisy and cant, to open the windows and let a little fresh air in. The people had prayed for release. When Arthur returned, it was my banner they rallied around. And do you know what the real beauty of it was? It was over a year before he learned he'd been overthrown."

Merlin shook his head. "You are so like your father! He too was an idealist—I know you find that hard to appreciate—a man who burned for the Right. We should have acknowledged your claim to succession."

"You haven't been listening!"

"You have a complaint against us. No one denies that. But, Mordred, you must understand that we didn't know you were the king's son. Arthur was . . . not very fertile. He had slept with your mother only once. We thought she was trying to blackmail him." He sighed piously. "Had we only known, it all could have been different."

I was suddenly embarrassed for him. What he called my complaint was the old and ugly story of my birth. Fearing the proof of his adultery—Morgawse was nominally his sister, and incest had both religious and dynastic consequences—Arthur had ordered all noble babies born that feast of Beltaine brought to court, and then had them placed in an unmanned boat and set adrift. Days later, a peasant had found the boat run aground with six small corpses. Only I, with my unhuman vigor, survived. But, typical of him, Merlin missed the horror of the story—that six innocents were sacrificed to hide the nature of Arthur's crime—and saw it only as a denial of my rights of kinship. The sense of futility and resignation that is my curse descended once again. Without understanding between us, we could never make common cause.

"Forget it," I said. "Let's go get a drink."

I picked up 476 to the Schuylkill. Shikra hung over the back seat, fascinated, confused, and aroused by the near-subliminal scent of murder and magic that clung to us both. "You haven't introduced me to your young friend." Merlin turned and offered his hand. She didn't take it.

"Shikra, this is Merlin of the Order of Ambrose, enchanter and master politician." I found an opening to the right, went up on the shoulder to take advantage of it, and slammed back all the way left, leaving half a dozen citizens leaning on their horns. "I want you to be ready to kill him at an instant's notice. If I act strange—dazed or in any way unlike myself—slit his throat immediately. He's capable of seizing control of my mind, and yours too if you hesitate."

"How 'bout that," Shikra said.

Merlin scoffed genially. "What lies are you telling this child?"

"The first time I met her, I asked Shikra to cut off one of my fingers." I held up my little finger for him to see, fresh and pink, not quite grown to full size. "She knows there are strange things astir, and they don't impress her."

"Hum." Merlin stared out at the car lights whipping toward us. We were on the expressway now, concrete crashguards close enough to brush fingertips against. He tried again. "In my first life, I greatly wished to speak with an African, but I had duties that kept me from traveling. It was one of the delights of the modern world to find I could meet your people everywhere, and learn from them." Shikra made that bug-eyed face the young make when the old condescend; I saw it in the rear-view mirror.

"I don't have to ask what you've been doing while I was . . . asleep," Merlin said after a while. That wild undercurrent of humor was back in his voice. "You've been fighting the same old battles, eh?"

My mind wasn't wholly on our conversation. I was think-ing of the *bons hommes* of Languedoc, the gentle people today remembered (by those few who do remember) as the Albigensians. In the heart of the thirteenth century, they had reinvented Christianity, leading lives of poverty and chastity. They offered me hope, at a time when I had none. We told no lies, held no wealth, hurt neither man nor animal—we did not even eat cheese. We did not resist our enemies, nor obey them either, we had no leaders and we thought ourselves safe in our poverty. But Innocent III sent his dogs to level our cities, and on their ashes raised the Inquisition. My sweet, harmless comrades were tortured, mutilated, burnt alive. History is a laboratory in which we learn that nothing works, or ever can. "Yes."

"Why?" Merlin asked. And chuckled to himself when I did not answer.

The Top of Centre Square was your typical bar with a view, a narrow box of a room with mirrored walls and gold foil insets in the ceiling to illusion it larger, and flaccid jazz oozing from hidden speakers. "The stools in the center, by the window," I told the hostess, and tipped her accordingly. She cleared some businessmen out of our seats and dispatched a waitress to take our orders.

"Boodles martini, very dry, straight up with a twist," I said.

"Single malt Scotch. Warm."

"I'd like a Shirley Temple, please." Shikra smiled so sweetly that the waitress frowned, then raised one cheek from her stool and scratched. If the woman hadn't fled it might have gotten ugly.

Our drinks arrived. "Here's to progress," Merlin said, toasting the urban landscape. Silent traffic clogged the far-below streets with red and white beads of light. Over City Hall the buildings sprawled electric-bright from Queen Village up to the Northern Liberties. Tugs and barges crawled slowly upriver. Beyond, Camden crowded light upon light. Floating above the terrestrial galaxy, I felt the old urge to throw myself down. If only there were angels to bear me up.

"I had a hand in the founding of this city."

"Did you?"

"Yes, the City of Brotherly Love. Will Penn was a Quaker, see, and they believed religious toleration would lead to secular harmony. Very radical for the times. I forget how many times he was thrown in jail for such beliefs before he came into money and had the chance to put them into practice. The Society of Friends not only brought their own people in from England and Wales, but also Episcopalians, Baptists, Scotch-Irish Presbyterians, all kinds of crazy German sects—the city became a haven for the outcasts of all the other religious colonies." How had I gotten started on this? I was suddenly cold with dread. "The Friends formed the social elite. Their idea was that by example and by civil works, they could create a pacifistic society, one in which all men followed their best impulses. All their grand ideals were grounded in a pragmatic set of laws, too; they didn't rely on good will alone. And you know, for a Utopian scheme it was pretty successful. Most of them don't last a decade. But. . . ." I was rambling, wandering further and further away from the point. I felt helpless. How could I make him understand how thoroughly the facts had betrayed the dream? "Shikra was born here."

"Ahhh." He smiled knowingly.

Then all the centuries of futility and failure, of striving for first a victory and then a peace I knew was not there to be found, collapsed down upon me like a massive barbiturate crash, and I felt the darkness descend to sink its claws in my shoulders. "Merlin, the world is dying."

He didn't look concerned. "Oh?"

"Listen, did my people teach you anything about cybernetics? Feedback mechanisms? Well, never mind. The Earth—" I gestured as if holding it cupped in my palm "—is like a living creature. Some say that it is a living creature, the only one, and all life, ourselves included, only component parts. Forget I said that. The important thing is that the Earth creates and maintains a delicate balance of gases, temperatures, and pressures that all life relies on for survival. If this balance were not maintained, the whole system would cycle out of control and . . . well, die. Us along with it." His eyes were unreadable, dark with fossil prejudices. I needed another drink. "I'm not explaining this very well."

"I follow you better than you think."

"Good. Now, you know about pollution? Okay, well now it seems that there's some that may not be reversible. You see what that means? A delicate little wisp of the atmosphere is being eaten away, and not replaced. Radiation intake increases. Meanwhile, atmospheric pollutants prevent reradiation of greater and greater amounts of infrared; total heat absorption goes up. The forests begin to die. Each bit of damage influences the whole, and leads to more damage. Earth is not balancing the new influences. Everything is cycling out of control, like a cancer.

"Merlin, I'm on the ropes. I've tried everything I can think of, and I've failed. The political obstacles to getting anything done are beyond belief. The world is dying, and I can't save it."

He looked at me as if I were crazy.

I drained my drink. " 'Scuse me," I said. "Got to hit up the men's room."

In the john I got out the snuffbox and fed myself some sense of wonder. I heard a thrill of distant flutes as it iced my head with artificial calm, and I straightened slightly as the vultures on my shoulders stirred and then flapped away. They would be back, I knew. They always were.

I returned, furious with buzzing energy. Merlin was talking quietly to Shikra, a hand on her knee. "Let's go," I said. "This place is getting old."

We took Passayunk Avenue west, deep into the refineries, heading for no place in particular. A kid in an old Trans Am, painted flat black inside and out, rebel flag flying from the antenna, tried to pass me on the right. I floored the accelerator, held my nose ahead of his, and forced him into the exit lane. Brakes screaming, he drifted away. Asshole. We were surrounded by the great tanks and cracking towers now. To one side, I could make out six smoky flames, waste gases being burnt off in gouts a dozen feet long.

"Pull in there!" Merlin said abruptly, gripping my shoulder and pointing. "Up ahead, where the gate is."

"Getty Gas isn't going to let us wander around in their refinery farm."

"Let me take care of that." The wizard put his forefingers together, twisted his mouth and bit through his tongue; I heard his teeth snap together. He drew his fingertips apart—it seemed to take all his strength—and the air grew tense. Carefully, he folded open his hands, and then spat blood into the palms. The blood glowed of its own light, and began to bubble and boil. Shikra leaned almost into its steam, grimacing with excitement. When the blood was gone, Merlin closed his hands again and said, "It is done."

The car was suddenly very silent. The traffic about us made no noise; the wheels spun soundlessly on the pavement. The light shifted to a melange of purples and reds, color Dopplering away from the center of the spectrum. I felt a pervasive queasiness, as if we were moving at enormous speeds in an unperceived direction. My inner ear spun when I turned my head. "This is the wizard's world," Merlin said. "It is from here that we draw our power. There's our turn."

I had to lock brakes and spin the car about to keep from overshooting the gate. But the guards in their little hut, though they were looking straight at us, didn't notice. We drove by them, into a busy tangle of streets and accessways servicing the refineries and storage tanks. There was a nineteenth-century factory town hidden at the foot of the structures, brick warehouses and utility buildings ensnarled in metal, as if caught midway in a transformation from City to Machine. Pipes big enough to stand in looped over the road in sets of three or eight, nightmare vines that detoured over and around the worn brick buildings. A fat indigo moon shone through the clouds.

"Left." We passed an old meter house with gables, arched windows and brickwork ornate enough for a Balkan railroad station. Workmen were unloading reels of electric cable on the loading dock, forklifting them inside. "Right." Down a narrow granite block road we drove by a gothic-looking storage tank as large as a cathedral and buttressed by exterior struts with diamond-shaped cutouts. These were among the oldest structures in Point Breeze, left over from the early days of massive construction, when the industrialists weren't quite sure what they had hold of, but suspected it might be God. "Stop," Merlin commanded, and I pulled over by the earth-and-cinder containment dike. We got out of the car, doors slamming silently behind us. The road was gritty underfoot. The rich smell of hydrocarbons saturated the air. Nothing grew here, not so much as a weed. I nudged a dead pigeon with the toe of my shoe.

"Hey, what's this shit?" Shikra pointed at a glimmering grey line running down the middle of the road, cool as ice in its feverish surround. I looked at Merlin's face. The skin was flushed and I could see through it to a manically detailed lacework of tiny veins. When he blinked, his eyes peered madly through translucent flesh.

"It's the track of the groundstar," Merlin said. "In China, or so your paperbacks tell me, such lines are called *lung mei*, the path of the dragon."

The name he gave the track of slugsilver light reminded me that all of Merlin's order called themselves Children of the Sky. When I was a child an Ambrosian had told me that such lines interlaced all lands, and that an ancient race had raised stones and cairns on their interstices, each one dedicated to a specific star (and held to stand directly beneath that star) and positioned in perfect scale to one another, so that all of Europe formed a continent-wide map of the sky in reverse.

"Son of lies," Merlin said. "The time has come for there to be truth between us. We are not natural allies, and your cause is not mine." He gestured up at the tank to one side, the clusters of cracking towers, bright and phallic to the other. "Here is the triumph of my Collegium. Are you blind to the beauty of such artifice? This is the living and true symbol of Mankind victorious, and Nature lying helpless and broken at his feet— would you give it up? Would you have us again at the mercy of wolves and tempests, slaves to fear and that which walks the night?"

"For the love of pity, Merlin. If the Earth dies, then mankind dies, too!"

"I am not afraid of death," Merlin said. "And if I do not fear mine, why should I dread that of others?" I said nothing. "But do you really think there will be no survivors? I believe the race will continue beyond the death of lands and oceans, in closed and perfect cities or on worlds built by art alone. It has taken the wit and skill of billions to create the technologies that can free us from dependence on Earth. Let us then thank the billions, not throw away their good work."

"Very few of those billions would survive," I said miserably, knowing that this would not move him. "A very small elite, at best."

The old devil laughed. "So. We understand each other better now. I had dreams, too, before you conspired to have me sealed in a cave. But our aims are not incompatible; my ascendancy does not require that the world die. I will save it, if that is what you wish." He shrugged as he said it as if promising an inconsequential, a trifle.

"And in return?"

His brows met like thunderstorms coming together; his eyes were glints of frozen lightning beneath. The man was pure theatre. "Mordred, the time has come for you to serve. Arthur served me for the love of righteousness; but you are a patricide and cannot be trusted. You must be bound to me, my will your will, my desires yours, your very thoughts owned and controlled. You must become my familiar."

I closed my eyes, lowered my head. "Done."

He owned me now.

• • •

We walked the granite block roadway toward the line of cool silver. Under a triple arch of sullen crimson pipes, Merlin abruptly turned to Shikra and asked, "Are you bleeding?"

"Say what?"

"Setting an egg," I explained. She looked blank. What the hell did the kids say nowadays? "On the rag. That time of month."

She snorted. "No." And, "You afraid to say the word menstruation? Carl Jung would've had fun with you."

"Come." Merlin stepped on the dragon track, and I followed, Shikra after me. The instant my feet touched the silver path, I felt a compulsion to walk, as if the track were moving my legs beneath me. "We must stand in the heart of the groundstar to empower the binding ceremony." Far, far ahead, I could see a second line cross ours; they met not in a cross but in a circle. "There are requirements: We must approach the place of power on foot, and speaking only the truth. For this reason I ask that you and your bodyguard say as little as possible. Follow, and I will speak of the genesis of kings.

"I remember—listen carefully, for this is important—a stormy night long ago, when a son was born to Uther, then King and bearer of the dragon pennant. The mother was Igraine, wife to the Duke of Tintagel, Uther's chief rival and a man who, if the truth be told, had a better claim to the crown than Uther himself. Uther begot the child on Igraine while the duke was yet alive, then killed the duke, married the mother, and named that son Arthur. It was a clever piece of statecraft, for Arthur thus had a twofold claim to the throne, that of his true and also his nominal father. He was a good politician, Uther, and no mistake.

"Those were rough and unsteady times, and I convinced the king his son would be safest raised anonymously in a holding distant from the strife of civil war. We agreed he should be raised by Ector, a minor knight and very distant relation. Letters passed back and forth. Oaths were sworn. And on a night, the babe was wrapped in cloth of gold and taken by two lords and two ladies outside of the castle, where I waited disguised as a beggar. I accepted the child, turned, and walked into the woods.

"And once out of sight of the castle, I strangled the brat."

I cried aloud in horror.

"I buried him in the loam, and that was the end of Uther's line. Some way farther in was a woodcutter's hut, and there were horses waiting there, and the wetnurse I had hired for my own child."

"What was the kid's name?" Shikra asked.

"I called him Arthur," Merlin said. "It seemed expedient. I took him to a priest who baptized him, and thence to Sir Ector, whose wife suckled him. And in time my son became king, and had a child whose name was Mordred, and in time this child killed his own father. I have told this story to no man or woman before this night. You are my grandson, Mordred, and this is the only reason I have not killed you outright."

We had arrived. One by one we entered the circle of light.

It was like stepping into a blast furnace. Enormous energies shot up through my body, and filled my lungs with cool, painless flame. My eyes overflowed with light: I looked down and the ground was a devious tangle of silver lines, like a printed circuit multiplied by a kaleidoscope. Shikra and the wizard stood at the other two corners of an equilateral triangle, burning bright as gods. Outside our closed circle, the purples and crimsons had dissolved into a blackness so deep it stirred uneasily, as if great shapes were acrawl in it.

Merlin raised his arms. Was he to my right or left? I could not tell, for his figure shimmered, shifting sometimes into Shikra's, sometimes into my own, leaving me staring at her breasts, my eyes. He made an extraordinary noise, a groan that rose and fell in strong but unmetered cadence. It wasn't until he came to the antiphon that I realized he was chanting plainsong. It was a crude form of music—the Gregorian was codified slightly after his day—but one that brought back a rush of memories, of ceremonies performed to the beat of wolfskin drums, and of the last night of boyhood before my mother initiated me into the adult mysteries.

He stopped. "In this ritual, we must each give up a portion of our identities. Are you prepared for that?" He was matter-of-fact, not at all disturbed by our unnatural environment, the consummate technocrat of the occult.

"Yes," I said.

"Once the bargain is sealed, you will not be able to go against its terms. Your hands will not obey you if you try, your eyes will not see that which offends me, your ears will not hear the words of others, your body will rebel against you. Do you understand?"

"Yes." Shikra was swaying slightly in the uprushing power, humming to herself. It would be easy to lose oneself in that psychic blast of force.

"You will be more tightly bound than slave ever was. There will be no hope of freedom from your obligation, not ever. Only death will release you. Do you understand?"

"Yes."

The old man resumed his chant. I felt as if the back of my skull were melting and my brain softening and yeasting out into the filthy air. Merlin's words sounded louder now, booming within my bones. I licked my lips, and smelled the rotting flesh of his cynicism permeating my hindbrain. Sweat stung down my sides on millipede feet. He stopped.

"I will need blood," said Merlin. "Hand me your knife, child."

Shikra looked my way, and I nodded. Her eyes were vague, half-mesmerized. One hand rose. The knife materialized in it. She waved it before her, fascinated by the colored trails it left behind, the way it pricked sparks from the air, crackling transient energies that rolled along the blade and leapt away to die, then held it out to Merlin.

Numbed by the strength of the man's will, I was too late realizing what he intended. Merlin stepped forward to accept the knife. Then he took her chin in hand and pushed it back, exposing her long, smooth neck.

"Hey!" I lunged forward, and the light rose up blindingly. Merlin chopped the knife high, swung it down in a flattening curve. Sparks stung through ionized air. The knife giggled and sang.

I was too late. The groundstar fought me, warping up underfoot in a narrowing cone that asymptotically fined down to a slim line yearning infinitely outward toward its unseen patron star. I flung out an arm and saw it foreshorten before me, my body flattening, ribs splaying out in extended fans to either side, stretching tautly vectored membranes made of less than nothing. Lofted up, hesitating, I hung timeless a nanosecond above the conflict and knew it was hopeless, that I could never cross that unreachable center. Beyond our faint circle of warmth and life, the outer darkness was in motion, mouths opening in the void.

But before the knife could taste Shikra's throat, she intercepted it with an outthrust hand. The blade transfixed her palm, and she yanked down, jerking it free of Merlin's grip. Faster than eye could follow, she had the knife in her good hand and—the keen thrill of her smile!—stabbed low into his groin.

The wizard roared in an ecstasy of rage. I felt the skirling agony of the knife as it pierced him. He tried to seize the girl, but she danced back from him. Blood rose like serpents from their wounds, twisting upward and swept away by unseen currents of power. The darkness stooped and banked, air bulging inward, and for an instant I held all the cold formless shapes in my mind and I screamed in terror. Merlin looked up and stumbled backward, breaking the circle.

And all was normal.

We stood in the shadow of an oil tank, under normal evening light, the sound of traffic on Passayunk a gentle background surf. The groundstar had disappeared, and the dragon lines with it. Merlin was clutching his manhood, blood oozing between his fingers. When he straightened, he did so slowly, painfully.

Warily, Shikra eased up from her fighter's crouch. By degrees she relaxed, then hid away her weapon. I took out my handkerchief and bound up her hand. It wasn't a serious wound; already the flesh was closing. For a miracle, the snuffbox was intact. I crushed a crumb on the back of a thumbnail, did it up. A muscle in my lower back was trembling. I'd been up days too long. Shikra shook her head when I offered her some, but Merlin extended a hand and I gave him the box. He took a healthy snort and shuddered.

"I wish you'd told me what you intended," I said. "We could have worked something out. Something else out."

"I am unmade," Merlin groaned. "Your hireling has destroyed me as a wizard."

It was as a politician that he was needed, but I didn't point that out. "Oh come on, a little wound like that. It's already stopped bleeding."

"No," Shikra said. "You told me that a magician's power is grounded in his mental somatype, remember? So a wound to his generative organs renders him impotent on symbolic and magical levels as well. That's why I tried to lop his balls off." She winced and stuck her injured hand under its opposite arm. "Shit, this sucker stings!"

Merlin stared. He'd caught me out in an evil he'd not thought me capable of. "You've taught this . . . chit the inner mysteries of my tradition? In the name of all that the amber rose represents, why?"

"Because she's my daughter, you dumb fuck!"

Shocked, Merlin said, "When—?"

Shikra put an arm around my waist, laid her head on my shoulder, smiled. "She's seventeen," I said. "But I only found out a year ago."

We drove unchallenged through the main gate, and headed back into town. Then I remembered there was nothing there for me anymore, cut across the median strip, and headed out for the airport. Time to go somewhere. I snapped on the radio, tuned it to 'XPN and turned up the volume. Wagner's valkyries soared and swooped low over my soul, dead meat cast down for their judgment.

Merlin was just charming the pants off his great-great-granddaughter. It shamed reason how he made her blush, so soon after trying to slice her open. "—make you Empress," he was saying.

"Shit, I'm not political. I'm some kind of anarchist, if anything."

"You'll outgrow that," he said. "Tell me, sweet child, this dream of your father's—do you share it?"

"Well, I ain't here for the food."

"Then we'll save your world for you." He laughed that enormously confident laugh of his that says that nothing is impossible, not if you have the skills and the cunning and the will to use them. "The three of us together."

Listening to their cheery prattle, I felt so vile and corrupt. The world is sick beyond salvation; I've seen the projections. People aren't going to give up their cars and factories, their VCR's and styrofoam-packaged hamburgers. No one, not Merlin himself, can pull off that kind of miracle. But I said nothing. When I die and am called to account, I will not be found wanting. "Mordred did his devoir"—even Malory gave me that. I did everything but dig up Merlin, and then I did that, too. Because even if the world can't be saved, we have to try. We have to try.

I floored the accelerator.

For the sake of the children, we must act as if there is hope, though we know there is not. We are under an obligation to do our mortal best, and will not be freed from that obligation while we yet live. We will never be freed until that day when Heaven, like some vast and unimaginable mall, opens her legs to receive us all.

The author acknowledges his debt to the unpublished
"Mordred" manuscript of the late Anna Quindsland.

GLACIER

Kim Stanley Robinson

"Glacier" was purchased by Gardner Dozois, and appeared in the October 1988 issue of IAsfm, *with an illustration by Janet Aulisio. Many excellent stories by Robinson have appeared in* IAsfm *over the last few years, under two separate editors, and we're pleased to be able to say that we have more in inventory. The story that follows is Robinson at his evocative best, a thoughtful and intensely rendered study of a boy's difficult coming-of-age in a future Boston caught in a deadly grip of ice. . . .*

Kim Stanley Robinson sold his first story in 1976, and quickly established himself as one of the most respected and critically acclaimed writers of his generation. His story "Black Air" won the World Fantasy Award in 1984, and his novella "The Blind Geometer," an IAsfm *story, won the Nebula Award in 1987. His excellent novel* The Wild Shore *was published in 1984 as the first title in the resurrected Ace Specials line, and was one of the most critically acclaimed novels of the year. Other Robinson books include the novels* Icehenge, The Memory of Whiteness, *and* The Gold Coast, *and the landmark collection* The Planet on the Table. *His most recent books are* Escape From Kathmandu, *a new collection, the hardcover novella* A Short, Sharp Shock, *and a new novel,* The Pacific Shore. *Upcoming is a trilogy of novels set on a future Mars. Robinson and his wife, Lisa, are back in their native California after several years in Switzerland, and have recently added a baby son to their family.*

"This is Stella," Mrs. Goldberg said. She opened the cardboard box and a gray cat leaped out and streaked under the corner table.

"That's where we'll put her blanket," Alex's mother said.

Alex got down on hands and knees to look. Stella was a skinny old cat; her fur was an odd mix of silver, black, and pinkish tan. Yellow eyes. Part tortoise-shell, Mom had said. The color of the fur over her eyes made it appear her brow was permanently furrowed. Her ears were laid flat.

"Remember she's kind of scared of boys," Mrs. Goldberg said.

"I know." Alex sat back on his heels. Stella hissed. "I was just looking." He knew the cat's whole story. She had been a stray that began visiting the Goldbergs' balcony to eat their dog's food, then—as far as anyone could tell—to hang out with the dog. Remus, a stiff-legged ancient thing, seemed happy to have the company, and after a while the two animals were inseparable. The cat had learned how to behave by watching Remus, and so it would go for a walk, come when you called it, shake hands and so on. Then Remus died, and now the Goldbergs had to move. Mom had offered to take Stella in, and though Father sighed heavily when she told him about it, he hadn't refused.

Mrs. Goldberg sat on the worn carpet beside Alex, and leaned forward so she could see under the table. Her face was puffy. "It's okay, Stell-bell," she said. "It's okay."

The cat stared at Mrs. Goldberg with an expression that said *You've got to be kidding.* Alex grinned to see such skepticism.

Mrs. Goldberg reached under the table; the cat squeaked in protest as it was pulled out, then lay in Mrs. Goldberg's lap quivering like a rabbit. The two women talked about other things. Then Mrs. Goldberg put Stella in Alex's mother's lap. There were scars on its ears and head. It breathed fast. Finally it calmed under Mom's hands. "Maybe we should feed her something," Mom said. She knew how distressed animals could get in this situation; they themselves had left behind their dog Pongo, when they moved from Toronto to Boston. Alex and she had been the ones to take Pongo to the Wallaces; the dog had howled as they left, and walking away Mom had cried. Now she told Alex to get some chicken out of the fridge and put it in a bowl for Stella. He put the bowl on the couch next to the cat, who sniffed at it disdainfully and refused to look at it. Only after much calming would it nibble at the meat, nose drawn high over one sharp eyetooth. Mom talked to Mrs. Goldberg, who watched Stella eat. When the cat was done it hopped off Mom's lap and walked up and down the couch. But it wouldn't let Alex near; it crouched as he approached, and with a desperate look dashed back under the table. "Oh Stella!" Mrs. Goldberg laughed. "It'll take her a while to get used to you," she said to Alex, and sniffed. Alex shrugged.

Outside the wind ripped at the treetops sticking above the buildings. Alex walked up Chester Street to Brighton Avenue and turned left, hurrying to counteract the cold. Soon he reached the river and could walk the path on top of the embankment. Down in its trough the river's edges were crusted with ice, but midstream was still free, the silty gray water riffled by white. He passed the construction site for the dam and came to the moraine, a long mound of dirt, rocks, lumber, and junk. He climbed it with big steps, and stood looking at the glacier.

The glacier was immense, like a range of white hills rolling in from the west and north. The Charles poured from the bottom of it and roiled through a cut in the terminal moraine; the glacier's snout loomed so large that the river looked small, like a gutter after a storm. Bright white iceberg chunks had toppled off the face of the snout, leaving fresh blue scars and clogging the river below.

Alex walked the edge of the moraine until he was above the glacier's side. To his left was the razed zone, torn streets and fresh dirt and cellars open to the sky; beyond it Allston and Brighton, still bustling with city life. Under him, the sharp-edged mound of dirt and debris. To his right, the wilderness of ice and rock. Looking straight ahead it was hard to believe that the two halves of the view came from the same world. Neat. He descended the moraine's steep loose inside slope carefully, following a path of his own.

The meeting of glacier and moraine was a curious juncture. In some places the moraine had been undercut and had spilled across the ice in wide fans; you couldn't be sure if the dirt was solid or if it concealed crevasses. In other places melting had created a gap, so that a thick cake of ice stood over empty air, and dripped into gray pools below. Once Alex had seen a car in one of these low wet caves, stripped of its paint and squashed flat.

In still other places, however, the ice sloped down and overlaid the moraine's gravel in a perfect ramp, as if fitted by carpenters. Alex walked the trough between dirt and ice until he reached one of these areas, then took a big step onto the curved white surface. He felt the usual quiver of excitement: he was on the glacier.

It was steep on the rounded side slope, but the ice was embedded with thousands of chunks of gravel. Each pebble, heated by the sun, had sunk into a little pocket of its own, and was then frozen into position in the night; this process had been repeated until most chunks were about three-quarters buried. Thus the glacier had a peculiarly pocked, rocky surface, which gripped the torn soles of Alex's shoes. A non-slip surface. No slope on the glacier was too steep for him. Crunch, crunch, crunch: tiny arabesques of ice collapsed under his feet with every step. He could change the glacier, he was part of its action. Part of it.

Where the side slope leveled out the first big crevasses appeared. These deep blue fissures were dangerous, and Alex stepped between two of them and up a narrow ramp very carefully. He picked up a fist-sized rock, tossed it in the bigger crack. *Clunk clunk . . . splash.* He shivered and walked on, ritual satisfied. He knew from these throws that at the bottom of the glacier there were pockets of air, pools of water, streams running down to form the Charles . . . a deadly subglacial world. No one who fell into it would ever escape. It made the surface ice glow with a magical danger, an internal light.

Up on the glacier proper he could walk more easily. Crunch crunch crunch, over an undulating broken debris-covered plain. Ice for miles on miles. Looking back toward the city he saw the Hancock and Prudential towers to the right, the lower MIT towers to the left, poking up at low scudding clouds. The wind was strong here and he pulled his jacket hood's drawstring tighter. Muffled hoot of wind, a million tricklings. There were little creeks running in channels cut into the ice: it was almost like an ordinary landscape, streams running in ravines over a broad rocky meadow. And yet everything was different. The streams ran into crevasses or potholes and instantly disappeared, for instance. It was wonderfully strange to look down such a rounded hole: the ice was very blue and you could see the air bubbles in it, air from some year long ago.

Broken seracs exposed fresh ice to the sun. Scores of big erratic boulders dotted the glacier, some the size of houses. He made his way from one to the next, using them as cover. There were gangs of boys from Cambridge who occasionally came up here, and they were dangerous. It was important to see them before he was seen.

A mile or more onto the glacier, ice had flowed around one big boulder, leaving a curving wall some ten feet high— another example of the glacier's whimsy, one of hundreds of strange surface formations. Alex had wedged some stray boards into the gap between rock and ice, making a seat that was tucked out of the west wind. Flat rocks made a fine floor, and in the corner he had even made a little fireplace. Every fire he lit sank the hearth of flat stones a bit deeper into the otherwise impervious ice.

This time he didn't have enough kindling, though, so he sat on his bench, hands deep in pockets, and looked back at the city. He could see for miles. Wind whistled over the boulder. Scattered shafts of sunlight broke against ice. Mostly shadowed, the jumbled expanse was faintly pink. This was

because of an algae that lived on nothing but ice and dust.
Pink; the blue of the seracs; gray ice; patches of white, marking
snow or sunlight. In the distance dark clouds scraped the top of
the blue Hancock building, making it look like a distant serac.
Alex leaned back against his plank wall, whistling one of the
songs of the Pirate King.

Everyone agreed the cat was crazy. Her veneer of civilization
was thin, and at any loud noise—the phone's ring, the door
slamming—she would jump as if shot, then stop in mid-flight
as she recalled that this particular noise entailed no danger;
then lick down her fur, pretending she had never jumped in
the first place. A flayed sensibility.

She was also very wary about proximity to people; this
despite the fact that she had learned to love being petted.
So she would often get in moods where she would approach
one of them and give an exploratory, half-purring mew; then,
if you responded to the invitation and crouched to pet her, she
would sidle just out of arm's reach, repeating the invitation
but retreating with each shift you made, until she either let
you get within petting distance—just—or decided it wasn't
worth the risk, and scampered away. Father laughed at this
intense ambivalence. "Stella, you're too stupid to live, aren't
you," he said in a teasing voice.

"Charles," Mom said.

"It's the best example of approach avoidance behavior I've
ever seen," Father said. Intrigued by the challenge, he would
sit on the floor, back against the couch and legs stretched ahead
of him, and put Stella on his thighs. She would either endure
his stroking until it ended, when she could jump away without
impediment—or relax, and purr. She had a rasping loud purr,
it reminded Alex of a chainsaw heard across the glacier. "Bug
brain," Father would say to her. "Button head."

After a few weeks, as August turned to September and the
leaves began to wither and fall, Stella started to lap sit voluntarily—but always in Mom's lap. "She likes the warmth,"
Mom said.

"It's cold on the floor," Father agreed, and played with the
cat's scarred ears. "But why do you always sit on Helen's lap,

huhn, Stell? I'm the one who started you on that." Eventually the cat would step onto his lap as well, and stretch out as if it was something she had always done. Father laughed at her.

Stella never rested on Alex's lap voluntarily, but would sometimes stay if he put her there and stroked her slowly for a long time. On the other hand she was just as likely to look back at him, go cross-eyed with horror and leap desperately away, leaving claw marks in his thighs. "She's so weird," he complained to Mom after one of these abrupt departures.

"It's true," Mom said with her low laugh. "But you have to remember that Stella was probably an abused kitty."

"How can you abuse a stray?"

"I'm sure there are ways. And maybe she was abused at home, and ran away."

"Who would do that?"

"Some people would."

Alex recalled the gangs on the glacier, and knew it was true. He tried to imagine what it would be like to be at their mercy, all the time. After that he thought he understood her permanent frown of deep concentration and distrust, as she sat staring at him. "It's just me, Stell-bells."

Thus when the cat followed him up onto the roof, and seemed to enjoy hanging out there with him, he was pleased. Their apartment was on the top floor, and they could take the pantry stairs and use the roof as a porch. It was a flat expanse of graveled tarpaper, a terrible imitation of the glacier's non-slip surface, but it was nice on dry days to go up there and look around, toss pebbles onto other roofs, see if the glacier was visible, and so on. Once Stella pounced at a piece of string trailing from his pants, and next time he brought up a length of Father's yarn. He was astonished and delighted when Stella responded by attacking the windblown yarn enthusiastically, biting it, clawing it, wrestling it from her back when Alex twirled it around her, and generally behaving in a very kittenish way. Perhaps she had never played as a kitten, Alex thought, so that it was all coming out now that she felt safe. But the play always ended abruptly; she would come to herself in mid-bite or bat, straighten up, and look around with a forbidding expression, as if to say *What is this yarn doing draped over me?*—then lick her fur and pretend the preceding minutes hadn't happened. It made Alex laugh.

Although the glacier had overrun many towns to the west and north, Watertown and Newton most recently, there was surprisingly little evidence of that in the moraines, or in the ice. It was almost all natural: rock and dirt and wood. Perhaps the wood had come from houses, perhaps some of the gravel had once been concrete, but you couldn't tell that now. Just dirt and rock and splinters, with an occasional chunk of plastic or metal thrown in. Apparently the overrun towns had been plowed under on the spot, or moved. Mostly it looked like the glacier had just left the White Mountains.

Father and Gary Jung had once talked about the latest plan from MIT. The enormous dam they were building downstream, between Allston and Cambridge, was to hold the glacier back. They were going to heat the concrete of the inner surface of the dam, and melt the ice as it advanced. It would become a kind of frozen reservoir. The melt water would pour through a set of turbines before becoming the Charles, and the electricity generated by these turbines would help to heat the dam. Very neat.

The ice of the glacier, when you got right down to look at it, was clear for an inch or less, cracked and bubble-filled; then it turned a milky white. You could see the transition. Where the ice had been sheared vertically, however—on the side of a serac, or down in a crevasse—the clear part extended in many inches. You could see air bubbles deep inside, as if it were badly made glass. And this ice was distinctly blue. Alex didn't understand why there should be that difference, between the white ice laying flat and the blue ice cut vertically. But there it was.

Up in New Hampshire they had tried slowing the glacier— or at least stopping the abrupt "Alaskan slides"—by setting steel rods vertically in concrete, and laying the concrete in the glacier's path. Later they had hacked out one of these installations, and found the rods bent in perfect ninety-degree angles, pressed into the scored concrete.

The ice would flow right over the dam.

• • •

One day Alex was walking by Father's study when Father called out. "Alexander! Take a look at this."

Alex entered the dark book-lined room. Its window overlooked the weed-filled space between buildings, and green light slanted onto Father's desk. "Here, stand beside me and look in my coffee cup. You can see the reflection of the Morgelis' window flowers on the coffee."

"Oh yeah! Neat."

"It gave me a shock! I looked down and there were these white and pink flowers in my cup, bobbing against a wall in a breeze, all of it tinted sepia as if it were an old-fashioned photo. It took me a while to see where it was coming from, what was being reflected." He laughed. "Through a looking glass."

Alex's father had light brown eyes, and fair wispy hair brushed back from a receding hairline. Mom called him handsome, and Alex agreed: tall, thin, graceful, delicate, distinguished. His father was a great man. Now he smiled in a way Alex didn't understand, looking into his coffee cup.

Mom had friends at the street market on Memorial Drive, and she had arranged work for Alex there. Three afternoons a week he walked over the Charles to the riverside street and helped the fishmongers gut fish, the vegetable sellers strip and clean the vegetables. He also helped set up stalls and take them down, and he swept and hosed the street afterwards. He was popular because of his energy and his willingness to get his hands wet in raw weather. The sleeves of his down jacket were permanently discolored from the frequent soakings—the dark blue almost a brown—a fact that distressed his mom. But he could handle the cold better than the adults; his hands would get a splotchy bluish white and he would put them to the red cheeks of the women and they would jump and say My *God*, Alex, how can you stand it?

This afternoon was blustery and dark but without rain, and it was enlivened by an attempted theft in the pasta stands, and by the appearance of a very mangy, very fast stray dog. This dog pounced on the pile of fishheads and entrails and disappeared with his mouth stuffed, trailing slick white-and-red guts. Everyone who saw it laughed. There weren't many stray dogs left these days, it was a pleasure to see one.

An hour past sunset he was done cleaning up and on his way home, hands in his pockets, stomach full, a five-dollar bill clutched in one hand. He showed his pass to the National Guardsman and walked out onto Weeks Bridge. In the middle he stopped and leaned over the railing, into the wind. Below the water churned, milky with glacial silt. The sky still held a lot of light. Low curving bands of black cloud swept in from the northwest, like great ribs of slate. Above these bands the white sky was leached away by dusk. Raw wind whistled over his hood. Light water rushing below, dark clouds rushing above . . . he breathed the wind deep into him, felt himself expand until he filled everything he could see.

That night his parents' friends were gathering at their apartment for their bi-weekly party. Some of them would read stories and poems and essays and broadsides they had written, and then they would argue about them; and after that they would drink and eat whatever they had brought, and argue some more. Alex enjoyed it. But tonight when he got home Mom was rushing between computer and kitchen and muttering curses as she hit command keys or the hot water faucet, and the moment she saw him she said, "Oh Alex I'm glad you're here, could you please run down to the laundry and do just one load for me? The Talbots are staying over tonight and there aren't any clean sheets and I don't have anything to wear tomorrow either—thanks, you're a dear." And he was back out the door with a full laundry bag hung over his shoulder and the box of soap in the other hand, stomping grumpily past a little man in a black coat, reading a newspaper on the stoop of 19 Chester.

Down to Brighton, take a right, downstairs into the brightly lit basement laundromat. He threw laundry and soap and quarters into their places, turned the machine on and sat on top of it. Glumly he watched the other people in there, sitting on the washers and dryers. The vibrations put a lot of them to sleep. Others stared dully at the wall. Back in his apartment the guests would be arriving, taking off their overcoats, slapping arms over chests and talking as fast as they could. David and Sara and John from next door, Ira and Gary and Ilene from across the street, the Talbots, Kathryn Grimm, and Michael Wu from Father's university, Ron from the hospital. They would settle down in the living room, on couches and chairs and floor, and talk and talk. Alex liked Kathryn especially, she could talk twice as fast as anyone else, and she called everyone darling and laughed and chattered so fast that everyone was caught up in the rhythm of it. Or David with his jokes, or Jay Talbot and his friendly questions. Or Gary Jung, the way he would sit in his corner like a bear, drinking beer and challenging everything that everyone read. "Why abstraction, why this distortion from the real? How does it help us, how does it speak to us? We should forget the abstract!" Father and Ira called him a vulgar Marxist, but he didn't mind. "You might as well be Plekhanov, Gary!" "Thank you very much!" he would say with a sharp grin, rubbing his unshaven jowls. And someone else would read. Mary Talbot once read a fairy tale about the Thing under the glacier; Alex had *loved* it. Once they even got Michael Wu to bring his violin along, and he hmm'd and hawed and pulled at the skin of his neck and refused and said he wasn't good enough, and then shaking like a leaf he played a melody that stilled them all. And Stella! She hated these parties, she spent them crouched deep in her refuge, ready for any kind of atrocity.

And here he was sitting on a washer in the laundromat.

When the laundry was dry he bundled it into the bag, then hurried around the corner and down Chester Street. Inside the glass door of Number 21 he glanced back out, and noticed that the man who had been reading the paper on the stoop next door was still sitting there. Odd. It was cold to be sitting outdoors.

Upstairs the readings had ended and the group was scattered through the apartment, most of them in the kitchen, as Mom had lit the stovetop burners and turned the gas up high. The blue flames roared airily under their chatter, making the kitchen bright and warm. "Wonderful the way white gas burns so clean." "And then they found the poor thing's head and intestines in the alley—it had been butchered right on the spot."

"Alex, you're back! Thanks for doing that. Here, get something to eat."

Everyone greeted him and went back to their conversations. "Gary you are so *conservative*," Kathryn cried, hands held out over the stove. "It's not conservative at all," Gary replied. "It's a radical goal and I guess it's so radical that I have to keep reminding you it exists. Art should be used to *change* things."

"Isn't that a distortion from the real?"

Alex wandered down the narrow hall to his parents' room, which overlooked Chester Street. Father was there, saying to Ilene, "It's one of the only streets left with trees. It really seems residential, and here we are three blocks from Comm Ave. Hi, Alex."

"Hi, Alex. It's like a little bit of Brookline made it over to Allston."

"Exactly."

Alex stood in the bay window and looked down, licking the last of the carrot cake off his fingers. The man was still down there.

"Let's close off these rooms and save the heat. Alex, you coming?"

He sat on the floor in the living room. Father and Gary and David were starting a game of hearts, and they invited him to be the fourth. He nodded happily. Looking under the corner table he saw yellow eyes, blinking back at him; Stella, a frown of the deepest disapproval on her flat face. Alex laughed. "I knew you'd be there! It's okay, Stella. It's okay."

They left in a group, as usual, stamping their boots and diving deep into coats and scarves and gloves and exclaiming at the cold of the stairwell. Gary gave Mom a brief hug. "Only warm spot left in Boston," he said, and opened the glass door. The rest followed him out, and Alex joined them. The man in the black coat was just turning right onto Brighton Avenue, toward the university and downtown.

Sometimes clouds took on just the mottled gray of the glacier, low dark points stippling a lighter gray surface as cold showers draped down. At these times he felt he stood between two planes of some larger structure, two halves: icy tongue, icy roof of mouth. . . .

He stood under such a sky, throwing stones. His target was an erratic some forty yards away. He hit the boulder with most of his throws. A rock that big was an easy target. A bottle was better. He had brought one with him, and he set it up behind the erratic, on a waist-high rock. He walked back to a point where the bottle was hidden by the erratic. Using flat rocks he sent spinners out in a trajectory that brought them curving in from the side, so that it was possible to hit the concealed target. This was very important for the rock fights that he occasionally got involved in; usually he was outnumbered, and to hold his own he relied on his curves and his accuracy in general, and on a large number of ammunition caches hidden here and there. In one area crowded with boulders and crevasses he could sometimes create the impression of two throwers.

Absorbed in the exercise of bringing curves around the right side of the boulder—the hard side for him—he relaxed his vigilance, and when he heard a shout he jumped around to look. A rock whizzed by his left ear.

He dropped to the ice and crawled behind a boulder. Ambushed! He ran back into his knot of boulders and dashed a layer of snow away from one of his big caches, then with hands and pockets full looked carefully over a knobby chunk of cement, in the direction the stone had come from.

No movement. He recalled the stone whizzing by, the brief sight of it and the *zip* it made in passing. That had been close! If that had hit him! He shivered to think of it, it made his stomach shrink.

A bit of almost frozen rain pattered down. Not a shadow anywhere. On overcast days like this one it seemed things were lit from below, by the white bulk of the glacier. Like plastic over a weak neon light. Brittle huge blob of plastic, shifting and groaning and once in a while cracking like a gunshot, or grumbling like distant thunder. Alive. And Alex was its ally, its representative among men. He shifted from rock to rock, saw movement and froze. Two boys in green down jackets, laughing as they ran off the ice and over the lateral moraine, into what was left of Watertown. Just a potshot, then. Alex cursed them, relaxed.

He went back to throwing at the hidden bottle. Occasionally he recalled the stone flying by his head, and threw a little harder. Elegant curves of flight as the flat rocks bit the air and cut down and in. Finally one rock spun out into space and turned down sharply. Perfect slider. Its disappearance behind the erratic was followed by a tinkling crash. "Yeah!" Alex exclaimed, and ran to look. Icy glass on glassy ice.

Then, as he was leaving the glacier, boys jumped over the moraine shouting "Canadian!" and "There he is!" and "Get him!" This was more a chase than a serious ambush, but there were a lot of them and after emptying hands and pockets Alex was off running. He flew over the crunchy irregular surface, splashing meltwater, jumping narrow crevasses and surface rills. Then a wide crevasse blocked his way, and to start his jump he leaped onto a big flat rock; the rock gave under his foot and lurched down the ice into the crevasse.

Alex turned in and fell, bringing shoe-tips, knees, elbows and hands onto the rough surface. This arrested his fall, though it hurt. The crevasse was just under his feet. He scrambled up, ran panting along the crevasse until it narrowed, leaped over it. Then up the moraine and down into the narrow abandoned streets of west Allston.

Striding home, still breathing hard, he looked at his hands and saw that the last two fingernails on his right hand had been ripped away from the flesh; both were still there, but blood seeped from under them. He hissed and sucked on them, which hurt. The blood tasted like blood.

If he had fallen into the crevasse, following the loose rock down . . . if that stone had hit him in the face . . . he could feel his heart, thumping against his sternum. Alive.

Turning onto Chester Street he saw the man in the black coat, leaning against the florid maple across the street from their building. Watching them still! Though the man didn't appear to notice Alex, he did heft a bag and start walking in the other direction. Quickly Alex picked a rock out of the gutter and threw it at the man as hard as he could, spraying drops of blood onto the sidewalk. The rock flew over the man's head like a bullet, just missing him. The man ducked and scurried around the corner onto Comm Ave.

Father was upset about something. "They did the same thing to Gary and Michael and Kathryn, and their classes are even smaller than mine! I don't know what they're going to do. I don't know what *we're* going to do."

"We might be able to attract larger classes next semester," Mom said. She was upset too. Alex stood in the hall, slowly hanging up his jacket.

"But what about now? And what about later?" Father's voice was strained, almost cracking.

"We're making enough for now, that's the important thing. As for later—well, at least we know now rather than five years down the road."

Father was silent at the implications of this. "First Vancouver, then Toronto, now here—"

"Don't worry about all of it at once, Charles."

"How can I help it!" Father strode into his study and closed the door, not noticing Alex around the corner. Alex sucked his fingers. Stella poked her head cautiously out of his bedroom.

"Hi Stell-bell," he said quietly. From the living room came the plastic clatter of Mom's typing. He walked down the long hallway, past the silent study to the living room. She was hitting the keys hard, staring at the screen, mouth tight.

"What happened?" Alex said.

She looked up. "Hi, Alex. Well—your father got bad news from the university."

"Did he not get tenure again?"

"No, no, it's not a question of that."

"But now he doesn't even have the chance?"

She glanced at him sharply, then back at the screen, where her work was blinking. "I suppose that's right. The department has shifted all the new faculty over to extension, so they're hired by the semester, and paid by the class. It means you need a lot of students. . . ."

"Will we move again?"

"I don't know," she said curtly, exasperated with him for bringing it up. She punched the command key. "But we'll really have to save money, now. Everything you make at the market is important."

Alex nodded. He didn't mention the little man in the black coat, feeling obscurely afraid. Mentioning the man would somehow make him significant—Mom and Father would get angry, or frightened—something like that. By not telling them he could protect them from it, handle it on his own, so they could concentrate on other problems. Besides the two matters couldn't be connected, could they? Being watched; losing jobs. Perhaps they could. In which case there was nothing his parents could do about it anyway. Better to save them that anger, that fear.

He would make sure his throws hit the man next time.

Storms rolled in and the red and yellow leaves were ripped off the trees. Alex kicked through piles of them stacked on the sidewalks. He never saw the little man. He put up flyers for his father, who became even more distracted and remote. He brought home vegetables from work, tucked under his down jacket, and Mom cooked them without asking if he had bought them. She did the wash in the kitchen sink and dried it on lines in the back space between buildings, standing knee deep in leaves and weeds. Sometimes it took three days for clothes to dry back there; often they froze on the line.

While hanging clothes or taking them down she would let Stella join her. The cat regarded each shifting leaf with dire suspicion, then after a few exploratory leaps and bats would do battle with all of them, rolling about in a frenzy.

One time Mom was carrying a basket of dry laundry up the pantry stairs when a stray dog rounded the corner and made a dash for Stella, who was still outside. Mom ran back down shouting, and the dog fled; but Stella had disappeared. Mom called Alex down from his studies in a distraught voice, and they searched the back of the building and all the adjacent backyards for nearly an hour, but the cat was nowhere to be found. Mom was really upset. It was only after they had quit and returned upstairs that they heard her, miaowing far above them. She had climbed the big oak tree. "Oh *smart*, Stella," Mom cried, a wild note in her voice. They called her name out the kitchen window, and the desperate miaows redoubled.

Up on the roof they could just see her, perched high in the almost bare branches of the big tree. "I'll get her," Alex said. "Cats can't climb down." He started climbing. It was difficult: the branches were close-knit, and they swayed in the wind. And as he got closer the cat climbed higher. "No, Stella, don't do that! Come here!" Stella stared at him, clamped to her branch of the moment, cross-eyed with fear. Below them Mom said over and over, "Stella, it's okay—it's okay, Stella." Stella didn't believe her.

Finally Alex reached her, near the tree's top. Now here was a problem: he needed his hands to climb down, but it seemed likely he would also need them to hold the terrified cat. "Come here, Stella." He put a hand on her flank; she flinched. Her side pulsed with her rapid breathing. She hissed faintly. He had to maneuver up a step, onto a very questionable branch; his face was inches from her. She stared at him without a trace of recognition. He pried her off her branch, lifted her. If she cared to claw him now she could really tear him up. Instead she clung to his shoulder and chest, all her claws dug through his clothes, quivering under his left arm and hand.

Laboriously he descended, using only the one hand. Stella began miaowing fiercely, and struggling a bit. Finally he met Mom, who had climbed the tree quite a ways. Stella was getting more upset. "Hand her to me." Alex detached her from his chest paw by paw, balanced, held the cat down with both hands. Again it was a tricky moment; if Stella went berserk they would all be in trouble. But she fell onto Mom's chest and collapsed, a catatonic ball of fur.

Back in the apartment she dashed for her blanket under the table. Mom enticed her out with food, but she was very jumpy and she wouldn't allow Alex anywhere near her; she ran away if he even entered the room. "Back to square one, I see," Mom commented.

"It's not fair! I'm the one that saved her!"

"She'll get over it." Mom laughed, clearly relieved. "Maybe it'll take some time, but she will. Ha! This is clear proof that cats are smart enough to be crazy. Irrational, neurotic—just like a person." They laughed, and Stella glared at them balefully. "Yes you are, aren't you! You'll come around again."

• • •

Often when Alex got home in the early evenings his father was striding back and forth in the kitchen talking loudly, angrily, fearfully, while Mom tried to reassure him. "They're doing the same thing to us they did to Rick Stone! But why!" When Alex closed the front door the conversation would stop. Once when he walked tentatively down the quiet hallway to the kitchen he found them standing there, arms around each other, Father's head in Mom's short hair.

Father raised his head, disengaged, went to his study. On his way he said, "Alex, I need your help."

"Sure."

Alex stood in the study and watched without understanding as his father took books from his shelves and put them in the big laundry bag. He threw the first few in like dirty clothes, then sighed and thumped in the rest in a businesslike fashion, not looking at them.

"There's a used book store in Cambridge, on Mass Ave. Antonio's."

"Sure, I know the one." They had been there together a few times.

"I want you to take these over there and sell them to Tony for me," Father said, looking at the empty shelves. "Will you do that for me?"

"Sure." Alex picked up the bag, shocked that it had come to this. Father's books! He couldn't meet his father's eye. "I'll do that right now," he said uncertainly, and hefted the bag over one shoulder. In the hallway Mom approached and put a hand on his shoulder—her silent thanks—then went into the study.

Alex hiked east toward the university, crossed the Charles River on the great iron bridge. The wind howled in the superstructure. On the Cambridge side, after showing his pass, he put the heavy bag on the ground and inspected its contents. Ever since the infamous incident of the spilled hot chocolate, Father's books had been off-limits to him; now a good twenty of them were there in the bag to be touched, opened, riffled through. Many in this bunch were in foreign languages, especially Greek and Russian, with their alien alphabets. Could people really read such marks? Well, Father did. It must be possible.

When he had inspected all the books he chose two in English—*The Odyssey* and *The Colossus of Maroussi*—and put those in his down jacket pockets. He could take them to the glacier and read them, then sell them later to Antonio's—perhaps in the next bag of books. There were many more bagfuls in Father's study.

A little snow stuck to the glacier now, filling the pocks and making bright patches on the north side of every boulder, every serac. Some of the narrower crevasses were filled with it—bright white lines on the jumbled gray. When the whole surface was white the crevasses would be invisible, and the glacier too dangerous to walk on. Now the only danger was leaving obvious footprints for trackers. Walking up the rubble lines would solve that. These lines of rubble fascinated Alex. It looked just as if bulldozers had clanked up here and shoved the majority of the stones and junk into straight lines down the big central tongue of the glacier. But in fact they were natural features. Father had attempted to explain on one of the walks they had taken up here. "The ice is moving, and it moves faster in the middle than on the outer edges, just like a stream. So rocks on the surface tend to slide over time, down into lines in the middle."

"Why are there two lines, then?"

Father shrugged, looking into the blue-green depths of a crevasse. "We really shouldn't be up here, you know that?"

Now Alex stopped to inspect a tire caught in the rubble line. Truck tire, tread worn right to the steel belting. It would burn, but with too much smoke. There were several interesting objects in this neat row of rock and sand: plastic jugs, a doll, a lampbase, a telephone.

His shelter was undisturbed. He pulled the two books from his pockets and set them on the bench, propping them with rock bookends.

He circled the boulder, had a look around. The sky today was a low smooth pearl gray sheet, ruffled by a set of delicate waves pasted to it. The indirect light brought out all the colors:

the pink of the remarkable snow algae, the blue of the seracs, the various shades of rock, the occasional bright spot of junk, the many white patches of snow. A million dots of color under the pewter sheet of cloud.

Three creaks, a crack, a long shuddering rumble. Sleepy, muscular, the great beast had moved. Alex walked across its back to his bench, sat. On the far lateral moraine some gravel slid down. Puffs of brown dust in the air.

He read his books. *The Odyssey* was strange but interesting. Father had told him some of the story before. *The Colossus of Maroussi* was long-winded but funny—it reminded Alex of his uncle, who could turn the smallest incident into an hour's comic monologue. What he could have made of Stella's flight up the tree! Alex laughed to think of it. But his uncle was in jail.

He sat on his bench and read, stopped occasionally to look around. When the hand holding the book got cold, he changed hands and put the cold one in a pocket of his down jacket. When both hands were blue he hid the books in rocks under his bench and went home.

There were more bags of books to be sold at Antonio's and other shops in Cambridge. Each time Alex rotated out a few that looked interesting, and replaced them with the ones on the glacier. He daydreamed of saving all the books and earning the money some other way—then presenting his father with the lost library, at some future undefined but appropriate moment.

Eventually Stella forgave him for rescuing her. She came to enjoy chasing a piece of yarn up and down their long narrow hallway, skidding around the corner by the study. It reminded them of a game they had played with Pongo, who would chase anything, and they laughed at her, especially when she jerked to a halt and licked her fur fastidiously, as if she had never been carousing. "You can't fool us, Stell! We *remember*!"

Mom sold most of her music collection, except for her favorites. Once Alex went out to the glacier with the *Concerto de Aranjuez* coursing through him—Mom had had it on in the apartment while she worked. He hummed the big theme of the second movement as he crunched over the ice: clearly it was the theme of the glacier, the glacier's song. How had a blind composer managed to capture the windy sweep of it, the spaciousness? Perhaps such things could be heard as well as seen. The wind said it, whistling over the ice. It was a terrifically dark day, windy, snowing in gusts. He could walk right up the middle of the great tongue, between the rubble lines; no one else would be up there today. Da-da-da . . . da da da da da da, da-da-da. . . . Hands in pockets, chin on chest, he trudged into the wind humming, feeling like the whole world was right there around him. It was too cold to stay in his shelter for more than a minute.

Father went off on trips, exploring possibilities. One morning Alex woke to the sound of *The Pirates of Penzance*. This was one of their favorites, Mom played it all the time while working and on Saturday mornings, so that they knew all the lyrics by heart and often sang along. Alex especially loved the Pirate King, and could mimic all his intonations.

He dressed and walked down to the kitchen. Mom stood by the stove with her back to him, singing along. It was a sunny morning and their big kitchen windows faced east; the light poured in on the sink and the dishes and the white stove and the linoleum and the plants in the window and Stella, sitting contentedly on the window sill listening.

His mom was tall and broad-shouldered. Every year she cut her hair shorter; now it was just a cap of tight brown curls, with a somewhat longer patch down the nape of her neck. That would go soon, Alex thought, and then her hair would be as short as it could be. She was lost in the song, one slim hand on the white stove top, looking out the window. She had a low, rich, thrilling voice, like a real singer's only prettier. She was singing along with the song that Mabel sings after she finds out that Frederick won't be able to leave the pirates until 1940.

When it was over Alex entered the kitchen, went to the pantry. "That's a short one," he said.

"Yes, they had to make it short," Mom said. "There's nothing funny about that one."

• • •

One night while Father was gone on one of his trips, Mom had to go over to Ilene and Ira and Gary's apartment: Gary had been arrested, and Ilene and Ira needed help. Alex and Stella were left alone.

Stella wandered the silent apartment miaowing. "I *know*, Stella," Alex said in exasperation. "They're *gone*. They'll be back tomorrow." The cat paid no attention to him.

He went into Father's study. Tonight he'd be able to read something in relative warmth. It would only be necessary to be *very careful*.

The bookshelves were empty. Alex stood before them, mouth open. He had no idea they had sold that many of them. There were a couple left on Father's desk, but he didn't want to move them. They appeared to be dictionaries anyway. "It's all Greek to me."

He went back to the living room and got out the yarn bag, tried to interest Stella in a game. She wouldn't play. She wouldn't sit on his lap. She wouldn't stop miaowing. "Stella, shut up!" She scampered away and kept crying. Vexed, he got out the jar of catnip and spread some on the linoleum in the kitchen. Stella came running to sniff at it, then roll in it. Afterwards she played with the yarn wildly, until it caught around her tail and she froze, staring at him in a drugged paranoia. Then she dashed to her refuge and refused to come out. Finally Alex put on *The Pirates of Penzance* and listened to it for a while. After that he was sleepy.

They got a good lawyer for Gary, Mom said. Everyone was hopeful. Then a couple of weeks later Father got a new job; he called them from work to tell them about it.

"Where is it?" Alex asked Mom when she was off the phone.

"In Kansas."

"So we will be moving."

"Yes," Mom said. "Another move."

"Will there be glaciers there too?"

"I think so. In the hills. Not as big as ours here, maybe. But there are glaciers everywhere."

• • •

He walked onto the ice one last time. There was a thin crust of snow on the tops of everything. A fantastically jumbled field of snow. It was a clear day, the sky a very pale blue, the white expanse of the glacier painfully bright. A few cirrus clouds made sickles high in the west. The snow was melting a bit and there were water droplets all over, with little sparks of colored light in each drip. The sounds of water melting were everywhere, drips, gurgles, splashes. The intensity of light was stunning, like a blow to the brain, right through the eyes. It pulsed.

The crevasse in front of his shelter had widened, and the boards of his bench had fallen. The wall of ice turning around the boulder was splintered, and shards of bright ice lay over the planks.

The glacier was moving. The glacier was alive. No heated dam would stop it. He felt its presence, huge and supple under him, seeping into him like the cold through his wet shoes, filling him up. He blinked, nearly blinded by the light breaking everywhere on it, a surgical glare that made every snow-capped rock stand out like the color red on a slide transparency. The white light. In the distance the ice cracked hollowly, moving somewhere. Everything moved: the ice, the wind, the clouds, the sun, the planet. All of it rolling around.

As they packed up their possessions Alex could hear them in the next room. "We can't," Father said. "You know we can't. They won't let us."

When they were done the apartment looked odd. Bare walls, bare wood floors. It looked smaller. Alex walked the length of it: his parents' room overlooking Chester Street; his room; his father's study; the living room; the kitchen with its fine morning light. The pantry. Stella wandered the place miaowing. Her blanket was still in its corner, but without the table it looked moth-eaten, fur-coated, ineffectual. Alex picked her up and went through the pantry, up the back stairs to the roof.

Snow had drifted into the corners. Alex walked in circles, looking at the city. Stella sat on her paws by the stairwell shed, watching him, her fur ruffled by the wind.

Around the shed snow had melted, then frozen again. Little puddles of ice ran in flat curves across the the pebbled tar paper. Alex crouched to inspect them, tapping one speculatively with a fingernail. He stood up and looked west, but buildings and bare treetops obscured the view.

Stella fought to stay out of the box, and once in it she cried miserably.

Father was already in Kansas, starting the new job. Alex and Mom and Stella had been staying in the living room of Michael Wu's place while Mom finished her work; now she was done, it was moving day, they were off to the train. But first they had to take Stella to the Talbots'.

Alex carried the box and followed Mom as they walked across the Commons and down Comm Ave. He could feel the cat shifting over her blanket, scrabbling at the cardboard against his chest. Mom walked fast, a bit ahead of him. At Kenmore they turned south.

When they got to the Talbots', Mom took the box. She looked at him. "Why don't you stay down here," she said.

"Okay."

She rang the bell and went in with the buzzer, holding the box under one arm.

Alex sat on the steps of the walk-up. There were little ones in the corner: flat fingers of ice, spilling away from the cracks.

Mom came out the door. Her face was pale, she was biting her lip. They took off walking at a fast pace. Suddenly Mom said, "Oh, Alex, she was *so scared*," and sat down on another stoop and put her head on her knees.

Alex sat beside her, his shoulders touching hers. Don't say anything, don't put arm around shoulders or anything. He had learned this from Father. Just sit there, be there. Alex sat there like the glacier, shifting a little. Alive. The white light.

After a while she stood. "Let's go," she said.

They walked up Comm Ave. toward the train station. "She'll be all right with the Talbots," Alex said. "She already likes Jay."

"I know." Mom sniffed, tossed her head in the wind. "She's getting to be a pretty adaptable cat." They walked on in silence. She put an arm over his shoulders. "I wonder how Pongo is doing." She took a deep breath. Overhead clouds tumbled like chunks of broken ice.

DESTROYER
OF WORLDS

Charles Sheffield

*"Destroyer of Worlds" was purchased by Gardner
Dozois, and appeared in the February 1989 issue of
IAsfm with a striking cover and interior illustration
by Nicholas Jainschigg. One of the best contempo-
rary "hard science" writers, British-born Charles
Sheffield is a theoretical physicist who has worked
on the American space program, and is currently
chief scientist of the Earth Satellite Corporation. He
is a frequent contributor to IAsfm, and is also the
only person who has ever served as president of both
the American Astronautical Society and the Science
Fiction Writers of America. Here he presents us with
a scientific mystery, the unraveling of which, clue
by clue, leads us on a wild and suspenseful hunt
from Philadelphia to the remote hills of the Colorado
wilderness, and ultimately brings us face to face with
a deadly enigma that could spell the end of life
itself. . . .*

*Sheffield lives in Bethesda, Maryland. His books
include the bestselling non-fiction title* Earthwatch,
the novels Sight of Proteus, The Web Between the

Worlds, Hidden Variables, My Brother's Keeper, The McAndrew Chronicles, Between the Strokes of Night, The Nimrod Hunt, Trader's World, *and* Proteus Unbound, *and the collection* Erasmus Magister. *His most recent novels are* Summertide *and* Divergence.

"Neither snow nor rain nor heat nor gloom of night stays these couriers from the swift completion of their appointed rounds." Those words were not penned by a dedicated employee of the United States Postal Service. They were written by Herodotus, in about 450 B.C., and he was talking about the postal system of the Persians.

The first postage stamps in the world came long after the first postal service. They were introduced in Great Britain, in 1840. They were the Penny Black and the Twopenny Blue, and the picture on their face was based on the 1837 medal portrait of Queen Victoria engraved by W. Wyon.

A *reprint* is a stamp printed from the original plate after that stamp is no longer valid for use as postage. Its existence tends to depreciate the price to collectors of the original stamps.

Philately, as a term used to describe the collecting of postage stamps, was a word coined in 1865 by a Frenchman, Monsieur Herpin. Before that, stamp collecting was known by the less complimentary term of *timbromania*.

Everyone in the world knows these things. Don't they? That's what Tom Walton seemed to believe when I first met him.

I went to his shop on 15th Street in downtown Washington in early May, on a warm and pleasant afternoon. A reporter friend of mine had given me his name and the address of his store, and assured me that he knew more about stamps than any ten other people combined. To tell the truth, it was only faith in my friend Jill's opinions that persuaded me to go into that shop. The storefront was a hefty metal grating over dirty glass, and behind it on display in the window I saw nothing but a couple of battered leather books and a metal roller. It was a dump, the sort of shop you walk past without even noticing it's there.

The inside was no better. Narrow and gloomy, with a long wooden counter running across the middle to separate the customer from the shopkeeper. Bare dusty boards formed the floor and one unshaded light-bulb just above the counter served as the only illumination. Cobwebs hung across all the corners of the ceiling. As furniture there was one stool on my side and a tall armchair on the other. In that chair, peering through a jeweller's loupe at a stamp in its little cover of transparent plastic, sat a fat man in his early twenties. At the ring of the shop's doorbell he took the lens away from his eye and gave me a frown of greeting.

"Mr. Walton?" I said.

"Mmph. Yer-yes." A quiet voice, with the hint of a stammer.

"I'm Rachel Banks. I don't want to buy any stamps, or sell any, but I wondered if you could spare me a few minutes of your time. Jill Fahnestock gave me your name."

"Mm. Mmph. Yes."

It occurred to me that I should have asked Jill a few more questions. I hadn't, because there had been a fond tone in her voice that made me think Tom Walton might be an old boyfriend of hers. But seeing him now I felt sure that wasn't the case. Jill was one of the beautiful people, well-groomed and chic and dressed always in the latest fashions. Tom Walton was nice looking in a chubby sort of way, with curly fair hair, a beautiful mouth, and innocent blue eyes. But he hovered right at the indefinable boundary of fatness beyond which I cannot see a man as a physically attractive object. Also he hadn't shaved, his shirt was poorly ironed, and he was wearing a baggy cover-all cardigan that was as shapeless as he was. There was even a smudge of oil or something around his left eye that had come from the lens he had been using.

Not Jilly's type. Not at all.

"I have a question," I said. "About a postage stamp. Or what may be a postage stamp. Jill thought you might be able to help me."

"Ah." At least that was a positive sound, a tone approaching interest. But I still had to get the preliminaries out of the way. I'd been in trouble before when I didn't announce at once who I was and what I was doing.

"I'm a private investigator," I said. "Here's my credentials."

He hardly glanced at the card and badge I held out to him. Instead, a faint expression of incredulity crept across his face, while he stared first at my face, then at my purse.

"Hmph," he said. "Hmph."

Those particular "hmph" 's I could read. They meant, you don't look tough enough to be a private eye. Too young, too nervous. And anyway, where's your gun? (Raymond Chandler and Dashiell Hammett—I'd like to bring them back to life long enough to strangle the pair of them. Between them they ruined the image.)

"I'm investigating the disappearance of Jason Lockyer," I said. I *was* nervous, no doubt about it. Eleanor Lockyer had that effect on me.

"Jason Lockyer. Never heard of him."

"No reason you would have. Mind if I sit down?"

I took his silence for assent and perched on the stool. Tall and skinny I may be, but high chairs were made for legs like mine.

"Lockyer is a biologist," I went on. "A specialist in algae and slime molds and a number of other things I'm forced to admit I know nothing about. He's famous in his own field, a man in his early sixties, very distinguished to look at and apparently a first-rate teacher. He's on the faculty over at Johns Hopkins in Baltimore, as a full professor of an endowed chair, and he has an apartment there. But he also keeps an apartment here in Washington. Not to mention an apartment in Coral Gables and half an island that he owns in Maine. As you'll guess from all that, he's loaded."

With some people you can lose it right there. They resent other people's money so much, they can't work around them. Tom Walton showed nothing more than a mild disinterest in Jason Lockyer's diverse homes, and I went on: "He usually spent most of the week over on campus in Baltimore, and his wife is mostly down in Florida. So when he disappeared a couple of weeks ago she didn't even realize it for three or four days. She called me in last Friday."

"Why you? Why not the p-police?"

The question came so quickly and easily that I revised my first impression of Walton. Slob, maybe, but not dumb.

"The police, too. But Eleanor Lockyer doesn't have much faith in them. When she reported that he had disappeared, all they did was file a report."

"Yeah, I know the feeling. Same as they did when my shop was robbed last year."

"She expected more. She thought when she called them they would run off and hunt for him in all directions. As it was they didn't even come to search their apartment."

I was losing him. He was starting to fidget in the armchair and fiddle with the jeweller's loupe on the counter in front of him. It didn't look as though he'd had a customer in days, but I probably had only two more minutes before he made up a reason why he was too busy to listen to me.

I opened my bag and took out a 9 by 12 manila envelope. "But I did search the apartments," I said. "All four, the one here in Washington and the one in Baltimore and then the other two. No signs that he left in a hurry, no signs of any problem. A dead loss in fact, except for one oddity. An empty envelope in the Baltimore apartment, addressed to Jason Lockyer—didn't say Professor, didn't say Doctor, just Jason Lockyer—standard IBM Selectric II typewriter, but there was a very odd stamp on it. Here."

I took the photograph out of the envelope and slid it across the counter. It was an 8 by 11 color print and I was rather proud of it. I had taken it with a high-power magnifying lens, and after half a dozen attempts I had obtained a picture with both good color balance and sharp focus. The image showed the head of a black-faced doll with staring eyes and straight hair sticking up wildly like a stiff black brush. The doll was black and green and red, and an oval red border ran around it. At the bottom of the stamp was a figure "1" and the words, "One Googol."

My satisfaction at the work was not shared by Tom Walton. He was staring at the photo with disdain.

"It's a color enlargement," I said. "Of the postage stamp. And the picture in the middle there—"

"It's a golliwog."

That piece of information had taken me hours to discover. "How did you know? Until two days ago I had never even *heard* of a golliwog."

"I used to have a doll like this when I was a kid." He was a little embarrassed, but the sight of the picture had brought him to life. "Matter of fact, it was my f-favorite toy."

"I never knew a doll like that existed—I had to ask dozens of people before I found one who knew what it is. It started out as a character in children's books, you know, nearly a hundred years ago. How on earth did you get one to play with?"

"Aw, I guess it was a pretty old doll. Handed down, like."

"I know the feeling—all the clothes I ever saw came from my big sister."

For some reason he looked away awkwardly when I said that. I reached out and touched the photo. "This is a picture of the stamp, the best one I could take of it. I was wondering what you might be able to tell me about where it was made, maybe where it came from."

He hardly glanced at it before shaking his head. "You don't understand," he said. "This is useless. And it's not a stamp intended for use as real postage."

"How do you know?"

"Well, for a start you'll notice that it hasn't been post-marked. It was on an envelope but it was never intended to go through the mails. More important, a googol is ten to the hundredth. Making a stamp that says it has a value of 'one googol' is the sort of joke that the math class would have done back at Princeton."

It had taken me another half hour to discover what a googol was. "You went to Princeton?"

"For a while. I dropped out." His voice was unemotional as he went on: "There are plenty of interesting stamps that were never intended for postage and don't have currency value—Christmas seals, for example, that Holboll introduced in 1903 as part of an anti-tuberculosis campaign. Some people collect those. But what you have given me isn't a stamp at all. It's just a *picture* of a stamp, and that's a whole lot different. For instance, you missed off the most important piece."

"Which is?"

"The edges. You've blown the main picture up big, and that's good, but to get it you've cropped all four edges. I can't see how it's perforated. That's the first problem. Then there's the materials—the dyes and the gum, you can't tell one thing about them from a photograph. And what about the type of paper that was used? And the watermark. Look, you said you found the stamp in Lockyer's apartment. Don't you have it anymore?"

"I do."

"Then why on earth didn't you bring it with you? I've got all sorts of things in the back of my shop just for looking at stamps." He leaned closer across the counter. "If you would let me take a look at it here I'm sure I could squeeze out some information. There are analytical techniques available today that no one dreamed of twenty years ago."

Finally, some enthusiasm—and such enthusiasm! He was itching to get his hands on the golliwog stamp. I wanted to hear more, but whatever miracles he had in the back of the shop were apparently of no interest to my stomach. It chose that moment to give a long, gurgling groan of complaint. I had breakfasted on a cup of black coffee and lunched in mid-morning on a dry bagel, and it was now after five. Hunger and nerves. I put my hand on my midriff.

"Pardon me. I think that's trying to tell me something. Look, I'm sorry about not bringing the stamp. It's locked up in my safe. I've grown so used to protecting original materials—if I don't do it, the courts and the lawyers beat me into the ground. But if you'll let me pick your brains some more for the price of dinner . . ." He was going to say no, I knew it, and I hurried on, "—then I'll go get the stamp and bring it here in the morning. And if there's work for you to do—for God's sake don't destroy that stamp, though—I'll tell Mrs. Lockyer that I need you and I'll pay you at the same rate I'm being paid."

"How much?"

"Three hundred and fifty a day, plus expenses."

He didn't seem thrilled by the prospect, though it was hard to believe he made that much in a month in the store. I think it was the chance of getting a look at the stamp that sold him, because he finally nodded and said, "Let me lock up."

He turned to the unpainted inner door of the store and shielded the lock from me with his body while he did something to it.

"Not much in there to appeal to your average downtown thief," he said when he was done. He sounded apologetic. "No trade-in value, but a lot of the things are valuable to me."

Did Tom Walton spend everything he had on stamps? That idea was strengthened when we went out to his car, parked in the alley behind the store, and drove off to the Iron Gate Inn on N Street. He drove a 1974 white Dodge Dart rusted through at the bottom of the doors and under the fenders. I think cars are one of humanity's most boring inventions, but even I noticed that this vehicle was due for retirement.

I was a regular at the restaurant and I knew the menu by heart. He insisted on studying it carefully, a fixed stare of concentration on his face. I had the impression that he was more accustomed to food that came out of a paper bag.

While he read the menu I had an opportunity for a closer look at him. I changed my original estimate of his age. His innocent face said early twenties, but his hair was thinning at the temples. (Later, when I referred to him to Jill Fahnestock as "the Walton kid" she stared at me and said, "Kid? He's thirty-two—three years older than you." "But he looks—I don't know—brand-new." "You mean *unused*. I know. There's more to Tom than meets the eye.")

There was quite a bit of him that did meet the eye. "I'm on a diet," he explained, when he was ready to order.

"I see." Not before time, but I could hardly tell him that. "How long have you been dieting?"

"This time?" He paused. "Four years, almost."

Then he went ahead, quite unselfconsciously, to order and eat a vast meal of hummus, cous-cous, and beer. I couldn't complain, because he was also determined to earn his dinner. We talked about stamps, and only stamps. At first I made a feeble attempt to take notes but after a few minutes I concentrated on my own food. There was no way I would remember all that he said, and with him as my consultant I didn't need to.

Stamps are colored bits of paper that you lick and stick on letters, right?

Not to Tom Walton and a million other people. To the collectors, stamps are an obsession and an endless search. They spend their lives rummaging through dusty old collections, or bidding on large lots at auctions to get a single stamp, or writing letters all over the world for first-day covers. They have their own vocabulary—*double impressions* (where a sheet of stamps has been put through the press twice, and the second imprint is slightly off from the first one); *mint* (a stamp with its original gum undamaged and with an unblemished face); *inverted center* (when a stamp is made using two plates, and a sheet is accidentally reversed when it is passed through the second press, so the stamp's center is upside down relative to its frame); *tete-beche* (where a plate has been made with one stamp upside down in the whole sheet of stamps).

They also have their own versions of the Holy Grail, stamps so rare and valuable that only the museums and super-rich collectors can own them: the 1856 "One-Penny Magenta" stamp from British Guiana; the Cape of Good Hope "Triangle" from the 1850s; the 1843 Brazilian "Bull's-Eye," first stamp issued in the western hemisphere; the tri-colored Basle "Dove" issued in Switzerland in 1845; the 1847 Mauritius "Post Office" stamp.

And there are the anomalies, the stamps that are interesting because of some defect in their manufacture. Tom Walton owned a 1918 U.S. Airmail stamp, an example of an inverted center in which the plane in the stamp's center is flying upside-down. He told me it was very rare, with only one sheet of a hundred stamps ever reaching the public.

I don't know how much time he spent alone in that store of his but he was starved for company. He would probably have talked to me all evening, and to my surprise I was enjoying listening to him. But by the time we were onto baklava and a second cup of coffee my own preoccupations were beginning to take over.

"I'm sorry, Tom." I interrupted his description of the "$1.00 Trans-Mississippi" commemorative stamp, one of his favorites. "But I've got to pay the check and go now. I promised Mrs. Lockyer that I'd be over to see her this evening at her apartment."

He nodded. "Ready when you are, Rachel."

He seemed to assume that he was going with me. I hadn't intended it, but it made sense. If I were considering adding him to the payroll it was a near-certainty that Eleanor Lockyer would want to talk to him. (Though I was not sure that I wanted to expose *him* to *her*.)

The Lockyer apartment was out in yuppie-land on Massachusetts Avenue, far from any subway stop. Tom Walton's car received an incredulous look from the guard at the main entrance, but when we told him who we were going to see he couldn't refuse to let us in. We parked between a Mercedes 560 and an Audi 5000. Tom carefully checked that all his car doors were locked.

As we went inside and entered the elevator I decided that the second cup of coffee had been a mistake. I have an incipient ulcer, and my stomach hurt. Then I decided that the coffee was not to blame. What was getting to me was the prospect of another meeting with Eleanor Lockyer.

She was on the telephone when the maid ushered us in, and she took her time in finishing the conversation. We were not invited to sit down. She was obviously preparing to go out, because she was wearing a long dress and a cape that my year's income would not have paid for. I introduced Tom Walton as someone who was helping me with the investigation. She gave him the briefest of glances with bored grey eyes, dismissed him as a nonentity, and waved her arm at the table.

"Jason's mail for the past two days. I haven't looked at most of it, but you probably want to open it all and see what's there."

"I'll do that," I said. Tom Walton began to edge his way over to the stack of letters and envelopes.

"Right. You've been working on this for four days now. I hope you have results. What have you found out?"

"Quite a bit. We're making good progress." The tone in her voice was so critical I felt obliged to overstate what I had done. "First, we can rule out any possibility of kidnapping. Wherever he went, his trip was planned. The woman who cleaned the apartment in Baltimore is sure that there are a couple of suitcases missing, along with his clothes and toilet articles. She also thinks there are some spaces in the bookcases, but she can't remember what books used to be there, though they were in the middle of a group of books about single-celled plants and animals. Second, he's almost certainly still somewhere in this country. His passport was in his study here. Third—the absolute clincher, in my opinion—he left his notes for the rest of the semester with his Teaching Assistant at the university. Fourth—"

"But *where* is he?" she interrupted.

"I don't know."

"And you call that *progress?* You're telling me he could be anywhere in fifty states, millions of square miles, and you've no idea where, or how to find him. That's not what I'm paying you for. What good does that do me?"

"It's part of the whole investigative process. We have to rule out certain possibilities before I can explore others. For instance, now that we know he wasn't abducted against his will—Mrs. Lockyer, I don't know an easy way to ask this, but is there any chance that Jason Lockyer might have had a girlfriend?"

She didn't laugh. She sneered. "Jason? Why not ask a sensible question? He has the sex drive of a lettuce. One woman in his life is too much for him."

You'd be too much for most people. But that's the sort of thing you think and don't say. Fortunately I didn't have to ask a "sensible question" because we were interrupted by a loud whistle from Tom Walton.

"Look at this letter!" he said. "Professor Lockyer is going to be awarded the Copley Medal of the Royal Society, for his work on bacterial DNA transfer. That's really great."

It was a breakthrough, of sorts. It proved that Tom Walton was interested in something other than postage stamps.

But it did nothing for Eleanor Lockyer. She changed the direction of her scorn. "That's just the sort of nonsense I've had to put up with for five years. Bacteria, and worms, and slimes. If anyone deserves a medal it's *me*, having to live with that sort of rubbish." The buzzer sounded. She looked at her watch, then at me. "I must say, I'm most disappointed and dismayed by your lack of progress. You have to do better or I'm certainly not going to keep on paying you for nothing. Get to work. Look at this apartment again, and go over that mail with a toothcomb. When you are finished here Maria will let you out. I have to go. General Shellstock's limousine is waiting downstairs and the General asked me to be on time."

She was turning to leave when Tom Walton said quietly, "Walter Shellstock, by any chance?"

"Yes. He's visiting Washington for a few days."

"Say hello."

"Hello? You mean from *you?*"

"Sure. Wally Shellstock's my godfather."

It was a pleasure to watch Eleanor Lockyer's reaction. Her bottom lip went down so far that I could see the receding gum-line on her lower teeth, and she said, "*You.* You're . . . But who? . . ."

She had forgotten his name, or never registered it when I introduced them.

He realized her problem. "Well, in business I just use Tom Walton. But my full name is Thomas Walton Shellstock. Actually it's Thomas Walton Shellstock the Fourth, though I don't know why anyone would care about counting the numbers."

"The *Pennsylvania* Shellstocks?"

"That's right. Well, have fun with Wally." Tom turned back to the pile of letters, peering at each one and ignoring Eleanor.

I've never seen a woman so torn. The buzzer sounded again, this time more urgently. She turned toward the door, but then she hurried back and took Tom by the arm.

"Thomas, I'm having a small dinner party here next week. I'd love it if you could come."

"Send me an invitation. Rachel has my address."

"Of course. You and . . ." She turned to give me a look of frustration. It meant, I sure as hell don't want to have to invite *you*, you're the hired help—but I'm not sure what your relationship is to Thomas Walton Shellstock, and if you two are screwing I may have to include you just to get him.

"Both of you," she said at last. Tom didn't give her another look, and finally she went out.

"You'd really come to her dinner party?" I said. I had a lot of questions but that seemed like the most important one.

"What do you think? Saying 'send me an invitation' is a lot easier than saying no in person."

"What are the Pennsylvania Shellstocks? She almost dropped her teeth."

"Ah." He had finished looking at the stamps on the unopened letters, and now he was sitting idly at the table. " 'Old money, my d-dear,' " he said in a falsetto. " 'This only *real* kind of money.' That's what people like Mrs. Lockyer say—and that's why I don't use my full name. We happen to have rather a lot of it—money, I mean, no thanks to me. Isn't she revolting?"

"I wondered if it was just me. When I hear her talk about her husband it doesn't sound like she wants me to find him. It sounds like she wants me to prove he's *dead*."

"I don't understand why they're married at all. You said he's in his sixties, she can't be more than forty."

"Forty-five, if she's a day," I said. Pure malice. "His first wife died—he's got grown-up kids, and contacting them is on my agenda. Eleanor knew a good thing when she saw one. No responsibilities, lots of money—so she grabbed him."

"No children in this marriage?"

"Perish the thought. Children, my dear, they're such a *nuisance*. And having them is so *messy*."

He was laughing without making a sound. "And worse than that, my dear, I'm told it actually *hurts*. Rachel, it's none of my business but I think you have a problem."

"Mrs. Lockyer? Don't I know it."

"I wasn't thinking of that. From what you said it's quite obvious that Jason Lockyer disappeared because he wanted to disappear. If he intended his wife to know about it he'd have told her. So now you're trying to go against what he wanted, just to please her. Doesn't that give you fits?"

"Tom, she's my *client*."

"So drop her, my dear."

"Right. And find at the end of the month I can't pay the rent. I'm in a funny business, Tom. Some of my clients are people you'd cross the street to avoid meeting. And I won't even touch the worst cases, the bitter divorce settlements and the child abusers. But the nice, normal people of the world don't seem to have much need for detectives."

There was a conscience inside all that fat, because after a moment he shook his head and said, "I'm sorry. I shouldn't have said that, it's not my business."

"No, and it never will be. Know why, Tom? Because you're *rich*." I was angry but most of it was guilt. He was right; I shouldn't be hounding Jason Lockyer just to please Eleanor Lockyer. "You don't have the same pressures on you. I saw your face when I offered you three hundred and fifty dollars a day to work on this. A lousy three-fifty, you thought, that isn't worth bothering with. Why do you run that stamp store at all if you don't need money? Why don't you do something *important?*"

There must be a branch of etiquette that says you don't harangue near-strangers; but poor Tom Walton didn't feel like a stranger, so I unloaded on him.

After a few moments he sighed. "All right, all right. I'll help you look for Jason Lockyer. And why do I run the stamp store? I'll tell you, I do it to *avoid* conversations like this—with my own damned family. They're all over-achievers, and they went on at me for years, telling me to go out and change the world—run for public office, or buy a position on the New York Stock Exchange, or win a Nobel Prize." His voice was becoming steadily louder. "I don't want to do *any* of those things. I want a nice, peaceful life, looking at interesting things. And no one else is willing to let me do that! That's one nice thing about stamps. The family accepts that I'm running a business, they stay away and the stamps don't *harass* you."

That was the moment when I began to revise my opinion of Tom Walton. I had neatly pegged him as a pleasant, shy, introverted, and slightly kooky young man, preferring stamps to people, silence to speeches, and solitude to most types of company. I didn't think he knew how to shout. Now I saw another side of him, stronger and more determined. Anyone who got between Tom and what he wanted was in for a tough time.

Maria had heard the noise from another room of the apartment—she could have heard it from *any* room, and maybe out in the street. She appeared at the door and politely asked us if we were ready to leave. We were. Both of us became subdued. Thomas Walton Shellstock (the Fourth) drove me back to my apartment on Connecticut Avenue. We didn't speak.

As he stopped in front of the building he said: "I hate all this, Rachel. Really hate it. I'm not interested in looking for Jason Lockyer, and if I see his wife ever again that will be too soon."

I reached over and switched off the ignition key. "I know how you must feel," I said. "But I hope you'll decide to stick with it. It would be easy for you to say to hell with it, and quit. I feel the same way myself, but you know I can't do that. For one thing I need the money, and for another I could get a complaint that will cost me my license. And I need your help on this—you can see I'm floundering. Please, Tom. Don't back out now."

It was unfair pressure, and I knew it. After a couple of silent moments Tom lifted his head to look up at the front of the building.

"Oh, hell," he said. "If you want to, bring that lousy golliwog stamp around to my store tomorrow morning."

(Looking back, I see this as the critical moment when I began to use Tom Walton's essential niceness to ease him out of his shell. And if it was also the first step in saving or destroying the world, that's another matter—I certainly didn't suspect it at the time.)

I opened the door and stepped out. "Thanks, Tom," I said. "You're a real nice guy and I won't forget this. See you about ten o'clock. Good-night."

I walked away quickly. I wanted to be inside the lobby before he could tell me he had changed his mind.

I had taken the liberty of carrying Jason Lockyer's newly-arrived mail away in my purse from the Lockyer apartment. After all, Eleanor had just about ordered me to take it away and study it.

After two coffees and that conversation with Tom Walton I knew it was going to be difficult to go to sleep (yes, I have a conscience, too). I didn't even try. I spread out the mail on the kitchen table and began to go through it piece by piece. About half-past eleven I had a breakthrough, courtesy of the U.S. Postal Service. It's rare to thank the USPS for slow service, but I was ready to do it.

Although the letters had all been delivered to Lockyer's apartment that morning or the day before, one of them had been *mailed* nearly three weeks earlier. It should have reached Jason Lockyer long before he left for parts unknown, but of course it hadn't.

It bore a first-class postage stamp and a near-illegible postmark. I could make out the date and the letters "CO"—Colorado—at the bottom, but the town name was impossible. The handwritten envelope was addressed to Professor Jason Lockyer. Inside was a second envelope, this time with nothing written on it—but there was a golliwog stamp in the upper right corner. And inside *that* was the following typed message:

I think it's time to give you another progress report, even though it's sooner than I said. Seven and Eight are running along so-so, nothing much different from what you heard about in my last report. But Nine—you'd never believe Nine if you didn't see it for yourself. It's still changing, and no one can estimate an end-point. The crew are supposed to go inside in another week. Marcia says we'll be in no danger and she wants us to stay there longer than usual. She's done something new on the DNA splicing, and she believes that Nine is moving to a totally different limit, one with a Strange Attractor we've never seen before. She thinks it may be the one we've been searching for all along. Me, I'm afraid it may be the ultimate boss system—the real Mega-Mother. Certainly the efficiency

*of energy utilization is fantastic—more than double any of the
others, and still increasing.*

*I tell you frankly, I'm scared, but I'll have to go in there.
No way out of it. You told me that if I ever wanted advice
you'd give it. I think that's what we all need here, a new
look without any publicity. Any chance you can arrange to
come? I'll write again or telephone in the next few days to
keep you up-to-date. Then maybe you can tell me it's all my
imagination.*

The one-page letter was unsigned and undated, but I had the
date on the postmark. And I had the log of Jason Lockyer's
incoming long-distance phone calls at the university and at
each apartment. It should be straightforward to find out who
had written the cryptic note.

By half-past one I had changed my ideas about that. The
incoming log showed nothing from Colorado anywhere near
the right dates. As a final act of desperation I at last went to
the log of Jason Lockyer's outgoing calls, ones he had placed
himself. I had looked at this log before, but he made so many
calls to so many places that I had not been able to see anything
significant.

Sweet success.

It jumped out at me in the first ten seconds of looking. Six
days after this letter had been mailed, Lockyer had placed a
series of four phone calls in one day to Nathrop, Colorado.
One call had lasted for over forty minutes. I checked in my
National Geographic atlas. Nathrop was a small town about
seventy miles west of Colorado Springs. It lay on the Arkansas
River with the Sawatch Range of the High Rockies rearing up
to over fourteen thousand feet just to the west.

Nathrop, Colorado.

For the first time, I had a place to look for Jason Lockyer
that was smaller than the continental United States.

Within two minutes I knew I would be going to Nathrop
myself. Calling that telephone number was a tempting thought,
but there was a danger that it might make Jason Lockyer run
before I had a chance to talk to him face to face. The real
question was, would I tell Eleanor Lockyer what I was doing?
She was my client, so the natural answer was, yes, she had to

know and approve. But now I had to face Tom's question: did I *want* to find Jason Lockyer for her when he didn't want to be found?

I went to bed. I spent the rest of the night tossing and turning in mixed feelings of satisfaction and uneasiness.

I was standing at the door of Tom's shop on 15th Street by eight-thirty. Nice district. I was propositioned twice, and would have been moved on, too, if I hadn't been able to show the cops my license.

Tom's white Dodge wheezed around the corner at nine o'clock. He saw me and waved before he turned to park in the alley behind the building. He was eating an Egg McMuffin. I'm not a breakfast person, but I wished I had one.

"Got the stamp?" he said as soon as he came out of the alley. He was wearing a tan sports coat and matching flannels, and a well-ironed white shirt. His hair was combed and he was so clean-shaven his skin had a scraped look.

"Better than that. I have two of them."

I explained while he was opening the front door of the store.

"Good," he said. "It's nice to have a spare. It means I won't have to be quite so c-careful with the first one. And if you want my opinion, you ought to find Jason Lockyer and hear his side of the story before you tell Eleanor Lockyer a damned thing."

He went straight past the counter, unlocked the inner door, and waved me through.

It was just as well that I had learned the previous night that Tom was from a wealthy family. Otherwise, the word that would have entered my head when I stepped through the beige-painted wooden door into the rear of the store would have been: *drugs*. Money had been spent here, lots of money, and in downtown D.C. big money says illegal drugs more often than you would believe. At the back of the store was a massive Mosler safe, the sort of thing you'd normally see in a top-secret security installation or a bank vault. There was a well-equipped optical table along one wall and a mass of computer gear along another. Tom explained to me that it was an Apollo image analysis workstation, with a digitizer and raster scanner as input devices.

"I can view a stamp or a marking ink with a dozen different visible wavelength filters," he said. "Or in ultraviolet or multiband infrared. We can do chemical tests, too, on a tiny corner, so small you'd never know we'd touched it. I have verniers that will measure to a micron or better, and the raster scanner will create a digital image for computer processing. I can do computer matching against all the standard papers and inks."

"And the safe?"

"Stamps. They're negotiable currency, of course, but that's not the point. The old and rare ones have a worth quite unrelated to their face value."

Just like Tom Walton.

He took the envelope containing the first golliwog stamp and placed it carefully on a light-table. Those fat fingers were surprisingly precise and delicate. As he placed a high-powered stereo lens in position and bent over it, he said: "Why are you rejecting the most obvious reason of all for Jason Lockyer running off—that he c-can't stand his wife? Seems to me he has an excellent reason, right there."

"If he just wanted to get away from her he wouldn't need to disappear. He had good legal advice before they married. They have a marriage contract, and if they split up he knows exactly how much it would cost him. He can afford it. All he would have to do is stay over in Baltimore and tell his lawyers to go ahead with the separation papers. If he were to die, that's another matter. She gets a lot more. I think that's one reason why Eleanor is willing to pay me to find out what happened. She wants that money so bad she can taste it."

I watched as Tom grunted in satisfaction and straightened up. He fed the second envelope carefully into a machine that looked like a horizontal toaster.

"The thousand-dollar version of the old steam kettle," he said. "It takes the stamp off the cover with minimal damage to the mucilage. Here it comes." The stamp was appearing from the other side of the machine on a little porcelain tray. He removed it, placed it between two pieces of transparent film, and secured it in position on the scanner.

"There's one other reason why I'm sure Lockyer's not planning to stay away forever," I went on. "He didn't take any check books, and he hasn't used any credit cards. What will he do when he runs out of money?"

"What about coupon clipping?" asked Tom. And then, when I looked puzzled, "I mean dividends. If he's like me he gets dividend checks all the time, and he can cash them easily. All he would have to do is change the mailing address for receipt of those, and he could live off them indefinitely."

"Damn. I never thought of that. I'll have to check it."

He closed the cover on the scanner, leaned back, and stared at me. "It's none of my business, but how did you get into this detective work? And how long have you been doing it?"

"Six years. Two years on my own, since my uncle died. It was really his business, and I used to help him out in the summers when I was still in school. When I graduated a job was hard to find. Tell an employer you have a double degree in English and psychology and it's like saying you have AIDS and leprosy."

"But why do you *stay* in it?"

"Well, I've got an investment. There's a hundred-and-fifty-eight-dollar fee for the application for a D.C. license. And another sixteen-fifty for fingerprinting, and thirty for business cards. It adds up."

I was trying to tease him, but he was too smart and it didn't work.

"Do you make any money?" he asked.

He wasn't teasing at all, he was just making conversation while the scanner did its thing on the stamp. But unfortunately it *did* work. I've grown hypersensitive about what I do for a living. I broke up with my last boyfriend, Larry, over just this subject.

"I pay the rent," I snapped back at him. "And I bought your dinner last night. You say you're rich but I didn't see you itching to pick up the tab."

"I've been trained not to," he said quietly. "That's one of the things I was told at my mother's knee—everyone in the world will try to soak you for a loan or a f-free meal, as soon as they find out you're a Shellstock. I guess that's another reason why I'm Tom Walton. But I'll buy you dinner anytime you want to, Rachel."

Which of course left me feeling like the ultimate jerk. I hadn't bought him dinner—the Lockyers had, since it would be on my expense account. And he knew that, yet he offered to buy me dinner out of his own pocket. I'd slapped him and he was offering the other cheek.

"Let me tell you about the golliwog stamp," he went on. I was quite ready to let him change the subject. "There's more to be measured, but a few things are obvious already. First, look at the perforations on the edge of the stamp. Even without a lens you can see that only the top and bottom are perforated, with the sides clean. That means this stamp is from a vertical coil—a roll of stamps rather than a sheet, with the stamps joined at top and bottom, not at the sides. And even without measuring I can tell you this is 'perf 12'—twelve perforations in twenty millimeters. Nothing unusual about any of this, though horizontal coils are more common. What's more interesting is the way the stamp was produced. Take a look."

He moved me to the light-table and showed me how to adjust the binocular lens to suit my eyes.

"See the pattern of lines across the stamp? That's called a *laid batonné* paper, a woven paper with heavier lines in a certain direction. And there's no watermark—that's a pretty sure sign that these stamps were never intended for use as commercial postage."

"So what's the point of them?"

"My guess is that they were made to identify a certain group of people—like a secret sign, or a password. Put one of these on the envelope, you see, and it proves you're one of the inside group. I've seen it done before, though this is an unusually well-executed design for that sort of thing. The choice of a golliwog supports my idea because it's not a symbol I'd ever expect to see on a commercial stamp. Now, look at the actual design of the golliwog."

I stared at it and waited for revelation.

"There are five main processes used in manufacturing stamps," he went on. "First, engraved *intaglio*, where a design is cut directly into the surface of the plate—that's been used for as long as stamps have been made. Second, *letterpress*, in which the design is a *cameo*, a pattern raised in relief above the surface of the plate. Third, *lithography*, which uses water and an oily ink drawn on a stone, or actually on a metal surface prepared to simulate stone. Fourth, *embossed*, where a die is used to give the stamp a raised surface. Fifth, *photogravure*, where the lines are photographed onto a film covering the plate, and then etched onto the surface as though they were an engraving. Clearly, what you are looking at there is a photogravure."

Clearly. To him, perhaps. "I'll believe you. But I don't see where that takes us." I was losing interest in stamps and itching to head off for Colorado. I didn't have the gall to tell him, though, not when he thought what he was doing was important.

"It takes us to a very definite place." All signs of stammer had gone from Tom's voice. "To Philadelphia. You see, there aren't all that many people who do the design work for stamps. And I'm ninety-five percent sure I recognize the designer of that one you're looking at. I know his style. He likes vertical coils, and he likes to do intaglio photogravure. His name is Raymond Sines, and if you want me to I'll call Ray right now."

Why hadn't he told me that to start with, instead of giving me the rigmarole about *intaglio* and *cameo?* Because he liked to talk about stamps, that's why.

I stopped pretending to look at the golliwog. "I'm not sure what talking to Raymond Sines would do for me. How well do you know him?"

He hesitated. I was learning. Hesitation in Tom Walton usually meant uneasiness.

"So-so. I've met Ray a few times informally, at the Collectors' Club in New York City. He's a pretty peculiar guy. Very smart, and a terrific artist and designer. But when he gets away from stamps he's a one-subject talker. He's a space-nut, and a founder member of Ascend Forever—a group that designs space habitats."

"I don't see that taking us to Jason Lockyer. Do you realize that yesterday I had no leads and now I have two? And they go off in wildly different directions."

"Two's a lot better than zero. And I think you may need them both."

I saw his point. Nathrop showed a population of less than five hundred people, so if Lockyer was there I couldn't miss him; but it was also a wilderness area with hundreds of square miles of land and very few people. So if he *wasn't* in the town . . .

"I'm afraid you're right," I said. "It could be that whoever wrote the letter to Lockyer was just using the Nathrop post office mail-box and telephone. What do we do if we go there and find nothing?"

"We come back. Do you have the letter with you? If so, I'd like to see it for myself."

I handed it over and watched while he read it. "Make any sense to you?"

He shook his head. "Strange Attractor?"

"I know. I've never heard the phrase before."

"I have. I can tell you what it means at the *Scientific American* level. It's a math-physics thing, where you keep feeding the output of a system back in as a new input. Sometimes it converges to a steady state—an attractor; sometimes it goes wild, and ends up unstable or with total chaos; and sometimes it sort of wanders around a region—around a strange attractor. The type of behavior depends on some critical system variable, like flow rate or chemical concentration or temperature. It's obvious from this letter that the writer is involved in a set of experiments—but it's anybody's guess as to what field they're in. And *Mega-Mother?*" He placed the letter back on the light-table. "Maybe he's using 'Strange Attractor' to mean something different from what I've seen before. I don't think we're going to get much out of this."

"I'm not, that's for sure. And it's irrelevant. I'm trying to find Jason Lockyer, not solve puzzles. Useless or not, I guess I have to head for Colorado."

"Will you hold off for one day—so I can make a quick run up to Philly. Ray Sines has his own engraving shop there and I want to drop in on him."

"What do you think he can tell you?"

"If I knew, I wouldn't be going." Tom took a blank envelope over to the typewriter next to the safe and typed his own name on it. Then he removed the golliwog stamp from the scanner, placed a thin layer of gum on the back of it, and carefully stuck it on the envelope. Finally he placed the letter from Colorado inside it. "I'll call Ray now and tell him I'm interested in tracing works by an early American engraver. That's quite true, and he's bound to be interested. And during the meeting I want him to catch a look at this." He held up the envelope. "And we'll t-take it from there."

I had expected Eleanor Lockyer to quiz me about my proposed travel and give me a general hard time. Instead she was sweet and reasonable, and didn't ask me one question about where I was going, or why.

"Tell Thomas that the invitation is in the mail," she said. "It will be just a small, intimate group, no more than a dozen."

"I'll tell him." (I didn't.)

He wanted to drive to Philadelphia in the Dodge death-trap. I talked him out of it by suggesting that if we went by train we could fly straight to Denver after our meeting with Sines. Tom seemed surprised that I wanted to go with him, but he didn't seem to mind.

"Just don't say too much about stamps or engraving," he said.

The least of my worries.

Ray Sines was younger than I had expected, a thin, red-faced man of about thirty who suffered premature baldness. He was attempting the disastrous trick of training the remaining strands of hair to a pattern that covered his whole head, and every couple of minutes he ran his hand in a circular motion around his scalp. The top of his head looked like a rotary shoe-polisher. His office, above an industrial warehouse, reminded me of Tom's store, dusty and shabby and somehow irrelevant to what went on there.

He showed pleasure and no surprise at our visit, and he and Tom went off at once into their polite sarabande of talk about Gibbons and Scott and Minkus catalogs, the location of the printing equipment of the legendary Jacob Perkins of

Massachusetts, and the newly-discovered stamps of the 1842 City Despatch Post of New York City. I sat on the edge of my chair, drank four cups of coffee that I would later regret, and itched for Tom to get to the real business.

After about an hour and a half I realized the dreadful truth: he wasn't going to do it. The envelope and the golliwog stamp were there in Tom's case, standing by his leg—and they were going to stay there. He had had no trouble devising a theoretical plan to startle information out of Ray Sines, but when it came to the act he couldn't bring himself to begin.

Finally I reached down, hoisted the case, and placed it on Tom's lap. "The catalog. Don't you have a catalog in here that you want to show Mr. Sines?"

Tom glared at me, but he was stuck. He opened the case and peered inside. "I don't know if I remembered to bring it," he said. While Sines looked on he lifted out a layer of papers and placed them on the low table in front of us. On top was the envelope addressed to him, with its prominent golliwog stamp.

Sines stared at it and his face lit up. "I didn't know you were a member!" he said to Tom. Then he gave me a quick and nervous look.

"Yes," Tom started to say. "Both of us—"

"Member of what?" I rapped at Sines. If this were a secret organization any self-respecting member would check a stranger's credentials before admitting its existence.

For answer, Sines reached behind him and produced a whole roll of golliwog stamps. "My design," he said proudly. "I worked harder on this than on any commercial assignment. It's all right, you can talk to me. I was one of the first people that Marcia allowed in. When did you join?"

Tom looked at me beseechingly.

"I came in about four months ago," I said. "Tom's a recent acquisition, he joined just a month back."

"Terrific!" Sines leaned back in his chair and beamed at both of us. "If you haven't been out to the site already, there's a real treat in store for you."

I reached into my purse and waved our airline tickets at him. "We're on our way there now. Maybe you can tell us, what's the best way once we arrive at the airport?"

He frowned at me. "Isn't someone meeting you?"

We were moving onto tricky ground. I had an urge to get out quickly, but we needed information. "Everyone has their hands full," I said. "There seem to be problems with one of the systems—Seven, is it?"

"No, it's Nine." He relaxed again. "Yes, I hear it's still doing funny things. We'll get the right one eventually. Where are you flying to?"

"Denver."

"Pity. You should have flown to Colorado Springs. Either way, though, you'll have some pretty high driving ahead of you. Take Route 285 out of Denver until you meet Route 24 into Buena Vista. Go north from there and you should see the site on your left, up on the slopes of Mount Harvard."

"How far from Nathrop?" I asked.

"A few miles. But if you get there, you've gone the wrong way out of Buena Vista. Pretty good steak restaurant, though, if you do make the wrong turn." He frowned. "If you would like me to call ahead and try to arrange—"

"No. Please don't." I took Tom's arm and stood up. "We'd hate to make a nuisance of ourselves before we even arrive. And we'd better go now, our plane leaves in an hour and a half."

"You'll need a cab." He stood up, too. "I just wish I was going with you. Give me a call when you get back, tell me what you think of things out there. For me, it's the most exciting thing that's happened in my whole life."

He escorted us to the entrance of the building. "Ascend forever!" he said as we left, and raised his arm.

"Ascend forever!" I replied, but Tom said nothing. As soon as Sines was out of sight and sound he exploded at me. "I hate that sort of thing!"

"You think I enjoy it?" I had the caffeine shakes and I needed to go to the bathroom. "I know we lied to him, but what did you want me to do? Break down and explain to Sines that we went there to trick him?"

He didn't reply. But I suspected that it was not the lying that had him upset. It was me, pushing the attache case at him, pushing him to do something alien to his temperament. He'd never believe me, but I was as upset about that as he was.

Denver's Stapleton Airport is at five thousand feet; our drive south and west took us steadily higher. Within the hour we were up over nine thousand, with snow-capped mountains filling the sky ahead. I had never been to Colorado before and the scenery bowled me over—magnificent country, like moving to a different planet after the rampant azaleas and dogwoods of May in Washington.

Tom was less impressed. He had been here before—"skiing in Vail and Aspen, while I tried to persuade the family that they weren't doing me any favors by sending me. I finally managed to break a leg, and that did it."

On the plane and again in the car we beat to death what we learned from Ray Sines, and what we knew or surmised about its relevance to Jason Lockyer's disappearance.

"Ascend Forever is in the middle of this," said Tom. "Or perhaps it's a subgroup of them. More likely that, because they're going through a procedure to keep it a big secret, and that's quite impossible with too many participants."

"A pretty childish procedure, don't you think? I haven't run across special stamps and secret symbols and hidden messages since I was in high school."

"You'd never make a Freemason. And I knew a bunch of people at Princeton who were still into private codes. Let's go on. They have some project—"

"—a group of projects. Remember Seven, Eight, and Nine. Which also means there's probably a One through Six—"

"—Okay, at least nine projects, but they're probably all doing similar things. There is some sort of development activity associated with them and it's out in the Colorado mountains, west of Nathrop and Buena Vista. It's pretty big, visible from a fair distance. And it's in some sort of trouble—"

"—or part of it is. Remember, Seven and Eight are doing fine. It's Nine that's off, enough to want Jason Lockyer to come out and take a look at what's going on."

"And he's a famous biologist. But the projects have something to do with strange attractors. Not to mention the old

Mega-Mother." Tom shrugged. "You're the detective. Can you put it together?"

"Not a clue. Unless Jason Lockyer has other talents, and the group are calling on those to help them."

Grasping at straws. We both knew it and after a while we dropped it in favor of general chat. We uncovered a total of three common acquaintances, not counting Jill Fahnestock, and we agreed that except for Jill we liked none of them. He found out, to his horror, that the purple mark on my left forearm was the scar of a bullet-wound, inflicted when a man I approached in a child custody case fired at me without warning. ("Cocaine," I said. "He was carrying eight ounces of it, nothing to do with child custody. I was just unlucky—or lucky, depending on your point of view.") I found out, with equal horror, that Tom carried no health insurance of any kind and did not propose to get any. ("Health insurance is for people who don't have money. Obviously, it costs more on average to buy insurance than it does to be sick—otherwise, how could insurance companies stay in business. Health insurance is a bourgeois concept, Rachel." That last sentence was to annoy me, but this time I handled it better.)

He ate when he was happy. So did I. The fact that he was forty pounds overweight while I was too thin to please anyone but a clothes designer was lost on neither of us.

Eventually we stopped talking and simply sat in companionable silence. Tom was one of those people whose presence you can enjoy without speaking.

Buena Vista came finally into view, a town that couldn't be more than a couple of thousand people. For the past half hour we had scanned the mountains ahead of us for any anomalies, and seen nothing even though it was a glittering spring day and visibility was perfect.

I had been driving, because we were renting a Toyota Celica, and since I was considering buying one I wanted to see how it handled. When we reached Buena Vista I stopped the car at what looked like a general purpose store on the main through street.

"You need to buy something?" said Tom.

"Information. Want to come in with me?"

The bored youth behind the counter knew instantly what I was talking about. "The Observatory, you mean," he said. "You can see it from the road, but you have to look hard. Take the road north and look for a gravel cutoff to the left. That goes all the way on up, you can't miss it." He stared at us. "You'll be working there?"

"No. Just visiting."

"Ah. They say they're making a spaceship up there, one that's going off to the end of the universe."

"I don't know about that. We'll see." I bought two cans of Coke and we left.

"So much for the big secret," Tom said when we were back in the car. "They're practically running guided tours."

"If you want to hide something, disguise it as something else that local people don't much care about—like an observatory."

Tom up-ended his can of Coke. He inhaled it more than drank it, in one long gulp. "What about the spaceship?"

"Safe enough. No one in their right mind would believe it."

We had a major decision to make as we drove up the winding gravel-covered road. Would we barrel on up to the entrance, or would we leave the car and play Indian Scout?

We discussed it for another minute, then compromised. A complex of buildings stood on the south-facing slope of the mountainside. We parked the car three-quarters of a mile away, where the top of the blue Toyota would barely be visible over the top of the final ridge. I led the way as we walked until we had a good view. The location was well above ten thousand feet, and three minutes' walk up the slight incline left us gasping.

There were five major structures ahead. Three of them were large, hemispherical, geodesic domes, made of glass or plastic. Two of those were transparent, and we could see shadows inside where trees or shrubs seemed to be growing marked off by triangular support ribbing of painted metal or yellow plastic. The third dome was apparently of tinted material, and its wall panels gleamed dull orange-red. The three domes stood in roughly an equilateral triangle, each one sixty feet across, and at the center of that triangle were two more conventional buildings. They were white and square-sided, with the look of prefabricated or temporary structures. I counted seven cars parked outside the larger one.

A stiff breeze blew from the west, and even in the bright sunlight it was too cold to stand and watch for more than a few minutes. In that time no one appeared from any of the buildings or domes, nor was there evidence of activity within.

We went back to the car and sat inside. I put my hand on my stomach. The Coke had been a mistake. I had the jitters and a pain that ran from my solar plexus around the lower right-hand side of my ribs.

"What now?" said Tom. He looked like the detective, calm and confident. His question probably meant he had made up his mind what we ought to do.

I burped, in as ladylike a way as I could manage. "If Jason Lockyer is inside one of those buildings it won't do us any good to sit here. And if Jason Lockyer's *not* inside, and he's a thousand or two thousand miles away, it still won't do us any good to sit here."

"My thoughts exactly." It was his turn to reach out and turn a car's ignition key. "Let's do it, Rachel. Let's go up there and take the golliwog by the horns."

I eased up the slope at a sedate twenty miles an hour, all my attention on the road. Halfway there, Tom said, "Hold on a minute. Is something wrong with my eyes?"

I stopped the car. It took a few moments, then I saw it, too. The orange-red dome had changed color to a darker, muddier tone, with rising streaks of deep purple within it. Tom and I looked at each other.

"We'll never find out from here," I said. I let in the clutch—badly—and we jerked forward again. We crept all the way up to the larger building and parked in the line of cars. I did an automatic inventory. A new Buick, two old Mustangs, a Camaro that had been in an accident and needed body-work, two VW Rabbits, and an ancient Plymouth that made even Tom's car look fresh off the assembly line. The same sort of mix as I might expect to see in a Washington car park, but with a bit more Buy-American. The air was clear, the sunlight blinding, and there was not a sound to be heard. Living in the city you forget how quiet real quiet can be. We walked over to the building—aluminum-sided, I now saw—almost on tiptoe. My pulse rate was up in the hundreds, and I could feel it in my ears, the loudest sound in the world.

"Inside?" whispered Tom.

I nodded and he led the way. The front door was closed but not locked. It opened to a big lobby about twenty feet square, spotlessly clean and containing nothing but half a dozen metal-frame chairs. As we paused I heard a clatter of footsteps on the aluminum floor, and a man carrying a couple of thick notebooks came hurrying in. Tom and I froze.

"Well, thank Heaven," the new arrival said. "I didn't know anyone was coming out. We've been so short-handed this last week I've been on continuous double shifts."

New York accent, California tan. He was no more than twenty-two or twenty-three, and he was wearing an all-white uniform like a medical orderly. The first impression was of a clean-cut, clean-living lad who should have been carrying an apple for his teacher along with his notebooks. A closer look added something different. He had a spaced-out glassy stare in his eyes, a look that I had seen before only among the ranks of the Moonies and the Hare Krishnas.

"First visit?" he said.

Tom and I nodded. I hope I looked as casual and at ease as he did.

"Great. You'll love it here. I'm Scott."

"Rachel," I said. As I took his outstretched hand the inside of my head made its own swirling list of mysteries: vanished professor—golliwog stamp roll—observatory—spaceship—biology experiment—strange attractor—religion—sanctuary—lunatic asylum.

What was I missing?

"I'll tell Marcia you're here." Scott had shaken hands with Tom and was heading off along a passageway. "But let's settle you in first, and then find something for you to do."

We followed him to a long room with a dozen beds and a shower and toilet facility at the far end. "You'll sleep in here,"

Scott said. "Make yourselves comfortable. I'll be back in five minutes."

I sat down shakily on one of the beds. Hard as a rock. "Prison? Military barracks? Hospital? Tom, we were crazy to come here."

"Don't you want to find Lockyer?" Tom shook his head. "Not prison, not hospital. Boy Scouts, or the dorm in Vermont summer camp. Kids away from home for a big adventure, mummy and daddy miles away. But they've gone unisex."

"What *is* this place?"

"I don't know. Sounds like Marcia's the kingpin, whoever she is. Or queenpin. Or camp counselor. Everyone defers to her, even Ray Sines."

He went across to the window and stood gazing out of it. "My imagination, or is it changing again?"

I followed his pointing finger. The third dome was now a mottled and virulent green. A flowing column of darker color seemed to be rising steadily through the paint on the dome. Before we could discuss what we were seeing Scott came hurrying back in.

"Right," he said. "A quick look around, then introductions will have to wait until tonight. We'll need uniforms."

He led us to an array of tall lockers at the end of the room. While he watched—no thoughts of privacy here—Tom and I took off our outer garments and replaced them with aseptic-looking white uniforms identical to the one that Scott was wearing. Tom had a little trouble finding one that fitted him; the members of Ascend Forever were presumably an undernourished group.

When we were dressed to Scott's satisfaction he took us to the entrance hall—and back outside the building. Tom gave me a quick glance. Why bother with sterile clothing if we were going to be outside? Answer: sterility was not the point; uniformity was.

We marched to one of the three domes and peered in through the transparent wall panels. I saw a sloping floor with a little fountain at the upper end, close to where we were standing. A trickle of water ran across the dome's interior and vanished at the other side. The rest of the floor was covered with dusty-looking plants, growing half-heartedly in a light-colored soil. The plants looked tired, and slightly wilted. In the center of the floor stood the skeleton of a much smaller dome, with only half its walls paneled, and within that structure three human figures were bending over what looked like a computer console.

A telephone handset hung on the outside of the dome, and Scott reached for it. "New arrivals," he said. "Any changes?"

The three figures inside straightened to stare out at us and waved a greeting. "Welcome aboard." The voice on the phone was young, friendly, and enthusiastic. "Nothing special happening here. We've been trying to find out what's wiping out the legumes, but we don't have an answer. Oxygen and nitrogen down a little bit more—still decreasing."

"Still trying changed illumination?"

"Just finished it. We're putting in a bit less power from the ceiling lights, we're making it longer wavelength. We won't know how it works for a while."

"No danger, though?"

"Not yet. No matter what, we'll have another couple of weeks before we begin to worry. But it's a pain to see it go this way. Three weeks ago we were pretty sure this one would make it."

"Maybe it will." Scott waved to the people inside. "We'll keep trying, too. Now that I have some help maybe I'll have time to run an independent analysis."

He hung the handset back on its closed stand and pointed to the panel next to it. "This is all new," he said. "And a real improvement. We have dual controls now, inside and outside. Temperature and humidity and lighting levels in the dome can be controlled from this panel here. When we started out, all the controls were inside and it was a real nuisance. If there was no crew we had to send someone through the airlock whenever we wanted to vary the interior environmental conditions."

He started towards the middle of the complex. "Anyway, that's Eight," he said as we walked. "Not going too good now. Seven is a lot better."

"What happened to One through Six?" asked Tom.

"They went to stable end-forms, but they weren't ones that humans could live in. So we brought the crews back outside, closed down the operations, and re-used the domes."

He didn't notice Tom's raised eyebrows, and went on, "But Nine's the interesting one! I'll warn you now, though, you won't see much of the inside of it from here. We've had to ship a TV camera to the interior, to supplement the audio descriptions, otherwise we'd be short of data. But we'll take a look through the panels, anyway."

We were closing on the strangest of the domes, and now I could see that its wall panels were neither painted nor made of opaque materials. They were coated on the inside. Scott went to a telephone set in the wall—in that respect this was identical to the other dome.

"Marcia?" he said. "New arrivals. How about clearing a patch, so we can take a look inside Nine?"

The coating of the wall panels was close in color to the way we had first seen it, an orange-red with a touch of brown. While we stood and watched, a circular cleared patch began to appear on the wall panel closest to us. Soon we could see a hand holding a plastic scraper.

"Tough coating," said a woman's voice. "A good deal tougher than yesterday."

The clear patch was finished and about a foot across. In the middle of that patch a frowning black face suddenly appeared. It was that of a woman, with protruding eyes and black straight hair that stuck out wildly in all directions.

We hadn't found Jason Lockyer; but we had found the inspiration for the design of the golliwog stamp.

"New arrivals," said Scott again. The tone of his voice was quite different from the way it had been at the other dome. Now he was respectful and subdued, almost fearful.

This time there was no cheery wave. The golliwog face stared hard at me and Tom. "What chapter?" said a gruff voice through the handset.

We had no choice.

"Philadelphia," I said.

"Your names?"

"Rachel Banks and Tom Walton."

The way to the car was around the dome and then dead ahead. We could be in it in thirty seconds and driving down the mountain. On the other hand, Scott was acclimatized to ten thousand feet and we were not. I couldn't run more than fifty yards without stopping for breath, and overweight Tom was sure to be in worse shape . . .

While those thoughts were running through my head the face on the other side of the panel had disappeared. We stood there for about thirty seconds, while my instinct to run became stronger and stronger. I was all ready to shout at Tom to make a break for it when Marcia's face appeared again at the panel. Already the wall was partly coated, and she had to use the scraper again to clear it.

"I've told all the chapters," she said. "I have to approve any new members *in advance* of joining—and certainly in advance of being sent here. We must check on you two. And while that's being done we can't afford any risks. Building Two, Scott. You're responsible for them."

There was no doubt who was in charge. And I had waited too long. I half-turned, and found that Marcia had used her brief absence to call for reinforcements. Four men were on their way over to the dome, all young and tanned and fit-looking.

Tom looked to me for direction. I shook my head. Marcia's check on us was going to show that we were not members of whatever group she led, we could be sure of that. But this was not the time or place to look for an escape. I suddenly realized something I should have been aware of minutes ago: the car keys were in my purse—and my purse was back at the lockers with the rest of my clothes. Thank God I hadn't told Tom to run for it. I would have felt like the world's prize idiot, sitting inside the car while our pursuers came closer and I explained to him that I had no way to start the engine.

We were escorted, very politely, to the second and smaller of the two white buildings. I noticed for the first time that it had no windows.

"This is just part of the standard procedure," said Scott. He was embarrassed. "I know everything will be all right. I'll check as soon as I can with the group leader in Philadelphia, and then I'll come and let you out. Help yourself to any food you want from the refrigerator."

The door was thick and made of braced aluminum. It closed behind us. And locked.

We were standing in a room with three beds, a kitchen, and one other door. Tom went across to it.

"Locked," he said after a moment. "But padlocked on *this* side. Where do you think it leads?"

"Not outside, that's for sure. Probably upstairs. It wouldn't help, though—there are no windows there, either." I went across to the refrigerator and found a carton of milk. I had savage heartburn and what I would have really liked was a Mylanta tablet, but they were also in my purse. I was proving to be quite a klutz of a detective.

Tom was still over at the door. "It's wood, not aluminum. And nowhere near as strong as the one that leads outside."

"Good. Can you break the damned thing open?"

"Break it!" He stared at me in horror. "Rachel, this is someone's private property."

"It sure as hell is. Tom, I know you were brought up to regard personal property as sacred. But we're in a fix. That bloody golliwog woman is all ready to serve us on the half-shell, and I don't give a shit about property. Break it." I was drinking from the carton—most unhygienic, but I was past caring. "Whatever they plan to do with us, I doubt if adding a broken door to the list of crimes will make much difference. Have fun. Smash away."

"Well, if you really think we have to." Tom was still hesitating. "All right, I'll do it. With luck I won't need to do any actual smashing."

He wandered over to the kitchen area of the room and found a blunt knife. The door's padlock was held in position by four wood screws. It took him only three or four minutes to remove all of them. He swung the door open and we found we were looking at the foot of a tightly spiraling staircase.

"We can't get out this way," I said. "But there's nothing better to do. Let's take a look."

He went up the stairs in front of me, clutching the central support pole. On the second floor we came to another door, this one unlocked.

Tom opened it. We were looking at a carbon copy of the

room below, but with one important difference. At the table in the kitchen area sat a man with a loaf of bread and a lump of cheese—Edam, by the look of it—in front of him. Next to those stood a bottle of red wine, and the man facing us had a full glass in his hand and was sniffing at it thoughtfully. When the door opened he looked up in surprise.

I think I was more surprised than he was, though of course I had no right to be. I knew him from his picture. We were looking at Jason Lockyer.

The introductions and explanation of who we were and how we got there took a few minutes.

"And it seems we're all stuck here," I said.

"Well, there are worse places," said Lockyer. We had set a couple more chairs around the table and were all sitting there. "I ought to apologize, because of course this is all my fault. When I look back I can see I started the whole damned thing."

He was a small, neatly-built man with a good-humored face and the faint residual of a Boston accent. The fact that he was locked up, with no idea what was likely to happen to him next, did nothing to ruin his appetite. His only complaint was the quality of the wine. ("California 'burgundy,' " he said. "It shouldn't be allowed to use the name. It's no excuse to say wine like this is cheap. It ought to be *free*.")

"Three years ago," he went on, "I was invited to give a talk to the local chapter of Ascend Forever in Baltimore. I had no idea what to say to them, until one of my best students—Marcia Seretto—who was also a member of the society, mentioned the society's interest in establishing stand-alone colonies out in space. That would imply a completely stable, totally re-cycling environment. After that it was obvious what I had to talk about.

"Most people know that one fully re-cycling environment, driven only by energy from the sun, already exists. That's the biosphere of the planet Earth. What I pointed out—and what got Marcia so excited that she almost had a fit—was the existence today of other biospheres. They were small, and they only supported life at the microbe level, but they were—

and are—genuine miniature ecospheres, relying on nothing but solar energy to keep them going. The first ones were made by Clair Folsome in Hawaii in 1967, and they're still going."

"Small?" I asked. "How small?"

"You sound like Marcia. Small enough to fit in this wine bottle. The original self-sustaining ecospheres lived in one-liter containers."

"That's *small*," said Tom.

"You also sound like Marcia. *Too* small, she said. But she asked me if it would be possible to design an ecosphere that was big enough for a few humans to live in—and live off, in the sense that it would provide them with food, water, and air—but not much bigger than a house. I told her I didn't see why not, and I even sketched out the way I would go about designing the mix of living organisms to do it. You need something that does photosynthesis, and you need saprophytes that help to decompose complex organic chemicals to simpler forms. But with an adequate energy supply there's no reason why an ecosphere to support humans has to be Earth-sized.

"Marcia graduated, and I thought she had taken a job somewhere on the West Coast. I didn't worry about her, because she was the most charismatic person I had ever met. She seemed able to talk the rest of the students into doing anything. It turned out that I was right, but I had underestimated her. The next thing I knew, I had a letter from another one of my students. He wanted to know what end-forms were possible when you started an ecosphere with a given mix of organisms. The answer, of course, is that today's theories are inadequate. No one knows where you'll finish. But it was the first hint I had that something had gone on beyond my lecture. I sent him a reply, and a week later in my In-Box at the university I found a letter with an odd stamp on it, like a caricature of a black-faced doll."

"A golliwog," I said.

"So I learned. I also realized that it looked a lot like Marcia. The letter said that I was the official founding father of the Habitat League. I've seen stuff like that before, silly student jokes. So it didn't worry me. But *then* I began to receive anonymous letters with the same stamp. And when I read those, I began to worry."

"We saw one," I said. "It was sent to you but the mails fouled up the delivery."

"The person who wrote them said that Marcia had set up her own organization within Ascend Forever, with its own chapters and its own sponsors for funding. She had organized a camp in Colorado—this one—and they were following my advice on setting up self-sustaining ecospheres that could be used as a model for space habitats. I replied to him, saying the Colorado mountains were not a bad site, but they weren't the best."

"Why not?"

"Simulated space environment," said Tom, before Lockyer could answer. "If you want to match the spectrum of solar radiation in low earth orbit, you should go as high as you can and as near the equator as you can, where the sunlight is less affected by the atmosphere. Somewhere in the Andes near Quito would be ideal."

"You're a member of the Habitat League?" Lockyer was worried.

"Never heard of them until today. But I've read about space colonies and habitats."

"Then you probably know that you have to do things a lot differently than they're done in the Earth's natural biosphere. For example, the carbon dioxide cycle on Earth, from atmosphere, through plants and animals, and back to the atmosphere, takes eight to ten years. In the ecospheres that I helped to design, that was down to a day or two. And that means other changes—major ones. And *that* means unpredictable behavior of the ecosphere, and no way to know the stable end conditions without trying them. Sometimes the whole ecosphere will damp down to a low level where only microbial life forms can be supported. That happened in the first half dozen attempts out here. And there was always the possibility of a real anomaly, a thriving, stable ecosphere that seemed to be heading to an end-point equal in vigor to the Earth biosphere, but grossly different from it."

"Ecosphere Nine?" I said.

"You've got it. That one was first established four months ago, with its own initial mix of macro and micro lifeforms. Almost from the beginning it began to show strange oscillatory behavior—cyclic patterns of development that weren't exactly repeating. It reminded me when I saw it of the life cycle and aggregation patterns of the amoebic slime molds, such as *Dictyostelium discoideum*, though you may be more reminded of the behavior of the Belousov-Zhabotinsky chemical reaction, or of the Oregonator and Brusselator systems. They all have limit cycles around stable attractor conditions."

He must have seen the expression on my face. "Well, let's just say that the behavior of Ecosphere Nine originally had some resemblance to phenomena in the literature. But it isn't in a stable limit cycle. The man who wrote to me was worried by that, because he was one of the people who would live in Nine's habitat. He called me and asked if I would make a trip out here and look at Nine, without telling anyone back home where I was going—he had promised to keep this secret, just as all the others had.

"I agreed, and I must say I was fascinated by the whole project. When I arrived here, ten days ago, I was greeted very warmly—almost embarrassingly warmly—by Marcia Seretto, and shown Nine with great pride. In her eagerness to show me how my ideas had been implemented it did not occur to her immediately to ask why I was here. Nine was doing wonderfully well as a possible space habitat, easily sustaining the three humans inside it. But I realized at once that it hadn't stabilized. And it has still not stabilized. It is *evolving*, and evolving fast. I have no idea of its end state, but I do know this: the life cycles in Ecosphere Nine are more efficient than those on Earth and that means they are biologically more *aggressive*. I pointed that out to Marcia, and five days ago I recommended action."

A door slammed downstairs and I heard a hubbub of voices.

"What did you recommend?" asked Tom. He ignored the downstairs noise.

"That the human occupants of Nine be removed from it at once. And that the whole ecosphere be sterilized. I appealed to the staff to support my views. But I didn't realize at the time how things are run here. Marcia controls everything, and I think she is insane. She violently opposed my suggestions, and to prove her point that there is no danger she herself went into Ecosphere Nine. She is there now, together with the man who brought me out here. And she insisted that I be held here. No one will say for how long, or what will happen to me next."

There was a clatter of footsteps on the spiral staircase and Scott burst into the room followed by the other four who had brought us here. His face was pale, but he was obviously relieved when he saw all three of us quietly seated at the table.

"You lied," he said to me. "You have nothing to do with our Philadelphia chapter, or any other. You have to come with me. Marcia wants to talk to you. Both of you."

"What about me?" said Lockyer.

"She didn't say anything about seeing you."

"Well, I need to talk to her." He stood up. "Let's go."

"We're not supposed to take you."

"We won't go if Lockyer doesn't," I said quickly. "You'll have to drag us."

Scott and the others looked agonized. They weren't at all the types to approve of violence, but they had to follow orders.

"All right," said Scott at last. "All of you. Come on."

He led the three of us downstairs, with the others close behind. I expected to go back to the dome and peer in again through a cleared patch of wall panel, but instead we headed for the main building. I looked across at the dome. It was almost four in the afternoon and the sun was lower in the sky. The dome's internal lights must be on, for its panels were glowing now with a mottling of pale purples and greens.

When we had entered the main building earlier in the day it had seemed deserted. Now it swarmed with people. The entrance area had been equipped with a 48-inch TV projection screen, a TV camera, and about twenty chairs. Men and women were sitting on the chairs, staring silently at the screen. They were all in their early twenties and they all had the same squeaky-clean airhead look that we had first noticed in Scott.

As the main attraction we were led to chairs in the front row, and found ourselves staring up at the screen.

What we were looking at had to be the interior of Ecosphere Nine. There was a purple-green tinge to the air, as though it were filled with microscopic floating dust motes, and as the camera inside Nine panned across the interior I could see peculiar mushroom-shaped plants, three or four feet high, rising from the floor. And that floor was nothing like the soil we had seen in Ecosphere Eight. It was a fuzzy, wispy carpet of pale green and white, as though the whole area had been planted with alfalfa sprouts. As I watched, the carpet rippled and began to change color to a darker tone.

Lockyer grunted and leaned forward, but before the color change was complete the camera had zoomed in on three figures sitting on the floor near the far side of the dome. It focused still closer, so that only Marcia Seretto was in the field of view.

She must have been able to see exactly what was happening in the room we were in, because she at once pointed her finger at us. "I gave no instructions for *him* to be brought here," she said in a hoarse voice. The golliwog face was angry. "Can't you obey the simplest directive?"

"The other two refused to come without Professor Lockyer." Scott was close to groveling. "I thought the best thing to do was bring all three of them."

"I was the one who insisted on being here, Marcia," said Lockyer. He was not at all put out by her manner and he was studying her closely. "And I was quite right to do so. You have to get out of Nine—at once. Take a look at yourself, and listen to yourself. Look around you at the air. You're inhaling spores all the time, the air is full of them, and God knows what they'll do to you. And look at those fungi—if they are still fungi—like nothing you've ever seen before. The habitat is changing faster than ever."

She glared out of the screen at him. "Professor Lockyer, I respect you as a teacher, but on matters like this you don't know what you are talking about. I feel fine, the people in here with me feel fine. This is just what we have been looking for, a small habitat that will support humans and is perfect for use in space." She waved her arm. "Take a close look. We have more efficient energy utilization than we ever dreamed of, and that means we can make more compact living environments."

"Marcia, didn't you understand what I said?" Lockyer was not the type to raise his voice, but he spoke more slowly and clearly, as though to a small child. "You're not in a stable environment, as you seem to think. You are involved with a different attractor from any you've seen before, and everything in the ecosphere will be governed by it. You hear me? *The habitat is evolving.* And you form part of the habitat. If you remain there, neither I nor anyone else can predict what is going to happen. You have to get out—now."

She ignored him completely. "As for you two," she said to me and Tom. "I don't know why you came here and I don't much care. You represent a sheer nuisance and I'm not going to allow you to interfere with our work."

"So what are you going to do with us?" I asked.

"We don't owe you one thing. No one asked you two to come here, no one wanted you to come here. We'll decide if you leave and when you leave." Her protruding eyes bulged farther than ever and she rapped out: "What we're doing is more important than any individual. But I'll listen to you. If you can offer any reason why you shouldn't be held until we're ready to let you go, tell me now."

The force of personality, even through a TV link, was frightening. It made my nerves jangle and I could think of nothing at all to say. The surprise came from Tom.

"Professor Lockyer was your professor, wasn't he?" he said quietly. "The spiritual father of the Habitat League."

"What of it?"

"He provided you with the original idea for habitats, and the original designs for them. He's one of the world experts on microbial life forms, far more knowledgeable than anyone here. When he says it's dangerous in Nine, shouldn't you believe him?"

"I respect Professor Lockyer. But he has no experience with habitats of this size. And he's wrong about Nine." Marcia glared at us. "Anything else?"

When we did not speak she nodded and said, "Scott, take them back. All three of them. And then I want you here."

Within ten minutes we were back upstairs in the windowless

building and sitting again at the same table. The thick outer door on the ground floor had been locked, and two women members of the project had been left outside as guards. They had a radio unit with them, and knowing Marcia's style it wouldn't have surprised me if the two of them were expected to watch us all night.

Lockyer picked up his wine glass, still half-full from our rapid departure. "At least we know where we are with Marcia."

"She's a maniac," I said. "How long does she intend to stay in that habitat?"

"Maybe months. Certainly weeks."

"Continuously?"

He nodded. "She has to. That's the whole point about the habitat being a complete ecosphere. She's part of it, and if she leaves she upsets the thermal and material balance. Also, anyone who goes in and out provides a disturbance of another type, too: they carry foreign organisms. Even if it's only bacteria or viruses, every new living entry destroys the totally sealed nature of the habitat."

I was listening with half an ear and trying to think of ways we might get away. But Tom came to full attention and grabbed my arm hard enough to hurt. "Are you saying what I think you are?" he said to Lockyer. "When Marcia Seretto comes out of Ecosystem Nine, she'll bring out with her anything that happens to be in there."

"Roughly speaking. Of course, I'm talking mainly at a micro-organism level. She won't come out carrying plants and fungi."

"But you have no idea which part of the habitat is the 'aggressive' part. For all you know, when Marcia and the others step out of that habitat they'll be carrying with them the seeds of something that is more efficient and vigorous than the natural biosphere here on Earth. The damned thing could take over the whole planet. It'll be the Mega-Mother they talked about in that letter, wiping out the natural biosphere— and maybe we won't be able to live in it."

Lockyer put down his glass and frowned at the table. "I don't think so," he said at last. "The chances are, any ecosystem that works in the habitat won't be well-suited to control the Earth's biosphere. If it were, it should have occurred naturally during biological history."

Then he was silent for a much longer interval, and when he looked up his face was troubled. "But I am reminded of one thing. Marcia had an excellent understanding of recombinant DNA techniques. If she has been using them, to create tailored forms that provide efficient energy utilization and a more efficient ecosphere . . ."

"Then we'll all be in trouble when she comes out—and the longer she stays in there, the worse the odds." Tom jumped to his feet. "We can't risk wiping out Earth life, even if the chances are only one in a million that it will happen. We have to get the people out of Nine—and sterilize it."

"Sure. How do we get out of *here* for starters?" I said.

But Tom was already rushing down the spiral stairs. By the time I followed him he was hurtling towards the heavy outside door. He hit it at full speed, all two hundred and thirty pounds of him. It didn't cave in or fly open, but it certainly shivered on its hinges.

Tom hammered at it with both fists. "Open up!" he roared. "Open up!"

Only an idiot or a genius would expect jailers to respond to a command like that, but the Habitat League members were different—or maybe they were just used to obeying orders.

"What do you want?" said a nervous voice.

"We have to get out. There's a—a f-fire in here."

There was a scream of horror from the other side of the door, and a rattling of a key. Before the door could fully open Tom was pushing through. The two women were standing there, mouths gaping.

I tried to move past Tom. I knew what would happen next. He could never bring himself to hit a woman and he would just stand there. They had been foolish enough to let us out, but now they would either shout for help over the radio or run for the other building—and they were used to being at ten thousand feet. We would never keep up. It was up to me to stop them.

I had underestimated Tom. He reached out and grabbed the girls by the neck, one in each hand. While I watched in astonishment he banged their heads ruthlessly together and dropped the women half-stunned to the floor.

This was Tom, the gentlest of men! I stared at him in disbelief. I thought, *you've come a long way, baby*.

But he was off, blundering away in the semi-darkness towards the dome that housed Ecosystem Nine. "Take care of them," he shouted over his shoulder. "I need five minutes."

They didn't need much taking care of. They were down in the dirt, flinching away when I bent towards them. I picked up the radio and swung it by its strap against the wall of the building. The case cracked open and the batteries flew out. When I bent over one of the women and grabbed her arm, she moaned in fear and wriggled away from me.

"Inside," I said. With Lockyer's help—he had finally sauntered downstairs and out of the building—I pushed them through the door, slammed it, and turned the key. Then I walked—slowly, I might need my wind in a minute or two—towards the main building. Tom had said he needed five minutes. If anything had been sent over the radio before I destroyed it, I wasn't sure I could guarantee him five seconds.

I sneaked closer in the gathering darkness with Lockyer just behind me. The door of the building remained closed, and there was no sign of activity there. I crept forward to look in the window. Three people sat quietly reading.

"The dome!" said Lockyer in an urgent whisper. Then he moved rapidly away from me.

I looked after him. The third dome, the one that housed Nine, was glowing bright pink in the night. The internal lighting level had been turned way up.

After one more glance at the main building—all still quiet there—I headed after Lockyer. If one of the project teams happened to be outside, they would surely be drawn to the bright dome. I could help Tom better there than I could anywhere else.

He was standing by the dome controls and trying to peer in through one of the wall panels. The telephone was in his hand, but he was not using it.

"Can't get any response," he said when he saw me. "I called inside, told Marcia to get the hell out of there while they could.

But not a word back. Not one word."

I saw that the illumination level on the control panel had been turned to its maximum and the internal temperature was set at sterilization level—three hundred and twenty Celsius, hot enough to kill any organism that I knew about, hot enough even to destroy the Mega-Mother. The panel control knobs were broken off and lay on the floor.

"Tom, you'll kill them."

"I hope not. I warned them. I'm not going to stop. I won't stop until Ecosphere Nine is burned clean, and anyway I *can't* stop it—I buggered the controls here." He turned to Lockyer. "These people all respect you, they'll at least listen. Go back to the building where they have the TV, and see what's going on inside Nine. Tell them all that Marcia has to get out in the next ten minutes, otherwise she'll be cooked."

Lockyer didn't flap easily. He nodded and set off without a word. I stood around useless for a little while, and finally followed him. There was nothing to be done here and at least I could confirm what Lockyer said to the others.

The door was wide open when I got there and the building reception area was empty. Lockyer stood frozen in front of the big TV screen. It was still turned on, with the dome's camera set to provide a general view of the interior. The glare of lights at their maximum setting showed every detail.

Nine had changed again. No part of it resembled any Earth plant or animal that I could recognize. The floating spores were gone but the air was filled with tiny, wriggling threadworms, supported on gossamer strands attached to the walls and ceiling. The fuzzy carpet of green and white alfalfa sprouts had gone, too, passing through a color change and a riotous growth. The sprouts had formed long, wispy tendrils of purple-black, threading the whole interior and wriggling like a tangle of thin snakes across the floor and up the walls. They were connected to the squat mushroom plants, and small black spheres hung on them like beads on a necklace.

The increased lighting level seemed to be driving the whole ecosphere to a frenzy of activity. A crystalline silver framework of lines and nodes was forming, linking all parts of the dome into a tetrahedral lattice. The habitat pulsed with energy.

As I watched a new wave of black spheres began to inch their way towards the middle of the dome, where a great cluster of them sat on a lumpy structure near the dome's center.

It took me a few seconds to recognize that structure. It was formed of Marcia and her two companion crew members.

They sat quietly on the floor of the dome. Black spheres formed a dense layer over their bodies, and long tendrils of wriggling white grew from ears, mouths, and nostrils. Their skins had a wrinkled, withered look.

I grabbed at Lockyer's arm. "We have to get back to the dome," I exclaimed. "Turn off the heat. Marcia and the others are still inside and they're . . ."

They're still alive, I was going to say. But when I looked at them I could not believe it.

"No point now," said Lockyer in a hushed voice. "It's too late." And then, still capable of objective analysis, he added, "Drained. Drained and absorbed. They are on the way to becoming part of the ecosphere. It's evolving faster than ever, accepting everything. Look at the walls."

I saw that the dome's wall panels had an eroded, eaten look. Where the gossamer threads were attached, the hard panel material was being dissolved. In places the plastic support ribbing was almost eaten through. Given a little more time, Ecosphere Nine would break free of the dome's constraint and have access to the vast potential habitat of Earth.

But Nine would not be given time.

The internal temperature was rising rapidly. As we watched, the support tendrils began to writhe and convulse. The silver network shivered. Black spheres were thrown free and rolled around on the floor, pulping delicate filaments beneath them. As the mushroom structures split open, ejecting a black fluid that spattered across the interior, it was easy to see the ecosphere as one great organism, sucking in more and more energy from the blazing lights and fighting desperately for survival while the temperature went up and up.

(There was a clatter of footsteps and two men and a woman came into the room. Lockyer and I hardly noticed them. They sensed that something final and terrible was happening and they joined us, staring in horror at the TV screen.)

Ecosphere Nine was losing its battle. The black spheres inflated and burst, throwing off puffs of vapor like popping corn as the internal temperature rose above boiling point. Gossamer threads shriveled and fell to the floor, long tendrils writhed and withered. In the blistering heat the broken mushroom structures sagged and dwindled, sinking back to floor level.

Steam filled the interior, and in the final moments it was difficult to see; but I was watching when the last spheres fell away from Marcia and her companions, and the tendrils trailed limp from their open mouths. What remained was hardly recognizable as human beings. Their bodies were eaten away, corroded to show the staring white bones of chest and limbs.

And then, quite suddenly, it ended. Tendrils slowed and drooped, spheres lay on the floor like burst balloons. The silver lattice disappeared. Inside the dome, nothing moved but rising steam.

Lockyer felt his way towards one of the metal chairs and collapsed into it. The three camp members next to him clung to each other and wept.

I went outside and called to Tom. "Are you all right?"

"I'm fine, but I can't see into the dome. What's happening?"

"It's over," I said. "It's dead. They're all dead."

And then I leaned over in the cold Colorado night, and vomited until I thought I was going to die, too.

I thought that was the end, but of course it was just the beginning.

No one could think of sleep that night. There seemed to be a thousand things to do: police to be informed, families told, the interior of the dome inspected, the bodies recovered.

But none of this could begin until the morning, and some of it would take much longer; the dome needed at least forty-eight hours to cool before anyone could go inside.

Tom, Jason Lockyer, and I went back to our former prison and sat at the table, talking and drinking wine. I didn't ask the vintage or the pedigree, and I didn't care what it would do to my stomach or my liver. I sluiced it down—we all did.

"Thank God it's over," I said, after several minutes of silence.

Lockyer sighed. "Back to the real world. Pity in some ways; I quite like it here. You've no idea how complimented a professor feels when his students appreciate him enough to take his teaching and actually *implement* it. I'll be sorry to leave."

Not a word about wife Eleanor, waiting with her claws out back in Washington.

"I don't think you should leave," said Tom. "In fact, I don't think any of us should leave. It would be irresponsible."

He was sitting with his shirtsleeves rolled up and his hands in a bowl of cold water. There were great bruises on them, from where he had hammered on the metal door, and his fingertips were bloody from tearing off the dome's control knobs.

"But there's nothing to do here now," I said. "With Marcia dead the group will break up."

"I hope not. I hope they will all stay here." Tom looked at Lockyer. "The job's not finished, is it?"

Lockyer shook his head. "I think I know what you mean and no, it's not finished. There is no self-contained ecosphere that can support a human population."

"Who cares?" My mind was boiling over with a hundred dreadful images from the interior of Habitat Nine. I couldn't get out of my head the thought of Marcia and the others, invaded by the organisms of the habitat. Had she realized what was happening to her in those final few minutes before her mind and body succumbed? I hoped not.

"If I have the choice," I went on, "I'll never look at an ecosphere again—never. Let the Ascend Forever people have their fun, but keep me out."

"That's the problem," said Tom. "We can't stay out. No one can. We destroyed Ecosphere Nine, but this group isn't the only one trying to create self-contained habitats. There must be a dozen others around the world."

"At least that," said Lockyer. "The Habitat League used to send me newsletters."

"Fine." I didn't like the expression on Tom's face—all the softness had gone from it. "Let them play. That doesn't mean *we* have to."

"I'm afraid it does," said Tom. "If the endpoint for the biological forms of Ecosphere Nine is a stable attractor, it can arise from a whole variety of different starting conditions. So if people keep on experimenting, Nine can show up again. We were lucky. Nine didn't break free and come into contact with Biosphere One—the whole Earth—but it came close. If one did get free you couldn't sterilize the Earth the way we did with the chamber."

"But that seems like a case *against* fooling around any more with the ecospheres," I protested. "If more habitats are made here they'll add to the danger of a wild one getting loose."

Lockyer and Tom looked at each other. "She's right, of course," said Lockyer. "But so are you, Tom. We're damned if we do and we're damned if we don't. We have to keep working, so we'll understand ways that ecospheres can develop and learn how to handle dangerous forms."

"And we need to find a biosphere that people can live in in space," said Tom. "We're going to need it—if anything like Nine ever gets free on Earth."

That was two months ago. Tom, Jason Lockyer, and I went back to Washington, but only to clean up unfinished business that the three of us left behind. Then we returned to Colorado.

Amazingly, nearly half the staff of the project elected to stay on. They are a dedicated group, putting the project ahead of everything. Even before Marcia brainwashed them, they were all space fanatics. Thanks to them, the project picked up again with hardly a hitch. Ecospheres Ten, Eleven, and Twelve are already in operation. None of them looks particularly promising—and none looks anything like Nine.

Naturally, every aspect of ecosphere development is closely monitored. Jason Lockyer supervises every biological change and approves every technique used. It is hard to imagine how any group could be more careful.

And Tom runs the whole show—shy, introverted, overweight Tom Walton. But he is not the man I met in his stamp shop in Washington. He has lost thirty pounds, he doesn't stammer, he never mentions stamps. He does not have

Marcia's domineering manner, but he makes up for that with his sense of urgency. And if he pushes others, he pushes himself harder. Like Ecosphere Nine, he is still changing, developing, evolving. He will become—I don't know what.

I'm not sure I like the new Tom Walton—the Tom I helped to shape—as well as the old one. Sometimes I feel that I, like Marcia, created my own monster, so that now under his leadership we must all become God, the Builder of Worlds.

And also, perhaps, their annihilator.

(It was Jason Lockyer, the calmest and most cerebral of our group, who recalled Robert Oppenheimer's quotation of Vishnu from the *Bhagavad Gita*, at the time of the testing of the first atomic bomb: "I am become Death, the Destroyer of Worlds.")

Which brings my thoughts, again and again, to Marcia. How much did she understand, at the very end, as Nine took her for its own and the world around her faded? Surely she knew at least this much, that she had created a monster. But Nine was *her* monster, her baby, her private universe, her unique creation, and in some sense she must have loved it. Loved it so much that when logic said the ecosphere must be destroyed, she could not bring herself to do it. She must have somehow justified her actions. What did she say, what did she think, how did she *feel*, in those last minutes?

I hope that I will never know.

•

YOUR SCIENCE FICTION TRAVELS ARE ONLY BEGINNING.

Enjoy the same great science fiction authors throughout the year by subscribing to ANALOG SCIENCE FICTION/SCIENCE FACT MAGAZINE and ISAAC ASIMOV'S SCIENCE FICTION MAGAZINE. The choice is yours...Asimov emphasizes the world of fantasy, whereas Analog focuses on what is scientifically plausible.

- ❏ 8 issues of Asimov for only $14.95.
- ❏ 8 issues of Analog for only $14.95.
- ❏ 8 issues of Asimov & 8 issues of Analog for only $27.95.
- ❏ Payment enclosed
- ❏ Bill me.

Send your check or money order to:

> Davis Science Fiction Magazines
> Dept. MPLT-2
> P.O. Box 7061
> Red Oak, IA 51591

Name_____

Address_____

City/ST/Zip_____

OR CALL 1-800-333-4108

(Newsstand Price is $2.50 per copy)